Memory in the Flesh

Memory in the Flesh
Ahlam Mosteghanemi

Translated by Baria Ahmar Sreih
Revised translation by Peter Clark

Arabia Books
London

First published in Great Britain in 2008 by
Arabia Books
70 Cadogan Place
London SW1X 9AH
www.arabiabooks.co.uk

This edition published by arrangement with
The American University in Cairo Press
113 Sharia Kasr el Aini, Cairo, Egypt
420 Fifth Avenue, New York, NY 10018
www.aucpress.com

The words of Malek Haddad are taken from his novels
Le Quai aux fleurs ne répond and *Je t'offrirai une gazelle*

ISBN 978-1-906697-04-4
Printed in Great Britain by J. H. Haynes & Co. Ltd., Sparkford
1 2 3 4 5 6 7 8 9 10   14 13 12 11 10 09 08 07

Cover design: Arabia Books
Design: AUC Press

To the memory of Malek Haddad,
son of Constantine, who swore after the independence of
Algeria not to write in a language that was not his. The
blank page assassinated him. He died by the might of his
silence to become a martyr of the Arabic language and
the first writer ever to die silent, grieving, and
passionate on its behalf.

And to the memory of my father,
who may find someone there who knows Arabic
to read him this book, his book.

ONE

I STILL remember you once saying, "What went on between us was real love. What didn't happen was the stuff of love stories."

Today, now that it is all over, I can say, "If that's the case, we're lucky that it's just in a book. However, what didn't happen could fill volumes. We're also lucky in the beauty of the love we did have. What will not happen is also beautiful."

Before, I thought we could write about life only when we had recovered from our wounds; when we were able to touch old sores with a pen and not revive the pain; when we could look back free from nostalgia, madness, and a sense of grievance.

But is this really possible? We are never completely cut off from our memory. Recollection provides the inspiration for writing, the stimulus for drawing, and for some, the motivation even for death.

"Would you like some coffee?" 'Atiqa's voice drifts by, as if it was a question directed at somebody else. Apologizing wordlessly to the face of sadness I have been wearing for days. At that instant my voice deserts me.

I answer with a nod. She slips out silently and returns minutes later with a large, copper, coffee tray, bearing a pitcher, cups, sugar bowl, orange-flower water, and a plate of sweets. In other cities, coffee is served already poured in a cup with a piece of sugar and a spoon next to it. But Constantine is a city that abhors shortcuts. It puts everything on permanent display. It wears its entire wardrobe and says all it knows. Even grief is a public festival there.

I gather up the papers scattered in front of me, making room for the coffee—as if I am making space for you. Some are old, rough scribbles, others are blank sheets that have been around for days, waiting for just a few words to breathe energy into them and to bring them alive. Words are all that is needed to go from silence to speech, from memory to oblivion but . . . I leave the sugar at one side and sip my bitter coffee. I recall your love. I think of the tart taste of the unsweetened drink and feel able to write about you.

Nervously, I light a cigarette and chase through the smoke for the words that for years have seared my soul, words whose fire has never been quenched by ink. Is paper a dustbin for the memory, a place where we always deposit the ash of the last cigarette of nostalgia, the remnants of the final disappointment? Which one of us lights up or stubs out the other? I really do not know. Before you, I never wrote anything worth mentioning. Because of you, I put pen to paper.

Eventually I will find the right phrases. It is my right now to choose the way in which my tale is told. I have not chosen this story. It would not have been mine at all had destiny not inserted you in every one of its chapters.

How come this confusion? How is it that the white surface of these transformed pages is from the huge blank canvasses still leaning against a studio wall that was once mine?

Why do the letters of the alphabet run away just in the way colors used to desert me before, turning my world into a black-and-white television program? I see an old tape of my memory in the way television shows old silent movies.

I have always envied those artists who can switch effortlessly from painting to writing, simply as if they are moving from one compartment of the mind to another, or shifting to a new woman without seeing the previous one off. But I am not like that. I am a one-woman man.

Here is the pen then, at once a tool of vibes and jibes. Here is a tool that does not know how to lie, how to veil the truth, and is unable to gloss over a gaping wound.

Here are the words I have been deprived of, as naked as I want them to be, painful in the way that I want. So why does fear paralyze my hand and prevent me from writing? Am I only now realizing that I have swapped the brush for a dagger and that writing of you is as lethal as your love?

I sit down to sip your bitter coffee, this time with a wary pleasure. I feel almost as though I have found an introductory sentence for the book, a phrase that could be as a line from a letter. For example:

I'm writing to you from a city that bears your picture. I have come to resemble the city. Birds still swoop busily across those bridges, while I, hanging around here, have become another bridge.
Don't love bridges anymore . . .

Or something else, like this:

I thought of you while sipping a coffee. . . .
Fate decreed that you had to add a lump of sugar, just one.
So why do we need a fancy tray just for a single, bitter drink?

I could have written anything, because in the end, novels are just the letters and greeting cards we write for no special purpose; where we reveal the climate of our souls for those who care to take any interest in us.

The most beautiful novel is the one that starts with a sentence wholly unexpected by the reader who has lived through our storms and norms, and who might once have been the cause of our changing moods.

Sentences crowd up in my head, phrases you would never expect. Suddenly the memories pour back.

I gulp the coffee down and throw the window open to escape from you to the autumn sky, to the trees and bridges and the passers-by. To a city I have regained, this time for another reason, a city where you made an appointment for me.

This is Constantine. Here is everything: you.

Through that window that you knew years ago, there streams in the same call to prayer, the street cries of peddlers, the clattering footsteps of women clad in black, and songs that waft up from a loudspeaker that never wearies.

O apple, o apple . . . tell me why people adore you.

The banality of the fruit-seller's song stops me short.

It forces me face to face with my homeland. It reminds me without any glimmer of doubt that I am in an Arab city. The years I spent in Paris seem a fanciful dream.

Is singing to fruit an Arab phenomenon? Or is it because only apples still carry the flavor of our original sin and are so delicious that people in more than one Arab country sing to them?

And what if you were an apple?

But no, you were not an apple.

But you were the woman who seduced me into eating it. You were practicing the instinctive game of Eve and I was unable to resist. With you, I was as foolish as Adam.

"Hello, Si Khalid, how are you today?"

A neighbor gazes at me, peeling off layers of my melancholy, and greets me. He seems surprised at my morning appearance, standing at the back of a balcony of distraction. I follow his steps with an absentminded look as he heads to the nearby mosque, tramping in step with others, some sauntering and others with a determined stride, but all heading to the same destination.

The whole of my homeland is on its way to pray while a loud-speaker celebrates the eating of apples. The roofs around the minaret are littered with antennae that absorb foreign channels from the heavens. Every night, they cast onto the screen all manner of hi-tech ways of tasting forbidden fruit. Actually, I do not like fruit, least of all apples. I was in love with you, but what was my crime? Though your love came to me as a sin, why was I guilty?

"Hello there, how are you?" another neighbor calls as he heads for prayers. My tongue utters a few terse words in his direction before silently asking about you.

How am I? I am the result of what you have done to me,

4

madam. And how are you? You are the woman who cloaked my nostalgia with madness, who gradually assumed the features of a city and the contours of a country.

And then, when time was not looking, this woman became my world. It was as if I were entering compartments of my memory that had been deserted for years.

How are you?

You were Constantine's mulberry tree, every season in black. You were the city's love, its clothes, its joys, its misery, and its lovers.

Tell me, where are you now?

This Constantine has cold hands and feet, fervid lips and fevered moods.

That is the long and short of it.

You are so like the city today. If only you knew.

Let me close the window.

Marcel Pagnol used to say, "Think always of ordinary events, the kind that may actually happen."

Is not death, in the end, ordinary, just like birth, love, marriage, sickness, aging, being among strangers, going mad, and so on? How long is the list of ordinary events that we expect to be extraordinary until they actually occur? Such things that we think happen only to others and that life, for some reason, will spare us for the most part, until one day we find ourselves staring them in the face.

When today I look back through my life, I realize that the only truly exceptional event was meeting you. It was the only thing I could not have foreseen, because I did not then know that exceptional events carry in their train many ordinary occurrences as well.

Nonetheless, even now I wonder, after all these years, where I should place your love. Is it in the storehouse of ordinary things that may happen to any of us any day, like falling ill or tripping up or going insane?

Where do I place it?

As an exceptional event? As a gift from a planet that eluded even astronomers? As a tremor that did not register on any seismographic chart? Were you an accident or a jest of fate?

I skim through the morning paper looking for convincing answers to an ordinary event that changed the course of my life and brought me here. After all these years, I look at the pages of our misery, and the black ink of Algeria rubs off on my hands. The readers of some newspapers have to wash their hands after touching them, though not always for the same reason. One stains your hands and the other—better printed—pollutes your mind. Is it because newspapers always look like their owners? I think our newspapers start the day the same way the rest of us do, with sleepy features and a face hurriedly washed before rushing into the street without taking the trouble to comb their hair or put on the right tie.

October 25, 1988.

Banner headlines and a lake of black ink, much blood and little sensitivity. Some newspapers sell you the same pictures on their front page every day, adding just a new twist. Some papers sell you the same lies every day in a less intelligent way. Others sell you a ticket to escape from your own world—nothing more than that.

But since that is not possible anymore, I will fold up the paper and go and wash my hands. The last time any Algerian publication captured my attention was about two months ago. I happened to be scanning a magazine and was jolted by a picture of you filling up a whole page. There was an interview in which you talked about the launch of your new book. My eyes were glued that day to the picture. In vain, I tried to work out what you were saying. I read your words, but in my haste I stumbled over them and became confused. It was as if I was the one talking to you about myself and not you talking to others about a story that probably had nothing to do with us.

What kind of bizarre rendezvous did we have that day? How come I did not expect, after all those years, that you would make an appointment with me on paper between two pages of a magazine that I do not usually read? Murphy's law, right? Just my luck that I happen to buy a magazine I do not usually read that turns my life upside down.

And do you know why it is bizarre? Were you not a woman

of print? You loved and hated in print. You ran off and came back in print. You killed and revived to life at the stroke of a pen.

How could I not be confused when I was reading you? How could an electric shiver not run down my spine and send my heart into overdrive? It was as if I were in front of you, not in front of a picture of you. Every time I went back to look at that photograph, I wondered how you managed to come back into my life and haunt me. I am the one who avoided every road that led toward you.

So how did you come back?

The wound was just beginning to heal, and the heart that had been loaded with the memory of you was gradually liberating itself from you. You were packing up the baggage of love and leaving soon to take possession of the heart of another.

So you left my heart then. It was like a tourist leaving a city he has visited on a package holiday. Everything has been scheduled in advance, even the hour of departure. Every detail has been planned ahead of time, even the tickets for tourist attractions, the name of the play they are going to see and the shops where they will buy their souvenirs.

Was your trip that boring? There I was, in front of your picture, confused and bewildered, as if I was really looking at you. Your new hairstyle surprised me: it was short. Your hair used to be like a scarf that was so long it shut out the solitude of my nights. What did you do to it?

I stopped and gazed long at your eyes. I sought in them a memory of my first defeat at your hands.

Once there was nothing more beautiful than your eyes, but how they made me sometimes sad, sometimes happy! Have they changed as well, or is it the way I see you that has changed? I kept looking at your face for signs of my former madness. I almost failed to recognize your lips and your smile with its new lipstick.

How could I once have seen a resemblance to my mother in you? How could I have imagined you wearing her dress, kneading dough with those long polished nails, making bread the taste of which I have missed for years?

What kind of mad idiocy was that?

Has marriage really changed your expressions and your childlike laugh? Has it also changed your memory and the taste of your lips and the gypsy hue of your skin?

Did that impoverished prophet make you forget? The one who was stripped of the Ten Commandments on his way to you? The one who brought you only the Eleventh Commandment?

There you were in front of me, wearing the dress of a heretic. You have chosen another path and wear another face, one I no longer recognize, a face that looks out at us from magazines or from adverts in a shop window, draped to sell something. It could be toothpaste or anti-wrinkle cream.

Or maybe you wore that mask only to promote merchandise in the form of a book that you called *The Corner of Oblivion*, merchandise that could be the story of my life with you and the memory of my pain.

Of course, this could be just the latest method you have discovered of killing me again today, a method that avoids leaving your fingerprints on my neck.

I remember a conversation we had that day when I asked you why you chose specifically to write a novel. What you said amazed me. I could not figure out to what degree you were telling the truth and how much you were lying as you answered with a smile, "I had to put some order into my life and get rid of some old furniture. Our spirits also need refurbishing, just like any house we live in. I can't keep my windows closed indefinitely. The only reason we write novels is to kill off heroes and do away with people whose existence has become a burden. Every time we write about them we purge them from our system and breathe in fresh air."

You paused.

"In fact, every successful novel," you added, "is a kind of crime we commit against some memory and maybe against someone. We carry out a completely silent murder in full view of everyone and only the victim realizes that the lethal words are intended for him.

"Unsuccessful novels are merely botched crimes, and their authors should be banned from carrying a pen on the grounds that they don't know how to manipulate words. They might end up murdering the wrong person by mistake—including themselves. That, in addition to killing their readers with boredom."

Why did your sadistic tendencies not arouse my suspicions that day, and why did I not anticipate all those crimes that followed when you tried out all your other weapons? I did not expect then that one day you would point your arsenal in my direction. That is why I laughed at your words. Maybe I admired you in another way that day, because in such circumstances we cannot resist the mad folly of admiring our killer.

Anyhow, I expressed my surprise. "I used to think," I said, "that a novel was the way writers lived a love story a second time. Their way of giving immortality to those whom they had loved."

Apparently my reply surprised you as well. You looked as though you had come upon something you had not accounted for.

"That could be true," you said, "because in the end we kill only those we have loved. We give them a kind of literary immortality as compensation. That's fair, isn't it?"

Fair! Who can play around with tyrants about their sense of fairness or oppression? Who discussed matters with Nero on the day he burned Rome out of love and pyromania? And you, are you not like him? A woman whose professional craft shows an equally fiery passion? Were you even then anticipating my imminent demise and trying to console me in advance for my disaster? Or maybe you were playing with words as usual, observing their impact on me and secretly enjoying my constant amazement, my astonishment at your remarkable capacity for saying things that fit in with your contradictions.

Everything was possible.

For I might have been the victim of this novel of yours and also the corpse that you have sentenced to immortality, mummifying him with words . . . as usual.

But perhaps I was just the victim of my own illusion, and it was your lies that looked like honesty. Because only you know in the end, the answer to all these questions that have obsessed me with the stubbornness of someone searching vainly for the truth.

When did you write that book?

Was it before or after you got married? Before or after Ziad died? Did you write about me or about him? Did you write it to kill me off or to bring him back to life? Or to finish us both off, to kill us together in a single book, just as you left us both for the sake of another man?

When I read that news item a couple of months ago, I had absolutely no idea that you would return with your abiding presence, and that your book would become the center of my thoughts and a vicious solitary treadmill. After all that had happened, I was simply unable to go looking for it in bookshops, to hand over money to a bookseller just to buy my own story. Nor could I ignore it and carry on with my life as if I had never heard of it, or as if it did not concern me at all.

Did I not burn to read the rest of the story? You know, the one that ended when my back was turned? The one whose final chapters I did not know, chapters in which I was an absent witness after being the opening character of the book? It was just my luck to be always simply a witness and a victim in a story that had room for only one hero.

I have your book now. It is in front of me but I cannot read it today, so I have left it on my table, closed like a mystery, threatening me like a time bomb, its silent presence helping me to detonate a mine of words inside me and to jolt my own memory.

Everything in the book provokes me now. The title you chose is an obvious trick, and your smile in the photo takes no account of my distress. Your expression—devoid of all emotion—treats me as an ordinary reader, someone who does not know much about you.

Everything . . . even your name.

Maybe your name provokes me most because it leaps around in my memory even before the letters that spell it reach my eye. Your name is not one to be read, but to be heard, like music played on a solo instrument for an audience of one.

How can I read the book without feeling that it represents an episode from the incidental crossing of the destinies of our lives that day? The blurb on the back of the book says that its publication is a literary event.

I hide the book beneath a pile of notes I have written on in moments of delusion.

"It's time," I say to myself, "for you to write or to be silent forever, man, because what's happening these days is very strange."

Then suddenly the cold makes the decision for me. The Constantine night creeps up on me from my window of exile. I put the top back on my pen and slide under my blanket of loneliness.

I realized that every city gets the night it deserves, the night that reflects its character, showing the only thing that reveals the city's guilty secrets, casting off in the dark what it conceals during the day. Because of this, I resolve not to look out of the window after dark.

All cities lay themselves bare at night without realizing it, and silently disclose their secrets to strangers. Even when they lock their doors. And because cities are like women, some of them make us hasten the coming of the dawn but . . .

Soirs, soirs, que de soirs pour un seul matin . . .

How am I able to call to mind that line by Henri Michou? I repeat it to myself in more than one language.

Evenings, evenings, so many evenings for a single morning . . .

How am I able to call it to mind and when, I wonder, did I memorize it? Is it because for years I expected miserable evenings like this one that will have only a single morning? I dig into my memory for the whole poem from which this line is taken. I realize that it is called "Old Age."

My discovery suddenly scares me as if with it I am finding new features in my own face. Does old age overtake us in just one, single, long night? And in an interior darkness that slows us up in every way and makes us walk slowly with no clear direction? Could boredom, loss, and monotony be some part of the characteristics of old age or are they characteristics of this city? Is it me who is entering old age, or is the entire country now entering an era of collective decline? Does the country not hold some superior power both to make us grow old and to become old in a few months, sometimes in just a few weeks?

Until today I never felt the burden of years. Your love was my youth, my studio was my boundless solar energy, and Paris was an elegant city whose appearance one would be ashamed to ignore. But they pursued me and haunted me there in my exile and extinguished the flame of my passion and drove me all the way here.

Now we are standing on our country's erupting volcano. We have no longer any alternative but to become one with the lava flying from its mouth and to forget about our own small fires. Today, nothing is worthy of all this elegance and these manners. No longer is our country ashamed to present itself so ineptly.

There is nothing more difficult than to start writing at an age when others have finished saying everything. Writing for the first time after the age of fifty is something at once both sensual and insane, a reversion to adolescence. Something exciting but also dumb, resembling a love affair between a man in decline and a new pen! The former, confused and in a hurry, the latter an eager virgin that all the ink in the world would fail to satisfy.

Since that is the case, I reckon that what I have penned so far is just a preparation for real writing and an excess of lust for these sheets that I have for years dreamt of filling.

Maybe tomorrow I will start writing properly. I always like to relate important events in my life that then stir another memory.

This idea seduced me again when I was listening to the news this evening. I realized—I, who had lost all sense of time—I realized that tomorrow would be the first of November. How could I do other than start a book on such a date? On the first of November, thirty-four years ago, the first bullet in the War of Liberation was fired, and I arrived here three weeks ago on the anniversary of the date of the fall of the last group of martyrs.

One of those martyrs was the man whose body I brought here to be buried.

Between the first and last bullets, objectives changed. Aims changed and our country changed. That is why tomorrow will be a day of mourning for the loss of the dues that have already been paid. There will be no military parade, no receptions, no official commemorations. People will just hurl accusations at each other while we go and visit the graves.

I will not visit that grave tomorrow. I do not wish to share my grief with my country. I prefer the dignified silence of a piece of paper.

Everything is spurring me on tonight, and I feel as if I could at last write something striking and not tear it all up as I usually do.

How painful is the coincidence that brings me back here, after all these years, to the same place, to find the body of the one I used to love with the reliability of a first memory.

The past tonight returns to me, confusing me, surreptitiously leading me to the alleyways of my mind. I try to push it away, but will I be able to fight against that memory this evening?

I close the door of my room and open the window.

I try to see something other than myself, and I see the window looking at me. Forests of laurel and oak stretch out ahead of me. Constantine, covered with its old veil, crawls toward me with bushes and secret paths and slopes that I once knew, surrounding the city like a security cordon. The various paths lead you through its thickly wooded forests to the secret hideouts of the *mujahidin*, explaining to you, as it were, tree after tree, and cave after cave.

All the roads in this ancient Arab city lead to defiance. All the woods and the rocks here enlisted in the ranks of the revolution before you did.

Some cities do not choose their destinies. They are sentenced by history and geography not to surrender. And that is why their sons do not always have the choice. Is it strange that I look so much like this city—insanely so?

One day over thirty years ago, I followed these roads and chose these mountains to be my home and my private school where I learned the only subject that was not allowed to be taught. I knew then that among its graduates there my destiny would be determined in the slender gap between freedom and death. We had made the choice using another more attractive name, so we could go to it without fear and maybe with a secret lust, as if we were going to something other than our death.

Why did we then forget to give freedom more than one name? And how did we devalue the very concept of our freedom right from the start?

Death was then walking at our side, sleeping, then hastily eating bread with us. Just like patience, faith, and longing, an ambiguous joy never deserted us.

Death was walking and breathing at our side. Days came back harsh as always, different from the earlier days only in the tally of martyrs, mostly those who nobody ever expected to die, whose end, for some reason, nobody figured would be so near and so painful. That was the logic of death that I had not, till then, fully comprehended.

I still remember those whom we became accustomed to speaking about afterward in the plural, as if the plural in this case were not a collective abridgement, but used to show they had a precedence over us. They were not mass-produced martyrs. Each one was a martyr in his own right. One was killed in the first battle as if he came especially to die. Another fell only one day before setting out on a secret visit to his parents, after he had spent weeks studying and preparing the exact details of the visit. A third got married and returned to die a married man. Yet another was dreaming to come back one day to find a bride for himself, but never did.

In wars, the sad ones are not always those who die. The most wretched are those who are left behind, orphans, widows, and those with broken dreams. I discovered this fact early. One martyr after another, one account after another. At the same time, I discovered that I was probably the only one who left behind the fresh grave of a mother who died from sickness and a broken heart, one brother a few years younger, and a father too busy with the demands of a young bride.

The old adage—the orphan is not the one who loses his father but the one who loses his mother—is absolutely true.

I was an orphan, and I realized this profoundly all the time. Because the hunger for affection is a fearful and painful feeling that continues to tear you from the inside and stays with you until, one way or another, it finishes you off.

Did I join the national revolution at the time as a subconscious way of seeking death, a beautiful death remote from those feelings of nausea that were gradually filling me with hatred foreverything?

The revolution was entering its second year and I was in my third month as an orphan. I cannot remember now exactly when the country took over the character of motherhood and gave me an unexpected and strange affection and a compulsive sense of belonging.

It was probably the disappearance of Si Tahir from our

neighborhood in Sidi al-Mabruk a few months earlier that was a decisive factor in my haste in taking that sudden decision. It was no secret that he had moved to a hiding place in the mountains surrounding Constantine and had, with others, formed one of the first guerrilla cells of the armed struggle.

Why does the name Si Tahir come back to me tonight to add to my perplexity? And which one of you lured me to the other?

Where did he come back from? Did he really ever disappear? After all, two blocks from here a street bears his name. The power of the name. There are names that, when recalled, virtually compel you to pay attention or to put your cigarette out. You speak about them as if you are talking to them, with that same startled awe. And so, the name of Si Tahir still has some awesome effect on me. Habit has not killed it any more than being with him constantly. Experience of prison with him did not alter it, nor did the years of struggle make his name an ordinary one for a friend or a neighbor. Symbols always know how to surround themselves with that invisible barrier that separates the ordinary and the exceptional, the possible and the impossible in everything.

Here I am recalling his name on a night that was to be his.

As I take another puff of my last cigarette, the loudspeaker on the minaret blares away, announcing the dawn prayer, while from a room far away I hear the cry of a baby that awakens the whole household.

I envy the minaret. I envy newborn babies. Only they have the right to scream and the ability to do so before life tames their vocal chords and teaches them silence. I cannot remember who it was who said, "A man spends his first years learning how to speak, and the Arab regimes teach him silence for the rest of his life."

Silence could have become a blessing—especially tonight. It is like oblivion, because on occasions such as today, memory comes back not in installments, but like a cascade, sweeping you away to unknown slopes. How could you check them without hitting the rocks and breaking your neck? There you are, chasing after your memory to catch up with a past that in reality you have never really left, in pursuit of an idea that has become physically part of you.

Your mutilated body.

But then you know there are others right now, with one excuse or another, condemning a history of which they were a part. They do this in an attempt to follow the new wave before they are dragged off by the flood. All you can do is pity them. How miserable it is to live with wet clothes, as if you have just emerged from a swamp without even waiting for the clothes to dry.

Silent comes Si Tahir tonight.

Silent the way martyrs come.

Silent as is his wont.

Here you are, confused in his presence as usual. The fifteen years separating you were always greater than the actual number of years.

It was an age in itself, a symbol in itself, for a man who possessed more than that eloquence that is the hallmark of all those who went to Islamic societies and studied in Constantine. There was another eloquence—that of his presence.

Si Tahir knew when to smile and when to be angry. He knew how to speak and how to be silent. The expression on his face never ceased to inspire awe. Nor did the mysterious smile that inspired a myriad of different explanations. "Smiles are commas and full stops . . . and few are those who still know how to put commas and full stops into their worlds," wrote Malek Haddad.

In the al-Kudya prison I had my first encounter in the struggle with Si Tahir. It was an encounter charged with intense emotion and with the shock of being arrested for the first time, with its blend of dignity and fear.

Si Tahir, who had brought me day after day into the revolution, was mindful of his responsibility for my being there that day. And he may have secretly had some sympathy for my sixteen years, for my truncated childhood, and for my mother, whom he knew very well. He knew what the experience of my first arrest could do to her. But he hid all his sympathy from me, repeating, for those who wanted to hear, "Prisons were created for men."

Al-Kudya prison was, at the time, like all prisons in eastern Algeria, suffering all of a sudden from an excess of manhood. This was immediately after the demonstrations of May 8, 1945, when the cities of Constantine and Setif and their suburbs offered the first down payment for the revolution. Some thousands of martyrs fell in one demonstration, and tens of thousands of prisoners crammed the cells. This led the French to make one of their dumbest mistakes, mixing together political prisoners with criminals in the same cell and for months at a time. Sometimes cells had more than twenty men in them.

They made the revolution contagious, passing the message on to the criminals who discovered political consciousness and the chance to redeem their honor by joining the revolution, for the sake of which many were afterward killed in battles. Some of them are still alive, now living blameless lives as important people, the way historical leaders of liberation live, after history has taken care to rewrite the records to establish their state of innocence.

Some of the political prisoners found—in this imperialist stupidity—a chance to get to know others, and enough time to discuss and to think about the country's affairs and to plan the next stage.

Today when I remember that experience, with its intensity and the shock, the period seems longer than it was, even though for me it lasted only six months. I and two others were released because we were young and there were others who meant more to the French. So we were set free.

I went back to Constantine Secondary School. I had missed one year, but found the same syllabus, the same philosophy books, and the same French literature waiting for me. Some of the students were still absent, either prisoners or martyrs. Most of these were students in the senior grades who were expected to graduate among the first batch of real Algerian-French intellectuals and officials.

That was the privilege of those who had been marked by some as traitors, simply because they chose French culture and French secondary schools in a city where nobody could ignore the power of the Arabic language or the impact it had in the hearts and memories of the people.

Is it strange then, that among those who were imprisoned and tortured after those demonstrations there were many who, because of their exposure to western culture, enjoyed an early political awareness and were full of patriotic dreams? There were also those who realized, as the Second World War ended to the benefit of the French and their allies, that France had used Algerians to fight a war that was not their war. They had paid the price of thousands of lives in battles that did not concern them, only to return to their own slavery.

The chance of sharing a cell with Si Tahir was the stuff of legends. The experience of the struggle followed me with all its details for years. It might have had an influence on my fate. There are some men you meet and you feel as if you have come face to face with destiny.

Si Tahir was exceptional in everything. It was as if he had been preparing himself from the beginning to be more than a man. He was a born leader. There was something in him from the descendants of Tariq bin Ziad and the Amir 'Abd al-Qadir and of those who could change history with a single speech.

The French authorities who tortured him and locked him up for three years knew that very well, but they did not know that Si Tahir would exact his revenge years later, becoming the most wanted man after each operation undertaken by the *mujahidin* in eastern Algeria.

Coincidence or fate brought me back after exactly ten years to link me with Si Tahir, this time in armed struggle.

In September 1955, I joined the Front. My school friends were just starting a crucial new school year. I was in my twenty-fifth year starting a new life. I remember how surprised I was at the way Si Tahir welcomed me. He did not ask me about the details of my private life or about my studies. He did not even ask me how I had made up my mind to join the Front. Nor did he ask about the road I took to get to him. He examined me closely before hugging me warmly as if he had been waiting for me there for a whole year.

"You came!" he said.

"I came!" I answered with a strange blend of happiness and sadness.

This is the way Si Tahir was sometimes, abrupt even when he was happy. I, in my sadness, was also abrupt.

Later, he asked me about my family and especially about Mother. I told him that she had died three months before. I thought he understood everything because he said, "God rest her soul. She suffered so much."

Later on I envied that sudden tear in his eye that elevated Mother to the role of martyr. I never saw Si Tahir shed a tear except over the death of one of his men, and my wish for a long time after that was to lie as a corpse in his arms, to think that after my death there would be a tear in his eye.

Is that why he took the place of my whole family? I went on putting all the effort I could into proving my heroism to him as if I wanted him to witness my manliness or my death, to witness that I belonged to nobody else save this country, and that I was leaving behind nothing but the grave of a woman, my mother, and a younger brother for whom Father had already chosen a new mother.

I hurled myself at death all the time as if I were defying it or as if I wanted it to take me instead of my comrades who had left behind children and parents waiting for their return. But every time, I came back and others fell. It was as if death had decided to reject me.

After taking part in more than one successful battle, Si Tahir gradually started to count on me for tough assignments. He would charge me with the most dangerous missions, those that demanded direct encounters with the enemy. Two years later, he promoted me to the rank of officer, able to direct some of those battles myself and to take military decisions.

Only then did the revolution turn me into a man, as if the rank I was carrying had given me an authority that would liberate me from my memory . . . and my childhood. I was happy to achieve this mental tranquility and peace of mind. I did not realize then that my ambitions had nothing to do with what was waiting for me around the corner. I thought that nothing from then on would take me back to my former sadness.

Then came this furious battle fought on the outskirts of Batna that would turn my life upside down.

We had lost six *mujahidin* in that battle, and I was one of the wounded after two bullets penetrated my left arm. Suddenly my life changed when I found myself among the wounded who had to be transferred in a critical state to the Tunisian border for treatment. But the only solution for me was to have my left arm amputated: it was impossible to extract the bullets. There was no room for discussion or hesitation. The only talk was about the safe roads by which we could reach Tunisia, where the rearguard bases of the *mujahidin* were.

Here I lay facing another reality.

Destiny was throwing me out of my only refuge, the life of nightly battles, bringing me out from clandestinity and putting me in another battleground belonging not to life or death, but an arena only of pain. Henceforth, I could be only a spectator of what was happening on the field of battle. It was clear from what Si Tahir said that day that I might never return to the front again.

On that last day, Si Tahir tried to preserve his natural tone. He was bidding me farewell the way he would do every time before a new battle. Only this time he knew he was preparing me to deal with my own battle with destiny.

But, unlike other times, he was brief perhaps because there were no specific instructions given in these cases, or perhaps because he was suffering that day from the biggest human loss so far, ten of his best men among the dead and wounded. He was conscious of the value of each *mujahid*. The revolution was under siege, and each man was needed.

I did not say anything to him that day. I had that mysterious feeling that I had become an orphan again. Two tears stuck in my eyes. I was bleeding as if the pain in my arm was coursing through my whole body. There was a lump in my throat, a lump of pain, of disappointment, a fear of the unknown.

Events were happening fast in front of me, and fate was taking a new turn from one hour to the next. Only Si Tahir's voice giving me his final instructions was reaching me, becoming the only link with the world. In spite of all that, I still remember his last appearance when he came to check on me an hour before I set out. He put a small piece of paper in my pocket and some money. He leaned over as if he was saying goodbye secretly.

"I've put in your pocket the address of my family in Tunis," he said. Then, continuing in a whisper, "If you ever get there, I want you to call on them when you are better and give this money to my wife so she can buy a gift for the little girl. I want you to register her at the town hall if you can. It may be a long time before I can see them."

He came back moments later as if he had forgotten something.

"I chose this name for her," he added in some confusion, pro-nouncing that name for the first time. "Please register her whenever you can and give her a kiss for me, and give my best regards to my wife."

This was the first time I heard your name. I heard it as I was blee-ding, in a faint state between life and death. I clung to that name like a feverish man clinging to a word in a moment of delirium.

Like a messenger clinging to his message, afraid of losing it.

Like a drowning man clinging to the vestiges of a dream.

Between the first letter *alif* of the word *alam*, 'pain,' and the first letter *mim* of the word *mut'a*, 'pain,' was your name, Ahlam, 'dreams,' split in the middle by the letter *ha* of the word *hurqa*, 'burning,' and the *la*, meaning 'no': a warning. How could I have failed to be mindful of your name, born in the midst of those first fires, a small flame in that war? How could I not have been aware of a name that contains within itself its own opposite, beginning with the *Ah* of both pain and pleasure. How could I have failed to be aware of a name that was both singular and plural, like the name of this nation—Algeria, *al-Jaza'ir*, meaning islands. I realized this from the start, that the plural was always created only to be divided.

Between smiles and grief, it happens that I recall these instructions today. *Kiss her for me*, and I laugh at fate. I laugh at myself and at the weirdness of coincidence.

And then I become ashamed at the gravity of his voice, and of a rare veneer of weakness that covered that sentence of his. It was he who always wanted to appear before us as a strong and serious man with no worries save those of his country, and no family but his men.

He acknowledged that he was a frail man, a man of sentiment, who missed things, who might cry, albeit within the limits of timidity and always in secret, because symbols have no right to shed tears of sentimentality.

He never mentioned your mother, for instance. Do you not think he was missing her, that bride whom he enjoyed for only a few stolen months and then left pregnant? But why all this sudden rush? Why did he not wait for a few months to arrange a few days of absence and register your name himself? He waited six months so why could he not wait a few more weeks, and why *me*? What destiny made me go there at that time in your life? Every time I ask myself that question I am puzzled and believe more and more in the workings of Fate.

Despite his responsibilities, Si Tahir could have run away for a day or two to Tunis. Crossing the frontier with its reinforcement of guards, with their patrols and ambushes, would not have put him off. Not even crossing the lines of minefields between Tunisia and Algeria, from the desert to the sea. Later he crossed it three times, in spite of the dozens of *mujahidin* whose bodies were left there.

Was it Si Tahir's sense of discipline and respect for the law that made him so anxious after you were born? Did he realize helplessly that he was now a father and had been for months now, of a baby to whom he had not yet given a name and whose birth he had not registered? Or was he afraid? He, who waited for you for so long, was he afraid of losing you by not rooting your existence and your connection to him on an official paper that would be sealed by an official stamp?

Did he consider your unacknowledged illegal status as bad luck? Did he want to register his dreams at the town hall to ensure that they became real and that fate would not take them away from him? In the end, did he just dream of becoming a father like other men?

I did not know whether deep down Si Tahir would have preferred the newborn to have been a boy. Later on I learned that he had a boy's name ready, ignoring the possibility that it might be a girl. He may have done that because of his instinctive military background, and because of an unconscious patriotic preoccupation for extra manpower. All his plans and discussions started with a sentence I often heard him repeat: "We need more men, chaps."

Was that the reason Si Tahir seemed happy and optimistic about everything at that time? The tough guy had changed. He was becoming softer and had more of a sense of humor in his spare time. Something had changed inside him, making him more like other men, more appreciative of their personal circumstances.

More readily than before, he granted soldiers leave for quick visits to their parents, though he denied himself the same privilege. Late fatherhood changed him and was a welcome symbol for a rosier future.

A little miracle for hope. That was you.

Another morning.

Day breaks, surprising me with its usual din and sudden light forcing its brightness onto me. But I also feel it is taking something away from me.

At that moment I hate that curious and embarrassing aspect of the sun.

I want to write about you in the dark. My story with you is a film, and I fear that light will burn and erase it, because you are a woman who grew up in my innermost self. I can only write about you after I have drawn all the curtains and closed the windows of my room.

Nonetheless, looking through the papers piled up in front of me makes me happy. I filled them up yesterday, during a night dedicated to folly. I might still give them to you, nicely wrapped up in a book as a present.

And I know . . .

I know how much you hate such pretty things and how selfish you are! I also know that nothing concerns you in the end, outside your own boundaries and your own body.

But have some patience, madam.

Just a few more pages before I lay my other memories before you. A few necessary pages before I fill you with arrogance, lust, regret, and madness. In this, books are like meals of love. There must also be an introduction, though I admit this is not my real problem now as much as the problem I have finding a point where I can begin this story.

Where do I start my story with you?

Your story with me has so many unanticipated beginnings, so many tricks of fate.

When I talk about you, I wonder about whom I am talking. Is it a baby who was one day crawling at my feet, or a young woman who turned my life inside out twenty-five years later, or a woman who looks almost like you. I gaze at her on the dust jacket of an elegant book with the title *The Corner of Oblivion* and I wonder, "Is this really you?"

If I have to give you a name what could it be?

Should it be the name your father wanted for you, for which I went to the town hall on his behalf to register? Or should it be the first name you had for six months while waiting for a legal name?

Hayat! Meaning, 'Life!'

This is what I will call you. It is not your name anyway, but only one of your names. Let me then call you by that name since it is the one I have known you by, and the one that only I know, the name that no tongue has ever pronounced nor pen written on the pages of books or magazines or even on official documents.

The name you were once called in order to live, so that God would give you life. The one I killed one day by giving you another official name. It is my right to revive it today, it is mine and nobody before me has ever used it to address you.

Your infant name lingers on my tongue, as if it is you twenty-five years ago. Every time I pronounce it you are once more a baby sitting on my lap, playing with things I had and telling me things I did not understand. Only then can I forgive you and forget all your sins.

Every time I uttered your name I slipped back into the past, and you became as small as a doll. And there you are all of a sudden: my daughter!

Should I read your book to know how that little baby turned into a woman? But I already know that you will not write about your childhood, not even about your first years. You fill memory's gaps only with words, and you get over wounds by lying. Maybe that was the secret of your attachment to me. I know the missing links in your life. I know that father you only saw a few times in your life. I know that city where you used to live but that never inhabited you. The city whose alleys you regarded without passion and on whose memory you trampled. You became attached to me in order to discover what you did not know, and I did the same to forget what I knew. Was it possible for that kind of love to last?

Si Tahir was a third party in our story from the start, even when we did not talk about him. He was among us, present in his absence. So, would I kill him a second time only to be alone with you?

I wish you knew. I wish you knew how hard it was to hold the commandments even after a quarter of a century and how painful was that desire, blocked by all the attendant impossibilities and principles, which in the end made it only more desirable.

The question was there from the start.

How can I banish Si Tahir from my memory, erase his life from my life and give our love a chance? But what would remain then, if I were to put you out of our combined memories and turn you into an ordinary girl?

Your father was an extraordinary comrade, an extraordinary leader. He was exceptional in his life and in his death. How could I forget that?

He was not one of the *mujahidin* who rode the last wave to secure their fortune—the 1962 *mujahidin*, the heroes of the last battles. Nor was he one of the martyrs of the mischance—men who were surprised by death in random shelling or a stray bullet.

He was made from the same clay as Daydush Murad, as al-'Arabi bin Muhaydi and Mustafa bin Buleid: those who would go to death and not wait for death to overtake them.

Can I forget that he was your father, when your constant questioning keeps going back to his name, his prestige, in life or in martyrdom?

The heart that loved you madly was confused when you asked, "Tell me about him."

I will tell you about him, my love. There is nothing easier than talking about martyrs. Their history is already, like their endings, well-known. And their deaths absolve any mistakes they may have made. I will tell you about Si Tahir because only the history of martyrs can be written. Every history that comes afterwards is seized by the living to be written by another generation, a generation that does not know the truth but will figure it out automatically because there are other signs that cannot be mistaken.

Si Tahir died on the eve of independence with nothing in his hand save his weapon, nothing in his pocket save worthless papers, and nothing on his shoulders save the badge of martyrdom. Symbols carry their value in death. Only fakes carry their worth in their dignity, their medals, and what they filled their pockets with, secretly in hidden accounts.

Six hours of siege and concentrated shelling from a whole battalion, only for his killers to publish his photograph in the following day's newspapers as proof of their complete victory over one of the troublemakers whom France had sworn to get.

Was the death of that simple man really a triumph for a major power, a power that was to lose the whole of Algeria two months later? That was how he was killed in the summer of 1960, without even enjoying victory or harvesting its fruit. Here is a man who gave all he had to Algeria, but Algeria never gave him the chance of seeing his son walking at his side, or seeing you maybe a doctor or teacher, as he had dreamt. How much this man loved you: with the madness of becoming a father at forty, with the tenderness of one who concealed himself behind a screen of austerity, with the dreams of one whose dreams had been snatched away, with the pride of the freedom-fighter who realized that with the birth of his first child he would not completely die after that day.

I still remember the few times he came to Tunis to visit you in secret for a day or two. I used to rush to him, anxious to hear the latest news and of developments at the front. At the same time I would make an effort to avoid stealing from him those rare hours for which he was risking his life to spend some time with his small family. I was amazed then to discover in him another man, a man I had not known before, a man with different clothes, with a smile, with different words, seated in a way that made it easier for him to place you on his lap and cuddle you.

He lived every moment to the full, as if he were squeezing every drop of happiness from the brief time he had with you, or stealing from his life a few hours that he already knew were limited and giving you in advance enough tenderness to last a lifetime.

That was the last time I saw him. January 1960. He had come to attend the most important event in his life, meeting for the first time, Nasr, his second child. His secret wish had always been to have a son. For some reason, that day I watched him closely but spoke only a few words to him. I preferred to leave him to his joy, his stolen happiness. When I came back the next day I was told he had left for the front in a hurry, and that he would be back soon for a longer stay. But he never came back.

That was the last benevolent act of fate. Si Tahir was killed only a few months later without seeing his son again. Nasr was then eight months old, and you were nearly five years old. The country in the summer of 1960 was a volcano, dying to be born again every day, and with its death and rebirth there was more than one story, some painful, some amazing.

Some stories came late—like my story that encountered you one day.

A lesser, fateful story changed the course of my life. It could have been destiny, or it could have been insane passion. It was something surprising and came from an unexpected quarter and ignored all the principles and values we upheld. It was something that came at a moment when we do not expect anything anymore. Everything in us is turned upside down.

Was it possible for me, then, after time had severed communication between us, to write two stories at the same time? If I were to do that, I would do it just as I had lived them with and without you, after all those years full of desire, passion, dreams, grudges, jealousy, disappointment, and life-threatening disasters.

You loved to listen to me and flip me over as if you were skimming through an old exercise book. It was absolutely necessary for me to write that book for you, to tell you what I could not say to you, but there was not time.

I would talk to you about all those who loved you for various reasons while you betrayed them for other reasons.

I would tell you even about Ziad. Did you not love talking about him while pretending not to?

There was no need for any more pretense. Each of us had chosen our destiny. I would tell you about this city that was a partner to our love, and later became the cause of our separation, the place where the scene of our beautiful disaster ended.

So about whom, I wonder, are you talking?

Which one of us were you writing about, which one of us did you love, which one of us are you going to kill? To whom were you faithful, you who used to swap one love for another, one memory for another, and one impossible situation for another?

Where do I fit in the list of your lovers and victims? Do I occupy the first place because I am closer to the first edition, or am I the fake copy of Si Tahir, whose death did not lead to a replica of the original? Am I the counterfeit lover or the counterfeit love?

You are like this country, a past master in forging papers and changing them effortlessly.

Montherlant used to say if you are unable to kill those you claim to hate, do not say that you hate them because you would be debasing the word.

Let me admit to you that at this moment I hate you and that I have had to write this book to kill you. Let me borrow *your* weapons.

Maybe you are right. What if novels are really guns loaded with lethal words? What if those words are bullets? But I will not use a gun with a silencer as you do. A man who carries a gun at my age cannot take all these precautions. I want your death to be as noisy as I can make it, because in you I am killing more than one person. Someone has to have the courage to shoot all of them some day.

Therefore you must read this book to the end, and probably after that you will stop writing fantasy novels and read our story all over again.

One surprise after another, one wound after another. Our miserable literature has never known a story as good as this one, and never witnessed a disaster so beautiful.

TWO

THE DAY we met was amazing.

Destiny played more than a supporting role. It was a leading partner from the very start. Was it not destiny that had brought us from other cities, from another age, and another memory to bring us together in a gallery in Paris for the opening party of an art exhibition?

On this day I was the painter and you were, in different ways, a curious visitor.

You were not a girl with a passion for art, and I was not a man with a weakness for younger girls. What was it then that guided your steps there on that day? What made me fix my eyes on your face for so long?

I was a man fascinated by faces because only faces reflect our personality. Only they reveal us. And so I am capable of loving and hating because of a face. In spite of that, I am not so stupid as to say that I fell in love with you at first sight, but I can say that I was in love with you before that meeting.

There was something in you that I already knew, something attracting me to your features that were already dear to me, as if I had once loved a woman who looked like you, or as if I had always been ready to love a woman who looked exactly like you.

Your face was pursuing me among all the faces and your white dress was moving from one painting to another, becoming a color that aroused my curiosity and astonishment. And the color—so fulfilling in itself—filled that gallery crowded with more than one visitor and more than one color.

Can love be born also from a color that we do not necessarily like?

Suddenly the white color approached me and began to speak French to another girl I had not noticed before, probably because when White has long dark hair, it offsets the other colors.

White gazed at one painting.

"*Je préfère l'abstrait*," she said.

"*Moi, je préfère comprendre ce que je vois*," replied Colorless.

Colorless's stupidity did not surprise me in preferring to understand only what she saw. However, I was surprised by White, since it was not in that color's nature to prefer mystery.

Before that day, I was never predisposed to white. It was never my favorite color because I hated absolute colors. But I found myself predisposed towards you without thinking.

I found myself saying to that girl, as if I was taking up a point you had said, "Art is everything that touches us, and not necessarily just everything we understand."

You both looked at me in amazement, and before you said anything, your eyes were exploring, in a quick glance, the empty arm of my jacket and its sleeve slinking shyly in my pocket.

This was my personal documentation, my identification.

You held your hand out to me. "I must congratulate you on this exhibition," you said with a warmth that surprised me. And before your words reached me, my eyes were drawn to the bracelet that adorned the naked wrist you held out to me.

It was a piece of jewelry from Constantine, recognizable from the bright yellow of its gold and the distinctive engraving. It was a bracelet of the kind that, in the old days in eastern Algeria, could be seen on the wrist of every woman and in the trousseau of every bride.

I stretched out my hand to you without completely taking my eyes off it. And for a split second my mind went back a lifetime to my mother's wrist and the same bracelet that never left it.

I was overtaken by a strange feeling. When was the last time such a bracelet had caught my attention?

I could not remember. Probably more than thirty years earlier.

Very politely you pulled back the hand that I was squeezing unconsciously—as if I was clinging onto something.

You smiled at me, and I raised my eyes to you for the first time. Our eyes met in a half-look. You were examining my missing arm, and I was watching the bracelet on your hand. Each of us carried a memory, and we could have recognized each other just that way, but you were a mystery that additional details would only make more mysterious. So I responded to the challenge of discovering you by examining you, absorbed and distracted as if I had known you before and, at the same time, was still getting to know you.

You did not have that same astonishing old beauty, that beauty that would confuse and even alarm a person. You were an ordinary girl but with extraordinary details, with some kind of a secret hidden somewhere in your face.

Maybe on your high forehead and your thick eyebrows that were left in their natural shape, or maybe in your mysterious smile and your lips drawn with a light lipstick, a tacit invitation for a kiss. Or maybe in your wide eyes with their changing honey color.

I knew those details.

I knew them, but how?

Your voice came—in French—and took me out of my thoughts.

"It makes me very happy," you said, "to see an Algerian artist reaching such a pinnacle of excellence and creativity." Then you added shyly, "Actually I don't understand much about painting and I don't often come to exhibitions, but I do appreciate beautiful things. We need something new with a contemporary Algerian flavor like this. I was just saying this to my cousin before you surprised us."

Then the other girl stepped forward to shake hands and introduce herself, as if she wanted to be part of the company and the conversation from which she felt herself excluded. I had been unintentionally disregarding her.

"Miss 'Abd al-Mawla," she said, introducing herself. "I'm delighted to meet you."

On hearing that name I started, and I looked with surprise at the girl shaking my hand warmly and with a touch of arrogance.

I looked intensely at her, as if I was discovering her existence. I then switched to admiring you in the hope of finding something in the features of both of you that would answer my astonishment.

'Abd al-Mawla . . . 'Abd al-Mawla . . .

My mind went back searching for answers to that coincidence. I knew the 'Abd al-Mawla family very well. There were just two brothers. One of them was Si Tahir who had been killed more than twenty years before and left only a boy and a girl. The other was Si Sharif who had got married before independence and probably had many boys and girls by now.

So which of you is the daughter of Si Tahir? The one whose name I had carried clutched to my breast from the front to Tunis, the one whose father's place I took at the town hall to record her name officially in the registry of births. Which one of you is that little baby that I had kissed and spoilt in place of her father?

Which one? . . . You?

In spite of common features, I felt it was you and not her. Or at least that is what I wished as I was having a premature wild dream of a relationship that would bring us together.

I was amazed at this chance, because all of a sudden I had found a pretext for looking at your lovely face.

You were a copy of Si Tahir, but more attractive. You were female, but could you be the baby I last saw in Tunis in 1962 immediately after independence? I called to mind the details of your return to Algeria after Si Sharif contacted me from Constantine. He asked me to sell the house that no longer meant anything to him. Si Tahir had bought that house years before to provide a refuge for his little family. Then France had exiled him from Algeria in the 1950s, after imprisoning him for a number of months on the charge of political insurrection.

How old were you then? Is it possible that you have changed and grown up so much in twenty years?

I gazed at you again as if I was refusing to acknowledge your age and maybe denying my own and recognizing the man I had become since that time, a period that seemed to me that day like prehistory.

What brought you to this city and to this gallery at this precise moment? It was a day I had awaited so long for a reason that had nothing to do with you. A day for which I had made a thousand calculations, none of which included you, a day when I expected all kinds of surprises except that you would be my surprise.

Discovering who you were amazed me all of a sudden, and I was afraid to look you in the eye. Your eyes were contemplating my confusion with astonishment. So I decided to find things out indirectly and continued to talk to the other girl who had just introduced herself to me.

I realized that if I knew who she was, I would be able to solve the mystery and work out which one of you was you. One of you had a name I knew twenty-five years ago and I had only to meet its owner.

"Are you related to Si Sharif 'Abd al-Mawla?" I asked her.

"He is my father," she answered happily, learning of my interest. "He couldn't be here today because a delegation arrived yesterday from Algiers, but he told us a lot about you and made us curious enough to come along and attend this opening instead of him."

The girl's words, spontaneous as they were, gave me answers to two questions. First, she was not you, and, secondly, the reason for Si Sharif's absence. I had noticed this and had wondered why. Was the reason personal or political? Or was he for some reason avoiding being seen with me in public?

Our paths had crossed years before when he entered the arena of the political game and his only objective was to get a front seat. In spite of all that, I could not have ignored the fact that he was in the same city as I was. After all, he had been part of my youth and childhood: part of my memory. For that and for strictly emotional reasons he had been the only Algerian personality I had invited.

I had not met him for a number of years, but news of him had been reaching me since his appointment as attaché at the Algerian Embassy two years earlier. Of course, it was a post like many other overseas jobs that needed broad shoulders.

Si Sharif could have made his way to that job and to any higher one, simply with his history and with the name that Si Tahir had immortalized by his martyrdom. But it seemed that the past was not enough on its own to guarantee the present, and Si Sharif had to sway with all the winds to get there.

All this went through my mind as I was trying to adapt to the shocks and emotions that shook me in the few seconds that started when I wanted to shake hands with a beautiful girl visiting my exhibition. I was in touch with my memories.

Suddenly I go back to that first amazing encounter with you, to all the first details that drew me to you from the beginning. Actually, to the painting in front of which you stood for a long time. This was more than destiny, more than fate, more than a coincidence.

You . . .

Was it you in that gallery looking at my paintings, admiring some and stopping in front of others, returning to the catalogue in your hands to identify the names of the paintings that attracted your attention most?

You . . .

Were you another light shining on every painting you passed by? The lights on the painting looked as if they were focused on you, as though you were the original painting.

So, it is you, stopping in front of a small painting to which nobody else paid any attention, admiring it carefully, coming closer to it and looking for its name in the catalogue. A mysterious shiver went through my body at that moment and the artist's crazy curiosity was aroused within me.

Who are you, you, the one standing before my most beloved painting? I looked at you in confusion as you looked at it and saying something I could not make out to your companion.

What made you stop in front of it? It was not the most beautiful painting in the exhibition. It was simply my first painting, my first exercise in painting, but I had insisted that it be displayed in this most important exhibition of mine because, despite its simplicity, I considered it to be my little miracle.

I had painted it twenty-five years earlier, less than a month after my left arm was amputated. It was not an attempt at creativity, nor was it an attempt to enter history. It was only an attempt to escape from a life of desperation. I painted it like a student painting any view on a paper for his art exam in answer to an exercise set by his teacher.

"Paint what is closest to your soul."

This is the sentence that a Yugoslav doctor said to me, the doctor who had come with some other doctors from communist countries to Tunisia to treat wounded Algerians. He was the one who supervised the amputation of my arm and later monitored the developments of both my mind and my body.

He would ask me about my new interests every time I visited him, observing my chronic state of depression. I was not ill enough for the doctor to keep me in the hospital, and I was not sufficiently recovered to start on a new life. I was living in Tunis as a son of that country and a foreigner at the same time. I was a man rejected both by life and by death. I was a tangled ball of wool. How could that doctor find the end of the thread in order to unravel all my complexities? When he once asked me, trying to ascertain my level of education, if I liked to write or to paint, I held on to his question as if I were clutching at a straw that would save me from drowning. I immediately realized the prescription he was preparing for me.

"I have performed this operation dozens of times on wounded people," he said. "People who have lost an arm or a leg in combat. Although it is common to many people, still its psychological effects differ from one person to another depending on the age of the patient, his job, and his social background, but especially depending on his level of culture. Only an educated person can reassess himself and his relation with the world and the things around him on a daily basis, or if something changes in his life.

"I realized this from my experience in this field. I have been through more than one case of this kind and that's why I think losing your arm has caused you to have an unbalanced relationship with your environment. You've got to build a new bridge with the world through either painting or writing. You have to choose what is closest to your heart and sit down to write without restraint all that is going on in your mind. The qualities of these writings does not matter, nor does the literary standard. The important thing is writing in itself as a way of release and a tool for rehabilitation.

"If you prefer painting, then paint. It can reconcile you to things around you and to the world that has changed in your view because you yourself have changed and are looking at it, touching it with only one hand."

I could have answered him automatically that day, telling him that I loved writing. It was closest to my soul, since I had done nothing all my life except read, something that should naturally lead to writing. I could have answered him that way since my teachers had always forecast a successful future for me in French literature. This was probably why I answered him without thinking or maybe from a position that I discovered later on was really deep inside me, "I prefer to paint."

This brief answer failed to convince him and he asked me if I had painted before.

"No," I said.

"In that case start by painting what is closest to your soul. Paint something that you love the most."

And when he said goodbye to me, he said sardonically with the courtesy of a doctor who knows he can do no more.

"Paint. You might not need me anymore."

That day I hurried back to my room. I wanted to be by myself within the white walls of the extension to the al-Habib Thamir Hospital—until that time, the place I knew best in Tunis.

I started to look at walls in a different way, thinking of all the paintings I could hang on them, all the faces I loved, all the alleys I enjoyed walking through, and all I had left behind.

That night I slept badly. Perhaps I did not sleep at all. The doctor's voice kept coming to me in his broken French, waking me up, saying, "Paint."

I could see him in his white overalls bidding me farewell, squeezing my hand and saying, "Paint."

I shivered and recalled in my sleep the first revealed verse of the Holy Qur'an, when Gabriel appeared to the Prophet Muhammad for the first time and said, "Read."

The Prophet was shaken and asked him, "What should I read?"

"Read in the name of your God, your Creator," replied Gabriel who proceeded to recite to him the first verses of the Holy Qur'an. When he finished, the Prophet went back to his wife. His body was trembling, horrified by what he had heard, and as soon as he saw her, he cried, "Cover me up! Cover me up!"

That night I shivered in a cold fever. This was caused by the tension and anxiety after the meeting with the doctor, which I knew would be the last. But also probably because of a thin blanket, my only cover in that cold winter. That was all my stingy landlord would let me have.

I almost wept as I recalled the woolly blanket of my childhood bed that covered me in the cold Constantine seasons. I almost cried out loud every night when I was away from home.

"Cover me up, Constantine! Cover me up!" I cried.

But I did not say anything that night, either to Constantine or to the wretched landlord. I kept my fever and my cold to myself. It was difficult for a man who had just returned from the front to admit that he was cold, even to himself.

All I did was wait for the sun to rise so I could go and buy with what was left in my pocket some things I needed to do two or three paintings. I then stood like a man obsessed and hurriedly sketched the Rope Bridge at Constantine.

Was that bridge really the thing I loved most? To stand there and draw it unconsciously as if I was there about to cross it as usual. Or was it, I wonder, only the easiest thing to draw?

I do not know.

What I do know was that I painted it time and time again after that, as if every time was the first time, and as if it was what I loved most. Every time.

The painting that I called *Nostalgia* without a great deal of thought is now twenty-five years old. It is a painting made by a young man of twenty-seven years, with all his loneliness, sadness, and dejection. It is me.

And here I am today, with more loneliness, more sadness and dejection, but with the addition of a quarter of a century, during which I have had many personal disappointments and defeats, and just a few exceptional triumphs.

Here I am today, one of the great Algerian painters, probably the greatest of all according to columns written by Western critics whose testimonies I have copied in large letters onto the invitations.

Here I am today, a minor prophet who was inspired one autumn in a miserable small room in Bab Suwaiqa in Tunis.

Here I am, a prophet outside his homeland, as usual. Why

not? As the old saying has it, *A prophet is not without honor save in his own country.*

Here I am, an artistic phenomenon, and how could that not be when the fate of a handicapped man is to be a phenomenon, mighty even in his art.

Here I am, but where is that doctor? The doctor who told me on that occasion to draw, whose prophecy I believed, but whose help I did not need after that day. He was the only person missing in that enormous gallery where no Arabs had displayed their paintings before. Where was Dr. Capotsky? I wanted him to see what I had done with one hand and ask him what he had done with my other hand!

Here is *Nostalgia*, my very first painting, and next to it the date—Tunis, 1957—my signature, written for the first time at the bottom of a painting. It was the same signature I had put under your name and date of birth in the autumn of 1957 when I was registering you at the town hall.

Which one of you is my baby and which one is my love? The question never crossed my mind that day when I watched you standing in front of that painting for the first time.

A painting the same age as yourself, except that officially you are a few days older. The painting is actually a few months younger than you are.

A painting that launched me in two directions, first, when I took up my brush to start on my painting adventures, and then when you stood in front of it and I found myself having an appointment with destiny.

In a diary filled with insignificant appointments and addresses, I circled a day in April 1982, as if I wanted to set it off from the rest of the days. Before that day, I did not find anything worth noting in previous years. My days were like the pages of my diary, filled with scribbles not worth remembering. I would often fill them up rather than leave them blank. The color white always frightened me when it was on a vast sheet of paper.

Eight diaries for eight years, but there was nothing at all surprising in them. They were always one page for one day, with no history but alienation. An alienation I tried to summarize in a fake calculation where the eight years became just eight diaries still stacked in a cupboard one on top of another, registered not under the Muslim or Christian calendar, but the years of my voluntary exile.

I circled the date, as if I am closing up on you, enclosing you inside that circle, surrounding you and chasing the memory of you to get you into my circle of light forever.

I was acting on instinct, as if that date was going to be a turning point in memory, as if my other birth would be at your hands. I was fully aware then that being born at your hand, like trying to get to you, was something that would not be easy. Proof of that was the absence of your phone number or your address on that page which, in the end, bore nothing but the date of our meeting.

Did it make sense to ask for your phone number at this first encounter? But with what justification or excuse could I do that when every pretext looked dubious every time a man asked a beautiful girl for her telephone number?

I felt a great desire to sit with you, to talk and to listen to you, hoping to discover the other side of my memory, but how could I convince you to do that?

How could I explain to you in a few seconds that I knew so much about you?

I am the man you are meeting for the first time, whom you are addressing as a stranger, using the *vous* form. I can only answer in the same way, also using *vous*.

Words were tripping on my tongue that day as if I was talking to you in a language that was foreign to me and a language that was foreign to you. Was it possible to shake your hand after twenty years and to ask you coolly in French, "*Mais, comment allez-vous, mademoiselle?*"

"*Bien, je vous remercie,*" you answered in the same distant manner.

Memory almost burst into tears. Are you the crawling baby I once knew?

My one arm trembles, resisting a great desire to hold you tight and to ask you how you were in that old Constantine accent that I was missing.

How are you, you who have grown up when I was not looking?

How are you, strange visitor, who no longer knows me? A baby inside my memory and wearing on her wrist a bracelet that belonged to my mother.

Let me hold in you all those whom I have loved.

I look at you and recall Si Tahir's features in your smile and in the color of your eyes. How beautiful it is for martyrs to return that way in your looks! How beautiful for my mother to return in the bracelet on your wrist, and for my homeland to return today in your presence! How beautiful it is that you are you!

A man feels like crying every time he comes across beautiful things.

Meeting you by chance has been the most beautiful thing that has ever happened to me, but how can I explain all this to you, when we are standing in a crowd, full of eyes and ears? How can I explain to you that I have missed you without being aware of it, and have been waiting for you without believing it would happen?

It is inevitable that we meet.

I summarize the outcome of our first encounter.

During the fifteen minutes or more of our chat, I did most of the talking. A stupidity I greatly regretted later. I was really trying to detain you with conversation, but forgot to give you a better chance to talk.

I was delighted to discover your passion for art. You were ready to argue with me for a long time over each painting. Everything was subject to debate with you, while all I wanted was to talk about you. Your presence alone roused my appetite for talking.

But since there was not enough time to tell you the chapters of my story that was intertwined with yours, I just said two or three things about my old relationship with your father and your early childhood, and about a painting you said you loved. I also told you that it was your twin sister!

I chose sentences that were terse but intelligent. I left many pauses between my words to make you aware of the weight of a wordless silence. I did not want to rush the only chance I had with you.

I wanted to arouse your curiosity to know me more, to ensure that you would come to me again. When you asked me, "Will you be here throughout the exhibition?" I realized that I had passed the first test with you, by making you think of meeting me again. Then I answered in a steady voice that belied my internal turmoil, "I'll be here most afternoons."

I realized that this may not encourage you to come back, so I added, "I'll probably be here every day because of meetings with journalists and friends."

There was some truth in what I said, but I did not really have to be at the gallery all the time. I was just trying not to make you change your mind for some reason.

Suddenly you spoke to me as if you were an old friend. "I might come back and visit the gallery on Monday," you said. "It's the day I don't have any classes. In fact, I only came today out of curiosity, but I'll be happy to speak more to you."

Your cousin chipped in as if she was apologizing or feeling sorry she could not take part. "Unfortunately it's my busiest day," she said. "I won't be able to be with you, but I might return another day."

She then turned to me. "When does the exhibition end?" she asked.

"On April 25, ten days from now."

"Great," she shouted. "I'll find the opportunity to be back."

What a relief! I had to see you alone just once, then everything would be easier.

I took a last look at you as you shook my hand before leaving.

In your eyes there was an invitation to something . . .

There was some mysterious promise . . .

In them, there was some kind of exquisite drowning, and perhaps a look of advance apology for all the traumas that were going to afflict me later on.

I was aware at that moment—as White turned her back to me: she was wrapped in a black fur scarf and moved away to mingle with the Colorful—I was aware that whether I saw you or not after that day, I was in love with you, and that is the sum of it all.

So you left the gallery as you had entered, a beam of light brightly cutting a path as it passes through, as elegant in departure as in arrival, bringing in your wake more than one rainbow and the stuff that dreams are made of.

What do I know about you?

I kept talking to myself afterwards, persuading myself that you were not just a shooting star. You were not just passing by like a comet that lights up the summer evenings and disappears before astronomers have a chance to track it and give it a name for their encyclopedias of astronomy—the Fleeting Star.

No, you are not running away from me, disappearing easily into the streets and alleyways of Paris. At least I know that you are studying for a higher degree and that you are in your last year. I also know that you have been in Paris for four years, living at your uncle's since he got his appointment two years ago—trivial perhaps, but enough to track you down in one way or another.

The days between Friday and Monday seemed endless. I started the countdown the moment you left the gallery. I began by counting the days that separated Friday and Monday, reaching a total of four. Then I discounted Friday as it was almost over, and Monday when I would be seeing you. The gap seemed shorter and more bearable. Only two days, Saturday and Sunday. Next, I began to count the nights and that seemed to make it longer—three whole nights: Friday, Saturday, and Sunday.

I then asked myself how I would pass the time and I recalled the words of an old poet that I had never believed before, *I count the nights one after the other, and I have now lived for ages counting no nights.*

Is this how love always begins, when we start to adapt our own standards to the ones agreed upon by other people? This period seems to be part of a lifetime that is disconnected from the measurement of time.

I was happy to see Catherine that day coming into the gallery. She was late, as I expected, and also as elegant as I expected. In a light elegant dress that flapped around her like a butterfly. She kissed me on the cheek.

"I'm late," she said. "The traffic's always bad at this time of day."

She lived in one of the southern suburbs of Paris where the traffic doubled at weekends as Parisians used these roads to get to their weekend homes in the country. But this was not the only reason she was late. I knew how much she hated public gatherings and how she did not like to appear with me in public.

She was probably embarrassed lest some of her acquaintances see her with an Arab, ten years older and one arm missing.

She loved to meet me but always at my place or hers, away from the glare of publicity and the eyes of other people. Only then was she gay and relaxed with me, but as soon as we went out for a meal at the restaurant nearby she would change and become awkward, concerned only to get back home.

And so, every time she came over, I used to get enough food for a day or two. I no longer argued or suggested anything to her and that was easier for me. What was the point of an argument?

She spoke louder than usual as she held my arm and looked at the paintings she knew so well. "Bravo, Khalid," she said. "Congratulations! This is all so magnificent, darling."

I was somehow surprised this time, because she was talking as if she wanted other people to know that she was my girlfriend.

What was it that suddenly changed her behavior? Was it the crowd of celebrities from the art world and journalists who attended the opening? Or could it have been that she just realized that, without knowing it, she had been sleeping with a genius for two years and that the missing arm that irritated her now, in other circumstances, took on an artistic dimension that had nothing to do with aesthetic criteria?

I also discovered that during the twenty-five years I had lived with one arm, the only place where I could forget about my handicap was in exhibition galleries, where eyes would focus on my work rather than my missing arm.

It was probably also the same during the first years of independence when soldiers still enjoyed some respect and the war handicapped had some prestige among ordinary folk. They inspired admiration rather than pity. Nobody was expected to offer any explanations or to tell his story.

We carry our memory in the flesh and that required no explanation.

Today, a quarter of a century later, one is ashamed of the empty sleeve hidden timidly in the pocket of a jacket, as though trying to conceal a private memory and apologize for the past to those who have no past. The missing hand disturbs them and takes away their appetite.

This is not our time—the postwar period.

It is the time for elegant suits, smart cars, and big bellies. I am therefore often ashamed of this arm that accompanies me to the Metro, to the restaurant, to the café, to the airplane, and every party to which I go. People expect me to tell them my story every time. All the round eyes that look at you straight ask one question that lips are too shy to ask: "How did it happen?"

You feel distressed when you take the Metro and grab the strap with your one hand. Then you read on a few seats, "Reserved for the war handicapped and pregnant women."

But no . . . these places are not for you. What is left of your pride makes you prefer to stand up, hanging on with one arm. These places are reserved for other combatants. Their war was not your war, and their wounds may well have been inflicted by you.

As for your injuries, they are not recognized here.

It is an awkward contradiction, to live in a country that recognizes your talents but rejects your injuries, to belong to a country that respects your injuries but refuses the person. Which do you choose when the wounds and the man are one? You are the broken memory and this broken body is nothing but a display. I have never asked myself these questions before. It was easier to run away from them and bury myself in work, in constant creativity and an ever-burning internal anxiety.

Something inside me never rested or slept. Something continued to draw as if it wanted to run with me into the gallery where I could live for a few days like a normal human being with two arms, albeit maybe an extraordinary person. One who mocks this world with his one hand, one who can create something with one hand.

Here I am in this gallery, and here are my crazy things hanging on the walls for people to look at, for eyes to examine, and for mouths to explain however they please.

All I can do is smile as some of the diverse comments reach my ears, and I recall a sarcastic remark of Goncourt, "No greater follies can be heard than about a painting in an art gallery."

Catherine's voice could be heard, low this time, as if she was talking to me alone. "Strange, I look at these paintings and I don't recognize them. They look different here."

I had this urge to go on with my previous train of thought. I thought to myself, "Paintings have their moods and emotions too. They are like people. They change as soon as you put them in a gallery under the spotlight."

But instead all I said was, "A painting is a female too. She likes the bright lights and pretties herself up for them. She likes to be spoiled and looked at, adored and put in a place where the veil is withdrawn. She likes to be on display so that eyes can share her and admire her whether they like her or not."

Actually she hates to be ignored.

"It is true what you say," she said, thinking it over, "but where do you get these ideas from? You know, I love listening to you. I don't understand how it is we never find the time to talk when we are together."

Before I could make a convincing reply she laughed. "When will you finally treat me like a painting?" she said, her meaning clear.

I also laughed, surprised at her quick action and her unsatisfied lust.

"Tonight, if you wish," I said.

She took the keys of my flat from me and flew off like a butterfly in her yellow dress. As she approached the door, she said, as if she was suddenly jealous of all the paintings carefully hung on the wall still being gazed at by some visitors, "I'm a bit tired. I'll go on ahead."

Was she really so tired? Or did she suddenly become jealous for me or of me? Or was she already lusting for me when she arrived? I did not as usual try to understand any more than that. I only wanted her to help me forget. I was happy to shorten a day or two with her, waiting for you. Waiting for you! After a month of loneliness and dashing around dealing with the details of the exhibition, I needed a night of love.

An hour later, I followed Catherine. For many reasons I was tired. One reason was my strange meeting with you and all the emotional shocks of the day.

At the flat she said as she opened the door, "It didn't take you very long."

I gave her a cuddle. "I had a painting project in my mind so I came home early," I said. "You know that inspiration doesn't last long."

We laughed.

There was a kind of physical conspiracy that enveloped us with a shared joyfulness, a secret happiness that we practiced without any constraint but with crazy passion.

As I looked at her, sitting on the opposite sofa watching the news and quickly eating a sandwich, I felt that she was the woman who had almost been the love of my life; but now it would not be her. A woman who lives on sandwiches is a woman who suffers from emotional incapacity, excessive selfishness, a woman who cannot give a man the security he needs.

That night I pretended I was not hungry. In fact, I refused to eat, or perhaps I was unable to go along with the sandwich era.

Since meeting Catherine I had become used to not exploring the differences between us. I learned to respect her way of life and not to try to turn her into a copy of myself. I even thought that perhaps I loved her because she was so different from me, sometimes to the point of contradiction. There was nothing more beautiful than meeting our opposite because it was the only thing that enables us to discover ourselves. I admit that I owe Catherine many of my own self-discoveries because in the end, nothing brought that woman and myself together but our lust for each other and a shared love of art.

That was enough for us to be happy together. In time, we became accustomed not to bother each other with searching questions. At first I found it difficult to cope with that emotional style where there is no place for jealousy or possessiveness, but then I found a number of advantages in it, most importantly freedom and a lack of commitment to anyone.

We would meet once a week, but sometimes a few weeks might pass by before we saw each other, but we always met with renewed passion and desire for each other.

"We should not kill our relationship with habit," Catherine used to say. For that reason I made an effort not to get used to her and to be satisfied with being happy whenever she showed up, and not to think about her when she left.

This time, I tried to keep her in for the whole weekend and was happy when she accepted the offer with eagerness. I was actually afraid to be alone with my clock on the wall waiting for Monday.

Even though Catherine stayed until Sunday evening, time still seemed to drag, maybe even more slowly than usual because she was with me. I suddenly wanted her to go quickly, as if I would then be alone with you.

My thoughts revolved around one question.

What would I say to you if I were to be alone with you on Monday? How would I start the conversation, and how would I tell you this strange story, our story?

How would I tempt you to come back again and hear the rest of it?

On Monday morning, in anticipation of our meeting, I put on my best suit. I carefully selected a tie, put on my favorite scent and set off for the gallery at about ten. I had enough time to drink my morning coffee at a nearby café. I knew you would not come before then. Even the gallery did not open before ten.

I was the first to go in that morning. There was a strange melancholy in the air. There were no spotlights lighting up the paintings, no lighting at all. I glanced at the walls where my paintings were waking up one by one, like a woman, with that naked truth of the morning, no makeup or smartening up. A woman was leaning against the wall yawning after a heavy evening. I headed for my little painting, *Nostalgia*, examining it as if I was looking closely at you.

"Good morning, Constantine! How is my suspension bridge, my own sadness suspended for a quarter of a century?" I asked.

The painting answered me with its usual silence, but with a little wink this time. I smiled conspiratorially. The painting and I understood each other. As the Arab proverb has it, "People who are close understand each other with a wink." It was a homemade painting full of pride like its owner, noble like him, and capable of understanding even from half a wink!

I killed time by finishing some tasks that had been postponed, another way of gaining time so I could spend more of it with you later on. But a voice inside me kept chasing me, reminding me that you were coming soon, and preventing me from concentrating on anything.

She will come . . .

She will come . . . the voice kept repeating for an hour or two and more. The whole morning passed. Evening arrived and still you had not come.

I tried to keep myself busy with meetings and with a whole lot of ordinary details. I tried to forget that I was there only to wait for you.

I met one journalist and spoke to another, but my eyes never left the door. I expected to see you with every movement or step. Desperation mounted as time went by.

Suddenly the door opened and in came . . . Si Sharif! I went up to him and shook his hand while trying to hide my surprise. I recalled a French song that said, "I wanted to see your sister but I saw your mother as usual."

"Hello, my friend," he said, embracing me and warmly shaking my hand. "Long time, no see!"

In spite of my disappointment, I must admit I was never happier to shake hands with him than at that time. Before I had the chance to ask him how he was, he presented a mutual friend who was with him.

"Look who I've brought to you," he said.

I cried out as I moved from one surprise to another, "Si Mustafa, welcome! What do I see in front of me? It's so good to see you."

He held me too.

"Why is it," he said with warmth, "that we only get to see you when we come to Paris?"

I wanted to be courteous, so I asked in return how he was. I could tell he was doing well since he was fawning all over Si Sharif, a sign that he was a candidate for some ministerial post, as rumor had it.

"Is it possible, brother," Si Sharif said with a friendly though sincere admonition, "that we both live in the same city and you never think of calling on me? I have been here for two years and you've got my address."

Si Mustafa intervened to add, half in jest albeit with political overtones, "It seems you are boycotting us, or else there must be some other reason for your absence."

"Not at all," I replied in all sincerity. "But it isn't easy for a person haunted by exile to gather his things together just like that and go back. There is some truth in the saying that exile is a bad habit that we adopt. I have acquired more than one bad habit here!"

We laughed and touched on other subjects, fleetingly and courteously.

It was inevitable that they stopped later on in front of one of the paintings as they went round the exhibition. Only then did I learn the reason for Si Mustafa's visit. He wanted to buy one or two of my paintings.

"I would like to keep something from your work, for the sake of old memories," he said. "You remember you started painting when we were together in Tunis. I can still remember your first painting. I was the first person you showed your paintings to. You haven't forgotten that, have you?"

No, I had not forgotten, but how I wished at that moment that I had. I felt embarrassed as he took me back to those days.

Si Mustafa had been a friend of both Si Sharif and myself from the days of liberation. He belonged to a group that was working under the command of Si Tahir and, more than that, was one of the wounded who was transferred with me to Tunis for treatment. He spent three months there in the hospital, returned later to the front and stayed in the Army of Liberation until independence, reaching the rank of colonel.

He was a man of high combat ethics, a man of decency, and I used greatly to respect and admire him. Then his stock declined in my view as it rose in the views of others. In more than one way and in more than one currency. He was like all the others who went before, running after fat positions, having taken his turn in an assiduous sharing of the good things of life.

But I was concerned and particularly saddened in his case, because he had been my comrade in arms for two whole years. We had shared small intimacies that brought us together in the past, and that memory could not fade away in spite of everything.

Probably the incident that had had the greatest impact on me was when, as I was leaving the hospital, the nurse in Tunis handed to me the clothes he had been wearing when he had arrived wounded, covered with blood that had long since dried.

I found in his pocket his identity card, almost unreadable

because of the blood stains. I kept it, intending to give it back to him, but he returned to the front without even knowing I had it. He was heading for a place where he did not need an identity card.

Then in 1973 I came across that card by chance among some old papers of mine. I was sorting out my things preparing to leave. I hesitated for a moment, between retaining it and returning it. I realized that this identity card no longer represented his identity anymore, but I wanted to confront him with memory without making any comment. Perhaps, as I was about to go into exile, I also wanted to end my connection with a document that had accompanied me from one country to another since 1957. It was as if I was severing my relationship with my homeland, putting him and his concerns outside my memory.

Si Mustafa was astonished when I pulled that document out of my pocket and, after sixteen years, presented it to him.

Which of the two of us was more confused?

Once I had parted from it, I suddenly felt as if I had given him something that clung to me, become part of me, maybe my other arm or something else that I had possessed. It was myself. But I was consoled by his joy and the way he embraced me with that fundamental pride that had once brought us together. It was a testimony to memory, with the illusion of the possibility of rousing the other man in him.

Here stood Si Mustafa, years later, examining one of my paintings while I was examining him. The *other* man I knew in him was dead. How could I ever have counted on *him*?

At that moment nothing meant anything to him except owning one of my paintings, and he was probably prepared to pay any price for it. It was well known that he would not take much into calculation in such a case. He was also like some Algerian politicians and arrivistes who liked to possess paintings for reasons that had nothing to do with art, but rather with a mentality of art plunder and an obsession with being part of the elite.

He was probably more generous with me, for just the same reasons that made him that day more repulsive to me. He was changing that lousy identity card for an aquarelle to show off, but was blood the same as a watercolor? Even after a quarter of a century?

It was a relief afterward to get rid of him and of Si Sharif without having to be rude, and without surrendering a principle on account of which I was once hungry. I could not possibly eat rotten meat: some are born with an incurable allergy to all that is polluted.

In fact, I felt impatient and wanted to be free of them as soon as possible, worried that you might come in that second and find them there. I was so nervous and emotionally torn apart. Si Mustafa might be luring me back after all those years. I was apprehensive about your visit, for which I had been waiting for several days. I was exhausted. But you did not show up, then or later.

Why did I later feel so depressed?

My heavy feet took me home, downcast. Those same feet had taken me, as if in flight, to you that morning.

What if I were never to see you again? What if the exhibition came to an end and you did not return? And what if you had mentioned the possibility of coming simply to be polite, and I had taken it as something more?

How can I then catch hold of such a fleeting star?

Only that visiting card Si Sharif had handed to me as he was leaving brought some hope to my soul. For I knew those digits could put me in touch with you, and so I slept, thinking up a pretext for a phone call that might bring us together.

But love seeks no excuses, nor does it look for an appointment. So, the next morning, as soon as I arrived at the gallery and sat down to read my newspaper I saw you come in.

You were heading in my direction. Time stopped as I gazed in admiration at the way you looked. Love that had been ignoring me for a long time opened up and a fantastic story was under way.

THREE

AND SO we met . . .

"Hello!" she said, "Sorry, I'm a day late."

"Not to worry," I replied. "You came a lifetime too early for me."

"How long do you need to forgive me?"

"How long is a lifetime?"

The jasmine was seated before me.

You, the jasmine that bloomed hastily . . . not so much perfume, my love. Not so much.

I did not realize that memory had a beautiful scent, the scent of my homeland.

Bashful and confused, Homeland sat by me.

"Have you got a glass of water?" you asked.

Constantine exploded like a fountain inside me.

Drink out of my memory, my lady, until you quench your thirst. All this nostalgia is for you. Just leave a place at your side. I drank you in slowly, as coffee is drunk in Constantine.

We sat, each with a cup of coffee and a soft drink on the table. We did not have the same thirst but we did have the same desire to talk.

"I didn't turn up yesterday," you said apologetically, "because I heard my uncle arranging with someone over the phone to visit you, and I wanted to avoid meeting them."

I looked at you with the joy of seeing my shooting star, finally, in front of me.

"I was afraid you'd never come." I said, and then added, "Now I'm happy to have waited another day for you. Things we really want always come late."

A heavy silence filled the place, with the awkwardness of the first confession. Had I said more than I should have?

"Do you realize that I know a lot about you?" you said, as if you wanted to break the silence and to arouse my curiosity.

"Such as . . ." I said, both happy and surprised.

"Lots of things that you may have forgotten about yourself," you replied like a teacher who wished to embarrass his student.

A cloud of sorrow crossed my soul, "I don't think I've forgotten anything. In fact, my problem is that I never forget a thing!"

"Oh, my problem is that I always forget," you said, your voice coming so innocently, the full consequences of which I did not grasp at the time. "Can you imagine, yesterday I forgot my Metro ticket. It was in my other purse. A week ago, I left my keys inside my apartment and I had to hang around for two hours before someone came to open the door. It's crazy!"

"Thank you for remembering this rendezvous," I said with irony.

"It's not a date," you said in the same ironic tone. "It's more like a probable date. I must tell you how much I hate certainty in everything. I hate having to confirm things or to be committed to anything. I believe that most beautiful things are born as a probability, and they perhaps stay that way."

"Why did you come then?" I asked.

Your eyes were examining my face, looking for an answer to a sudden question. They were filled with promise and allure.

"Because you may be my probable certainty."

The feminine paradox of that phrase made me laugh. I did not know then that that was part of your character. But your eyes filled me with a male arrogance.

"As far as I'm concerned," I said, "I hate probabilities, and so I can confirm to you that I will be your certainty."

"It's a supposition," you said, insisting femininely on having the last word, "but it's also probable."

We laughed. I was happy as if I was laughing for the first time for many years. I expected other beginnings for us and had prepared many phrases and expressions for this first meeting, but I admit I never expected such a beginning. All I had prepared faded away the moment you arrived, and I, unlike you, was tongue-tied. I was amazed at the way you expressed yourself. You were fun and poetry at the same time. Your presence was spontaneous, simple, and almost childlike, without extinguishing an enduring femininity. You had that extraordinary capacity to break down the age barrier between us in one session. It was as if your youth and vitality had been transmitted to me. I was still under the charm of your behavior when you surprised me by saying, "Actually, I wanted to take a closer look at your paintings. They're not the same as when I share them with all the crowd. When I love something I prefer to be alone with it."

That was the most beautiful compliment a visitor could give to an artist, and the most beautiful thing you could have said to me that day. Before I could enjoy my happiness further or even have the chance to thank you, you added, "Apart from that, I've always wanted to meet you. My grandmother used to tell me about you, whenever she spoke about Father. I think she was very fond of you."

"How is she? I haven't seen her for ages."

"She died four years ago," you said, your face full of sadness. "That was when Mother moved to stay with my brother Nasr in Algiers and I came to Paris to study. Her death changed our lives somehow because she was actually the one who brought us up."

I had to make an effort to forget that bad news. Her death was another blow that day. She had had something of my own mother—her secret perfume, the way she covered her hair with a silk foulard, and hid valuable things in a tiny silver box in her bosom. She had that spontaneous warmth that mothers back home had in abundance, and was ready with words that gave you in one sentence enough tenderness for a lifetime. But it was no time for sorrow. At last you were with me, and it had to be a time only for joy.

"God rest her soul. I was also very fond of her."

Did you want to put an end to the cloud of sorrow that had taken us by surprise? Did you fear that it could sweep us to memories that we were not ready to face? Or did you just want to control the program of your visit by suddenly getting up and saying, "May I have a look at your paintings?"

I accompanied you and took time to explain the circumstances in which I painted some of them.

"You know, I like your style," you suddenly said, looking straight at me. "It's not a compliment, but I think if I ever drew, it would be like this. It seems as if both of us look at things with the same feelings. I have rarely felt like this about a work of Algerian art."

What confused me most now, I wonder? Was it your eyes that turned to another color under the light, looking into mine as if into another one of my paintings? Or was it what you had just said? Perhaps I wanted to believe that it was an emotional declaration rather than an artistic impression, or at least, that is what went through my mind. My sense of hearing stopped at the words "*both of us*," because in French these words take on a unique and emotional musical timbre. It is even the name of a romantic magazine in France, *Nous Deux*.

I hid my perplexity with a silly question, "Do you paint?"

"No, I write."

"What do you write?"

"Stories and novels."

"Stories and novels!"

I repeated the words, unable to believe my ears, and the doubt and surprise in my voice upset you.

"I published my first novel two years ago," you went on.

"What language do you write in?" I asked, moving from one surprising revelation to another.

"Arabic."

"Arabic!"

My tone irritated you, and you probably misunderstood what I meant.

"I could have written in French, but Arabic is the language of my heart. I can only write in Arabic. We write in the language in which we feel."

"But you speak in French."

"It's only a habit."

You continued to examine the paintings.

"The language in which we talk to ourselves is all that matters, and not the one we use to talk to others."

I was amazed, looking at you and trying to sort things out in my head. Could all these coincidences come together in one encounter. My constant convictions and the first dreams I have of my country are embodied in one woman, a woman who happens to be you, the daughter of none other than Si Tahir! I could not have imagined a more amazing encounter in all my life. It must be more than coincidence. It could only be destiny that made our paths cross in that way after a quarter of a century.

"You don't often paint portraits, do you?" you said examining one painting and bringing me back to reality.

"Look, let's only talk Arabic to each other. I'm going to change your habits."

"Will you be able to?" you answered in Arabic.

"I will, because I will change mine too."

"I will obey," you answered with the secret joy of a woman who, I learned later, liked to be given orders. "I like this language and I like your insistence. Just remind me if I happen to forget."

"I won't remind you. You won't forget."

I was making a great mistake there. Turning a language with which I had a passionate relationship into more than a means of affectionate conversation, but also into a partner in our complex story.

"What was that question of yours?" I asked in Arabic.

"I was wondering why there was only one portrait—of this woman's face—in this exhibition. Don't you draw faces?"

"I used to for a while, but then moved to other subjects. Small spaces become confining as an artist grows in age and experience. He moves on, looking for other means of expression."

In actual fact, I do not draw the faces I really love but rather what inspires me about them such as their appearance, the wavy movement of the hair, the sweep of a woman's dress, a piece of her jewelry.

I pause at these details that linger in our memory once we are separated from them, those features that take us to her without betraying her. I do not believe an artist is a photographer who is in pursuit of reality. His camera is hidden inside him, in a place of which he is himself unaware. He draws not with his eyes, but with his memory, his imagination, and with other tools.

You stared at a painting dominated by blond hair, leaving no place for any other color but wicked red lipstick.

"What about this woman?" you asked. "Why is she painted so realistically?"

"She cannot be painted in any other way," I laughed.

"Then why do you call it *Apology*?"

"Because I painted it as an apology to the person whose face it is."

Anger or private jealousy wiped out our recent agreement.

"I hope this apology satisfied her," you said in French. "It's really a pretty painting."

You then added with feminine curiosity, "Of course, it depends on the kind of offence you committed against her."

I did not feel like telling you the story in this, our first, meeting. I was worried that the story might have a negative impact on our relationship or might influence the image you had of me. I tried to avoid your comment that was very subtly obliging me to offer further explanations.

I ignored your stubbornness that made you stand quite a while in front of that painting. I was asking myself if there really was a way to resist the curiosity of a woman who insisted on finding out what she wanted to know.

"Behind this painting," I answered, "there is a rather funny story that reveals some of my complexes and age-old past. It is probably here for that reason."

For the first time, I went on telling the story behind that painting, which I had completed after attending a session at the School of Fine Art where I, along with some other artists, was invited by a colleague to meet some students and amateur painters—as happened from time to time.

The subject that day was to paint a young woman, a nude model. The students were busy painting her body from different angles. I was astonished at their capacity for painting the body of a naked woman with a neutral sexuality and with such an artistic perspective, as if they were doing a landscape or a vase on a table, or a statue in a town square.

It was clear that I was the only confused person in the room. I was looking for the first time at a naked woman under the arc lamps, moving simply and displaying her body with no embarrassment at all in the presence of dozens of eyes.

In an attempt to conceal my embarrassment I started to paint, but my brush carried so many complexes of a man of my generation that it refused to draw the lines of that body, out of prudery or pride—I really do not know. I found myself painting something else, nothing more than the face of that young woman as it appeared from my perspective.

When the session ended, the model put her clothes back on. It seems she was just another student. She went round, as usual, to see how she had inspired each of the students. She was shocked to observe that all I had painted was her face and saw in my painting a kind of humiliation of her femininity.

"Is this all I inspired in you?" she said.

"You have inspired in me much astonishment," I replied politely, "but I belong to a community where electricity has not yet invaded the dungeons of the soul. You are the first woman I have seen in this manner, naked under the lights, even though I am a professional painter. Forgive me. In a way, my brush is so like me. It, too, hates to share a naked woman with others, even in a painting session."

You were listening to me in bewilderment, as if suddenly you were discovering in me another man, not the one your grandmother had told you about. Something fresh appeared in your eyes, some mysterious look that seemed flirtatious. It was probably due to a jealousy of some unknown woman who had at one time stolen the attention of a man who had until that moment not meant much to you.

I was savoring that unexpected awkward situation. I was happy to contemplate that sudden silence imposed by jealousy, and that slight blush that invaded your cheeks and made your eyes expand with repressed anger. So I kept the rest of the story to myself and did not tell you that this incident had taken place two years earlier and that the woman was none other than Catherine. Nor did I tell you that later on I had had to present to her body another apology, an apology that was, it seemed to me, so convincing that from that time she has never been apart from me.

Today I recall with a sense of irony, the turn that our relationship was taking after telling you about that painting. How strange is the world of women! I expected you to fall in love with me and discover the secret relationship that bound you to my first painting, *Nostalgia*, a painting that matched you in age and identity. Instead, you became attached to me because of another painting that belonged to another woman who had crossed my memory by mistake.

Our first rendezvous ended at noon, but I had a feeling that I was going to see you again, perhaps the following day. I felt that we were at the beginning of something and that we were both in a hurry. There was much that we had not yet said. In fact, we did not in the end really say anything at all; we only seduced each other with a potential conversation. We were, naïvely or smartly, both playing the same game, so I was not entirely surprised when you asked as we said goodbye, "Will you be here tomorrow morning?"

"Of course!" I answered with the triumph of someone who has won a bet.

"Then I will come back tomorrow at about the same time. We'll have plenty of time to talk. Time has fled so quickly this morning—we didn't realize it."

I made no comment. I was aware that the only measurement for time was our hearts, because time ran for us only when our hearts ran too, breathless from one joy to another and from one thrill to another. I found in your words a statement of joyfulness, private and shared. I expected more of the same.

"Don't forget to bring your book tomorrow," I said at the door. "I want to read you."

"Do you read Arabic?" you asked, surprised.

"Of course. You'll see for yourself."

"I'll bring it then."

Then you added with a smile, with a lovable touch of feminine teasing, "Since you insist on getting to know me, I'll not deprive you of that pleasure!"

The door closed behind that smile of yours, without giving me the chance to grasp exactly what you meant by that.

You left with the same mystery with which you had entered. I stayed at the glass door that lead out and watched your steps mingle with those of other passersby and disappear for a second time, like a shooting star, leaving me thunderstruck and wondering if we had really met.

So we had met.

Those who say that only mountains do not meet are wrong. And those who build bridges between them so they can shake hands without leaning over or surrendering their pride do not understand anything about the laws of nature. Mountains only meet during major earthquakes but they do not shake hands then. They turn into a common pile of dust.

So we had met.

And the unexpected earthquake took place, because one of us was a volcano and I was the victim.

You are a woman who is an expert at fires, a volcanic mountain that sweeps away everything that comes its way and burns the last thing I hold onto.

From where did you get all this fire? And how could I be so careless with you: you were like the lips of a passionate gypsy.

How could I have been so careless with you, with your simplicity and fake modesty, that I failed to remember an old geography lesson? "Volcanic mountains have no peaks. They are mountains characterized by modest hills." Can *hills* do all this?

Many sayings allude to the depth of still rivers, but we still venture to stride into them. And a small splinter, to which at first we pay no attention, can in the end blind us.

More than one proverb in more than one language advises caution before leaping. But all the warnings will not stop us from committing even greater follies. Because outside folly and insanity, passion has no logic, and the more passionate we are, the greater our folly becomes.

Was it not Bernard Shaw who said you only realize you are in love when you start acting against your own interests?

My folly was that I started treating you like a tourist visiting Sicily for the first time. He races to Mount Etna and prays that the sleeping one-eyed volcano will wake up and drown the island with its fire, in sight of all those tourists with their cameras and their anticipated awe.

The spectator is always subject to some magnetic attraction, something similar to the appeal of the flame. It lures him and he stands there transfixed, trying to remember in his amazement all that he has read about the Day of Judgment, but with the folly of a passionate lover forgets that at the moment he is witnessing his own final hour.

The devastation around me today bears witness that I have loved you to death and have desired you infernally. I believed Jacques Brel when he said that there are scorched fields that provide you with more wheat than April can at its peak. So I placed all my bets on the spring of this lifetime and on the April of these desperate years.

You were a volcano that swept away all that was around me. Was it not insane to compete with the insanity of tourists and lovers, and all those who loved you before me? To move my home to the foot of your mountain, placing my memory at the foot of your volcano and sitting in the middle of fires, in order to paint you?

Was it not insane to refuse to heed the forecast of natural disasters and convince myself that I knew more about you than they all did? I completely forgot at the time that logic ended when love started. All that I knew about you had nothing to do with either logic or knowledge.

Mountains have met, then. We also have met.

A quarter of a century of blank pages, unfilled by you.

A quarter of a century of days that all seemed the same as I waited for you.

A quarter of a century for the first meeting between a man who was I and a baby playing on my lap who was you.

A quarter of a century for a kiss that I placed on your child's cheek, in the place of a father who had not seen you.

I am the handicapped one who lost his arm in forgotten battles, and his heart in closed cities.

I never expected you to be the battle where I would leave my body, the city where I would spend my memory, and the blank canvas before which my brush would surrender, remaining unsullied, as you in your colors carried within you all manner of paradoxes.

How did all that happen? I do not know anymore.

Time raced us from one appointment to another, and love took us from one sob to another, and I was becoming obsessed by you.

Loving you was my destiny, and may be my end, but can any force stand up to destiny?

We would meet almost every day in that same gallery and at different times of the day. What happy chance made my exhibition take place during the spring vacation when you had plenty of time to visit me every day, when you were free from attending any university courses? You had only to resort to some ruse, mostly with your cousin, so she did not come along with you.

I used to be anxious every time we parted, and repeat automatically, "See you tomorrow," wondering whether we were committing the utmost folly in becoming more attached to each other day by day. Maybe because I was older than you I felt responsible for that odd emotional situation and our quick and frightening slide toward love.

I tried in vain to stand up against that torrent that was carrying me away to you with all the force of love at fifty, with the madness of love at fifty, and with the appetite of a man who had not known what love was before that day. Your love was sweeping me along with youth and pride, taking me down to the point of illogic where, in the end, passion could almost touch madness or even death.

I used to feel, as I drifted down with you to those deep labyrinths inside me, those secret corridors of love and lust, those deep and distant parts where no woman had ever gone before, that I was gradually lowering my standards as well. I was unintentionally denying those ideals in which I had immoderately believed and had, all my life, refused to haggle over. Such values were for me something that could not be compartmentalized. In my book, there was no difference between political values and other values, and I became aware that, with you, I was beginning to deny one for the sake of convincing you of the other.

I often asked myself then if I was betraying the past by being alone with you, in an almost innocent meeting in a gallery full of paintings and memories.

Was I betraying the one man I loved more than any other man I knew? A man most honorable and generous, courageous and loyal?

Was I betraying Si Tahir, my leader and comrade and lifetime friend? Was I bringing disgrace to his memory, and stealing from him the only flower of his life, even his last will and testament?

Was it possible to do all this in the name of the past and while I was telling you of the past?

But was I really stealing anything from you, during these meetings where I could speak with you about him for a long time?

No, it did not happen. The prestige of his name was always present in my mind, binding me to you and detaching me from you at the same time. It was both a bridge and a barrier. My only pleasure at the time was to place in your hands the key to my memory and to open up to you the yellowing notebooks of the past, reading them in your presence, page by page, as if I was discovering them with you by listening to my own voice reading them for the first time.

We were silently discovering that we complemented each other in an alarming way. I was the past that you did not know, and you were the present that had no memory and onto which I was trying to unload the baggage that had weighed on my shoulders.

You were as empty as a sponge, and I was as deep and heavy as an ocean. You went on getting filled by me more and more every day.

I was unaware at the time that my own emptiness was being filled by you too, and that every time I offered you something from the past, I was making you a copy of myself.

By then, we had already been carrying a shared memory, shared roads and alleys, shared joys and griefs too. Both of us were victims of the war. Destiny had placed us in its pitiless quern, and we emerged, each carrying a different wound.

My wound was obvious and yours was hidden deep. They amputated my arm, and they amputated your childhood. They ripped off a limb of my body and snatched a father from your arms. We were the remnants of a war: two broken statues under elegant clothes.

I remember the day you asked me for the first time to tell you about your father, and you admitted with some nervousness that you visited me from the beginning with that intention. There was intense sadness in your voice and some bitterness that I was discovering in you for the first time.

"What is it to me," you asked, "to see a big street carrying Father's name, to carry the burden of his name when ordinary people, strangers, repeat it over and over in my presence every day? What is it to me if I don't know any more about him than they do, and if there isn't a single person among them who can really tell me something about him?"

"Didn't your uncle tell you anything about him?" I asked in surprise.

"My uncle doesn't have time for anything like that, and if he happens to mention him in front of me, his words seem more like a speech, as though he was laying out his brother's remarkable deeds before strangers. His words are not directed to me. He does not talk about a man who was, after all, my father.

"What I want to know about Father isn't a collection of ready-made slogans employed to glorify heroes and martyrs, words we use foreverybody on every occasion. As if death has suddenly made all martyrs equal, and that they have all become copies of one original.

"For me it's important to know something about his ideas, some details about his life, his mistakes, his qualities, his private ambitions, his private setbacks. I don't want to be the daughter of a legend, because legends are a Greek creation. I want to be the daughter of an ordinary man, with strengths and weaknesses, triumphs and defeats. Because I believe that in the life of every man, there are disappointments and setbacks that are the springboard for further triumph."

A heavy silence fell over us.

I was watching you and digging deep into myself. As I searched for the line separating my triumphs and setbacks, I wasn't a prophet at that moment. Nor were you a Greek goddess. We were just two ordinary statues with defaced limbs, trying to put it together with words, and I stood there listening to you disclosing your own destruction.

"I sometimes feel," you said, "like the daughter of a number, one number among millions of other numbers. Some could be bigger or smaller, or written in a different script. Smaller or bigger, all of them are numbers with their own tragedy.

"The fact that Father left me a big name," you went on, "doesn't mean a thing to me, because I've inherited misery with the weight of that name. It also left my brother with a permanent fear of failure. He lives haunted and obsessed by failure, as the only son of al-Tahir 'Abd al-Mawla. He doesn't have the right to slip back, either in his studies or in his life. Such symbols are not supposed to break down. As a result he gave up his university studies after discovering that there was no point in piling up qualifications when others were piling up millions. He may have been right: qualifications are the last thing that can get you a job.

"He saw his colleagues graduating before him and moving straight to unemployment or becoming minor officials with limited salaries and limited dreams. He decided to go into business. Even though I agree with him, I am saddened to see my brother turning into a small trader, running a little shop with a truck that, as the son of a martyr, he was privileged to get from Algiers. I don't think Father would have expected that kind of future for him."

I interrupted, trying to make light of your complaints, "He did not expect that kind of future for you either. You went beyond his dreams and inherited all his ambitions and principles. He was a man who used to see education and knowledge as a kind of religion. He adored the Arabic language. His dream was to see Algeria freed from the superstition and worn-out traditions that had oppressed and destroyed his generation. You don't realize the exceptional luck you have today, in a country that gives you the chance to be an educated woman, who can study, work and even write."

"I might owe my culture and education to Algeria," you replied with some irony, "but becoming a writer is another issue. It's not a gift from anybody. We write to recover what we've already lost or was filched from us. I'd have preferred an ordinary childhood and an ordinary life and to have had a father and a family like anybody else, instead of a group of books here and a bundle of notepads there. But Father became the property of the whole of Algeria. Only writing became my property, and nobody's going to take that away from me!"

I was surprised at what you said, and filled with conflicting emotions. I felt sad but not sorry for you. An intelligent woman does not evoke pity. She always earns admiration, even in grief. I admired you in your proud injuries and in your provocative style of challenging the nation. You looked like me, as I drew with one hand, as if it were compensating for the other. I would prefer to have been an ordinary man with two hands doing ordinary, everyday things and not to have turned into a genius with one arm that could only carry around drawings and paintings.

My dream was not to become a genius or a prophet, nor a defiant and rejected artist. I did not struggle for that. My dream was to have a wife and children, but destiny had other plans for me, so I was a father to other children and a husband to exile and the brush. My dreams too had been amputated.

"No one will take writing away from you," I said. "What is deep inside us is ours, and nothing can touch it."

"But inside me," you said, "is nothing but empty spaces, filled with press cuttings and silly books that have nothing to do with me."

Then you added as if you were confiding a secret to me, "Do you know why I loved my grandmother more than anybody else, even more than Mother? She was the only person who would find time to tell me about everything. She would return automatically to the past as if she refused to leave it. She dressed in the past, ate in the past, and enjoyed only the songs of the past.

"She used to dream of the past, at a time when others dreamed of the future. That was why she often spoke to me about Father without my asking. He had been the most beautiful thing of her transient feminine past. She never wearied of talking about him. It was as if she was bringing him back to us with words. She did that with the remorse of a mother who refused to forget that she had lost her firstborn son forever.

"But she never used to tell me any more about him than what a mother would say about her son. He was the most beautiful and the most wonderful son, the good boy who never hurt her feelings with a word.

"On Independence Day, my grandmother cried as she had never cried before. I asked her, 'Granny, why do you cry when Algeria is independent?' She said, 'I always waited for Independence Day so Tahir could come back to me. Today, I realize I'm no longer waiting for anything.'

"The day Father died, Granny did not go about trilling cries of joy as we read in the fictions about the revolution I read later on. Instead she stood in the middle of the house weeping loudly and shaking, bareheaded, repeating in a primitive grief, 'Oh sorrow! Oh, blackness and pain! Oh, my dear Tahir, why have you abandoned me?'

"My mother was crying silently, trying to calm her down. I was watching both of them, crying myself without really understanding that I was crying over a man I had seen only a few times, a man who was my father."

Why was it that every time you mentioned Umm al-Zahra, the name infused me with strange emotions that had been warm and beautiful before, but now became suddenly so painful that I was reduced to tears?

I still remember the face of that dear old woman who loved me as much as I loved her. I had spent the years of my boyhood running about, between her house and ours. That woman had only one way of loving. I discovered later that it was a common way among all our mothers at home. She loved through food. She would prepare your favorite meal and pursue you with food, loading you with sweets and bread and cakes that she had just made.

She belonged to a generation of women who devoted their

lives to the kitchen. They lived for feasts and weddings as if they were love-feasts where they would give to the world, among other things, their excessive femininity, their tenderness, and their secret yearning that found no other form of expression but in providing food for others.

In reality, they used to feed more than one table every day, and more than one terrace full of people. They would go to sleep every night without anyone paying attention to their own hunger, a hunger that went back generations. I realized this only recently when, perhaps out of loyalty to them, I found myself unable to love a woman who lived on fast food and had no zest for food except for what concerned her own body.

In flight from these memories, like my flight from the scars of my distant childhood, I asked you about your mother.

"You've never told me about her and how she spent her life after Si Tahir's death."

"She rarely spoke about him," you replied. "Maybe deep in her heart she blamed those who married her off to him, for they were celebrating her marriage to a martyr, not to a husband.

"She knew in advance of his political activities and knew he would be joining the front straight after their marriage, entering that secret life of his. She knew he could only visit her secretly from time to time, and she knew that he would probably only return to her as a corpse, so what did the marriage have in it for her? But it had to be gone through: there was a deal in the air. Her parents were proud to have a big name like Si Tahir 'Abd al-Mawla as a son-in-law, and it made no difference to them if she would be his second wife or even his future widow. Grandmother may have known that he was born to be a martyr, so she went round all the tombs of the saints, praying and weeping, and begging them to endow her son with offspring. She had done the same when she was pregnant with him, and asked that the baby be a boy."

"How come you know all these stories?" I asked.

"She told me herself, and Mother told me things too. Can you imagine that when Grandmother was pregnant with Father, she never left the shrine of Sidi Muhammad al-Ghurab in Constantine? She almost gave birth to him there—that's why she called him Muhammad al-Tahir in order to obtain his blessings. Later on I learned that half the men in the city were given those names, and that people attached great importance to these names. Most boys were named after prophets and saints. She almost called me 'Lady' after the Lady Manubia who she used to visit in Tunis, carrying with her different kinds of candles, carpets, and prayers. When she got there, she would go from the shrine of Lady Manubia to that of Sidi 'Umar al-Fayyash. You may have heard of him. He was a holy man who used to live completely naked. The Tunisian authorities used to tie one of his legs to an iron chain to prevent him going around the place naked. And so he lived in chains, moving around and screaming in a room that was empty except for women who raced to visit him, some seeking his blessings and others just to gaze at his manhood that was displayed for all to see, exposed to the curiosity of women in veils who assumed a modesty that was phony."

"Did you visit him yourself?" I laughed.

"Sure, I visited him afterward with each of them separately. I also visited the Lady Manubia, after whom I was nearly named, but Mother saved me from that disaster and decided to call me 'Hayat' instead. She gave me that name while she waited for Father to come home and make the final decision."

My heart stopped a beat on hearing that name and my memory raced backwards. My tongue tripped when I pronounced that name after exactly a quarter of a century. My next question surprised you.

"Would it make you happy if I called you Hayat?"

"Why would you do that?" you replied in surprise. "Don't you like my real name? Isn't it nicer?"

"Yes, it is nicer. But I was surprised how a name like that occurred to your father. I had heard it years ago, and I knew of nothing in his lifetime that would inspire him to give you such a beautiful name. But in spite of all that, I'd like to call you Hayat, because I may be the only person apart from your mother who knows about that name today. I want it to be a secret between us, to remind you of our unique relationship and that you are also, in a way, my baby."

You laughed. "You know, you've never emerged from that

revolutionary generation," you said. "That's why you have this urge to give me a name that goes back to the time of struggle, to a time before you loved me, as if you are enrolling me as an undercover agent. I wonder what mission you have in mind for me."

I laughed. You surprised me with your detached attitude. Were you getting to know me to that extent?

"Listen, you apprentice revolutionary," I said. "You've got to learn that there must be more than one test before you're sent on a suicide mission. I'll have to start by examining your special abilities so I can find out how prepared you are!"

Only then did I feel that it was the right time to tell you the story of my last day at the front, the day Si Tahir pronounced your name before me for the first time. He was bidding me farewell when he charged me with the task of registering you on his behalf if I managed to get to Tunis alive.

As I crossed the frontier between Algeria and Tunisia with a feverish body and a bleeding arm, I kept repeating your name to myself. I was having hallucinations. Your name became, amidst all my struggles and wounds, the title of the last mission Si Tahir assigned to me. I wanted to fulfill his last request successfully and give you a legal and official name that had nothing to do with legends and saints.

I remember the day I stood for the first time knocking at your door in al-Tawfiq Street in Tunis. I recall that visit with all its detail, as if my memory had foreseen what was destined for us, as if there was an empty space in my memory for it.

I waited in front of the green metal door on that September day. Then Umm al-Zahra opened the door after a wait that seemed very long. I still remember the surprise in her eyes, as if she was expecting someone else.

She stood there, examining my sad gray coat and my slim pale face. Her eyes paused at my one arm, clutching a box of pastries, while the other empty arm of my coat hid timidly for the first time inside the pocket of my coat.

Her eyes were filled with tears even before I uttered a word, and she went on crying without thinking of inviting me in. I bent forward to kiss her for all the years of absence during which I had not seen her, for all the love that her son had sent to her with me, and all the love I still had for my own mother, whom I had not seen for two and a half years, after a separation which I had not yet got used to.

"How are you, Umm al-Zahra?" I said.

Her cry became even louder. She held me tight.

"How are you, my son?" she asked in return.

Was she crying because of happiness at seeing me, or because she was sorry for me, seeing my amputated arm for the first time? Was she crying because she had expected to see her own son and was seeing me instead? Or was it just because someone had finally knocked at her door, bringing happiness and some news to a house where no man had entered for several months?

"Thank God you are safe. Come in, my son. Come in," she finally said, opening the door wide and wiping away her tears. Then she said louder as she walked ahead of me, "Come in, come on in!" as a signal to your mother who ran off, on hearing these words. All I saw of her was the flap of her dress as she hurried away and disappeared behind a door that closed quickly behind her.

I loved that house, with the vine branches climbing the walls of the tiny garden and stretching out to drop like black chandeliers over the center of the terrace.

The jasmine tree threw itself against the wall like a curious woman, constrained by the outside walls of the enclosure. It stretched, checking to see what was going on outside, and enticing passersby to pick its flowers or gather up what had fallen onto the ground. I also loved the smell of food that brought an inspiring serenity and a mysterious warmth that made one want to linger.

Umm al-Zahra went ahead to a room overlooking the middle of the terrace. "Sit down, my son. Sit down," she repeated, taking the white pastry box and putting it on a round copper tray that stood on a wooden table.

I had barely sat on that woolen blanket on the floor when you appeared at the other end of the room, as tiny as a doll. You quickly crawled to the white box, trying to pull it to the ground and open it. Before I could interfere, Umm al-Zahra had removed it and put it somewhere else saying, "Bless you, my son. You didn't have to bother yourself, Khalid. Seeing your face is enough for us."

Then she yelled at you when she saw you heading towards the wooden stool that stood above a tin container of burning coal, where your little clothes were hung to dry. You tottered towards me in two hesitating steps. Your tiny hands reached out to me appealingly. I realized the awfulness of what had happened to me only at that moment, when I stretched out my one arm to try to grab you. I was unable to catch you with my single shaky arm, to put you on my lap and play with you, without you slipping away from me.

Is it not strange that my first encounter with you should also have been my first test too? My first complex and even my first humiliation was at your hands. It was the most difficult experience I had gone through since I had become one-armed.

Umm al-Zahra came back with the coffee tray and a plate of sweets. "Tell me, Khalid, my son, God bless you, how is al-Tahir?"

She said these words even before she had sat down. There was a hint of tears in her question, and in her throat, the choke that feared the answer. I tried to comfort her, so I told her that I was under his command and that he was in the frontier region at that time. I also told her that he was in good health, but unable to come home these days because of the difficulty of the situation and the many heavy responsibilities on his shoulders.

I did not tell her that the battles were getting more and more difficult and that the enemy had decided to surround all the mountain districts and burn all the forests to make it easier for their planes to monitor our movements. I did not tell her that Mustafa bin Buleid had been captured along with a group of senior commanders and *mujahidin.* I did not tell her that thirty of them had been sentenced to death and that I had come to Tunis for treatment with a bunch of wounded and limbless soldiers, two of whom had died on the way.

My appearance told her more than a woman of her age could

handle. So I tried to change the subject. I gave her the small amount of cash that Si Tahir had sent along and asked her–as he had requested–to buy you a gift. When I made a promise to come back soon and register your birth with the name he had chosen for you, Umm al-Zahra repeated it with difficulty and astonishment, but made no comment. To her, whatever Si Tahir said, was sacrosanct.

It was as if you suddenly noticed that the conversation had something to do with you. You climbed on to my knees to sit on my lap with a childlike spontaneity. I could not keep myself from holding you with my one hand.

I held you close to me, as if I was holding the dream for which I had lost my other arm. It was as if I was afraid it would run away from me, and along with it the dreams of a man who had not had the joy of holding you close to him.

I was kissing you, in the midst of my tears, my happiness, my pain, and all sorts of conflicting emotions, on behalf of Si Tahir and other comrades who, since they joined the front, had not seen their children. Also on behalf of those who died while dreaming of a simple moment such as this, when they would hold not rifles, but children who had been born and raised where their eyes would never see them.

I forgot, then, to kiss you for myself.

To weep in your presence, for myself.

On behalf of the man who would be totally transformed at your hands a quarter of a century later.

It slipped my mind to write my name next to yours to ask for your memory and your future, to stop you getting older and to put a break on the years that were carrying me at speed to my twenty-seventh year, while you were just entering your seventh month!

I forgot to keep you on my lap forever playing and fondling things and saying words neither you nor I understood.

Not once did you interrupt me as I told you this story, intentionally brief, leaving the details to myself. Your life stopped on that date, September 15, 1957, when I stood there inscribing your name onto an official document. You asked no questions and offered not a single word in comment on a story that nobody had ever told you before. Perhaps because no one found in it anything worth telling.

You were listening to me in a frightening silence, astonished, with arrogant clouds hiding your eyes from me.

For the first time you were crying in my presence. It was the same you, the one who had laughed so much with me in that same place.

Did we realize that all of a sudden, when we laughed to sidestep a painful truth, we were avoiding something we had been simultaneously looking for and putting off?

I looked at you through a mist of tears. I wanted at that moment to hold you with my one arm like I had never held a woman before, like I had never had a dream before. But I did not. We both stayed fixed as we were, facing each other, two haughty mountains bound by an invisible bridge of sentiment and love, and clouds that carried no rain.

The word bridge caught my attention and I remembered that painting. It was as if I had remembered the most important chapter of the story I was telling you—and perhaps telling myself as well—hoping to believe its strangeness. I stood up and said, "Come, I want to show you something."

You followed me without a question.

You stood in front of that painting, waiting, with a look of anticipation in your eyes, for what I was about to tell you.

"You know," I said, "when I saw you standing before this painting on that first day, a cold thrill went through my body. I felt a kind of affinity between you and this painting. I knew nothing about it before, but I was sure of that affinity. That is why I came to greet you, hoping to discover how right or wrong my senses were."

"Were your feelings right?" you asked with surprise.

"Haven't you noticed the date on the painting?"

"No, I haven't," she said and bent down to look at the lower corner.

"It's very near the day of your birth. You are two weeks older than this painting. It's your twin sister if you like."

"Strange! All this is very strange."

You gazed at the painting as if you were searching for yourself in it.

"Isn't this the Rope Bridge?" you asked.

"It's more than just a bridge. It's Constantine, and this is the other affinity that links you to this painting. The day you came into this gallery, you brought Constantine along. Constantine came along with your looks, with your walk, in your accent, and in the bracelet you were wearing."

"Ah, you mean that *miqias* bracelet?" you said after a few seconds. "Well, it happens I wear it for some occasions, but it's heavy and hurts my wrist."

"Memory is always heavy. My mother wore one for years on end and never complained of its weight. She had it on her wrist when she died. It's just a habit."

I was not criticizing you. There was remorse in my voice, but I did not say anything. You belonged to a generation that found everything heavy to carry, and so swapped the old Arab dresses for modern ones made of just one or two pieces of cloth.

Your generation also cut down on old jewelry to wear lighter pieces that could be put on and taken off quickly. They summarized all history and memory in a couple of pages in the school textbooks, and only one or two names in Arabic poetry. I do not blame you, for we belong to nations that only wear their memory on occasions, from one news bulletin to the next. They quickly take it off as soon as the lights go out and as soon as the photographers withdraw, just like a woman who takes off her jewelry.

"I'll wear the bracelet for you if you wish," you said as if you were apologizing for an unintended mistake. "Would that make you happy?"

Your words surprised me. The situation somehow seemed sad. Even though it was spontaneous, it was probably funny in a sad way.

I felt as if I was offering you fatherhood, and that you were offering motherhood. You were the girl who could have been my daughter and, without realizing it, you became my mother!

At that moment, I could have answered you with one word that summed up all the contradictions of our situation. A word that summed up all the excessive and intense feelings I had for you, but instead I said something else.

"It makes me very happy, and it makes me even happier that you wear it for yourself. You must realize that you will not understand anything of the past you are looking for, nor of the memory of the father you never knew, unless you understand the traditions of Constantine and adhere to them. We don't discover our memory by looking at a picture postcard or even a painting like this one."

We only discover it when we touch it, when we wear it and live by it, like this bracelet for example, with which my relationship has suddenly become emotional. It was a symbol of motherhood, without my realizing it; in my memory, I only discovered this when I saw you wearing it, and how could it be that you would not wear it? All those feelings that this bracelet aroused inside me have been dormant in the realms of oblivion. Do you understand now that memory too needs to be awakened?

Oh, how stupid I was, unaware that I was rousing within me a monster that had been sleeping for years. I was turning you, in the fever of my insanity, into a city. You were listening to me like a pupil, absorbing my words as though I had put you into a trance, willing to obey orders from a master and to follow his wishes.

That day I also discovered how I could tame you and control your burning fire. In my heart, I decided to make you my fine city, full of pride, ancient and beautiful, where no pirate or dwarf was admitted.

I condemned you to be my Constantine, and sentenced myself to insanity.

We spent much more time together that day, and we parted psychologically shaken and charged with extreme emotions after four hours of nonstop conversation. We said much, sometimes with tears and at other times with frightening silence. I was happy perhaps because I saw you crying for the first time. I despise people who have no tears; they are either giants or hypocrites and either way they do not deserve respect.

You were the woman with whom I wanted to laugh and cry and that was the most magnificent thing I had discovered that day. I remembered our first meeting. On that day I remembered a cynical French saying that the shortest way to a woman's heart is to make her laugh. Seeing you laugh I thought, "I've won her over effortlessly."

Today I realize the folly of that saying. It encourages quick returns and a one-night stand, though the woman who laughed at the beginning may be crying in the end.

I did not win you with a laugh. But I did on the day when you cried at my side, listening to your story that was mine as well. Or maybe when one of my paintings obviously impressed you, and you all but planted a kiss on my cheek, or when you almost held me tenderly in a moment of sudden passion. Almost.

We departed as always, shaking hands, fearing that a quick peck on the cheek would stir sleeping volcanoes to life.

We understood each other in silence. Your presence aroused my masculinity, your perfume provoked me and drove me crazy, your eyes disarmed me until they shed tears of sadness. And your voice! Oh, how I loved it! Where did it come from? And what language was yours, what music!

I was constantly amazed, completely enthralled. Was it possible that you could have been my daughter, when logic would not let you be anything else?

I resisted you by inventing imaginary obstacles between us, over which you would leap at a glance in one bound, because you were a mare made for challenges and triumphs. Your eyes wandered all over me, pausing here and there and finally resting at my eyes or at my shirt button that was as usual open.

"There is something of Zorba in you," you once said, "his build, his color, his hair of ordered chaos, but you could be a bit more handsome."

"You may also add," I answered, "the same age and the same frenzy and extremism. Deep down I have some of his loneliness as well, his sorrow, and the triumphs that always turn into setbacks."

"You know a lot about him," you said with surprise. "Do you love him?"

"Maybe."

"You know, Zorba is the man who has impressed me most in my life?"

I was taken aback by your confession and thought it could be due to one of two things: either you did not know many men, or you had not read many books.

But before I could reply you continued enthusiastically, "I love his unexpected reactions and his madness. His strange relationship with that woman and his philosophy about love and marriage, about war and worship, all these have impressed me. I like him most when he drives his own emotions to reach their opposite.

"He has a strange way," you went on, "of curing himself of things that enslave him. Like the story of cherries. At first he didn't like being fond of them, so he decided to eat them until he threw up. After that, cherries were like any other food to him."

"I don't remember that story."

"Do you remember that dance of his, in the middle of what he calls 'the beautiful destruction'? It's amazing when a man reaches the point of dancing because of disappointment and pain. He stood out even in his defeats. Setbacks are not in everybody's reach. You've got to have extraordinary dreams and extraordinary joy and ambitions to get to the opposite emotions in this way."

I was enjoying listening to you, and instead of detecting in that 'beautiful destruction' that you described to me with such enthusiasm something that might have alarmed me as some sadistic tendency in you, I got carried away by the beauty of the thought.

"True and beautiful . . . I didn't know you loved Zorba so much!" I said without a lot of thought.

"Let me confess to you," you said with a laugh, "this story confused me so much when I first read it. I was thrilled but sad at the same time. I wanted to love a man like him or write a novel like that. But since it wasn't possible, the story will haunt me forever, until I find some way to exorcize it."

"I'm pleased you find something in common between him and me. You can make both wishes come true," I said sarcastically.

You looked at me with an adorable impishness and said, "With you, I only want to make one of the wishes come true."

You did not give me the chance to ask which one.

"I won't write anything about you," you said.

"Oh, yes . . .why?"

"Because I don't want to kill you. I'm happy to have you! We only write novels to kill those who have become a burden to us. We write to finish them off!"

We argued at length that day about your *criminal* theory of literature.

"May I see your first novel, or first crime?" I asked as we parted.

"Of course, but on one condition," she laughed.

"Which is?"

"You must promise not to become a criminal investigator or a part of the story."

Were you predicting what lay ahead? Did you already know that I was no longer going to be an impartial reader?

The next day you brought the book and handed it over to me.

"I hope you'll get some pleasure from reading it," you said as you gave it to me.

"And I hope the number of your victims doesn't spoil my pleasure," I joked.

"Don't worry, I hate mass graves."

How could I forget this last sentence?

When I remember it now I become convinced that this new story of yours that was being promoted by magazines and newspapers would have in it only one grave for one hero—Ziad or myself. Which of us would be the lucky victim?

Only your book would carry an answer to this question and to other questions that were on my mind.

I wonder why everything you write arouses within me more than one question? Why do I feel involved, as though I was an integral part in all your novels, be they novels of realism or novels of fantasy? Even those you wrote before we met.

Is it because I feel as if I have some historic claim to you? Or is it because when you gave me that first book of yours, you did not write anything in it for me? Instead you made a strange comment that I will never forget, "We only write things like that for strangers. The place of those we love isn't on the first blank page, but inside the pages of the book."

That night I rushed home and read the book voraciously in two evenings. I raced breathlessly from one page to the next, as if I was looking for something other than what I was reading. Something, for instance, you could have written for me in advance, even before we had met. Something that could bring us together in a story that was not ours.

I know full well how crazy this is, but life is full of amazing coincidences. That painting I did, on a particular day in 1957, standing there waiting for you a quarter of a century later without my realizing that it was yours or that it was even you yourself!

Nothing but an illusion. You did nothing for me in that book of yours except create bitterness, pain, and stupid jealousy, whose venom I tasted for the first time. A mad jealousy of a paper man who might have been real in your life. He could also be merely a creature of your imagination that you used in order to furnish the emptiness of your days and the blank pages of your book. But then, where is the line that divides illusion from reality? You never once answered that question of mine. You went on adding to my confusion by giving answers even more mysterious, such as when you said, "What is important in what we write is only what we write, because only writing is literature and that is what lasts. Those we have written about are like a car accident. People we have stood by some day, and then continued on our journey either with them or without them."

"The relationship between the writer and his muse can't be that simple," I said. "The writer is nothing without someone to give him inspiration; the writer owes them something."

"What does he owe?" you interrupted. "What Aragon wrote about the eyes of Elsa is far more beautiful than the eyes of Elsa herself that will grow old and fade. And what Nizar Qabbani wrote about the hair of Bilqis is surely more beautiful than a shock of thick hair that was condemned to go white and fall out. And what Leonardo painted in one smile of his Mona Lisa doesn't take its value from her naïve smile, but from the artist's amazing capacity to render conflicting emotions, an ambiguous smile that combines joy and sadness at the same time. So tell me then, who owes glory to whom?"

Our talk was taking a direction different from what you

intended, maybe in an attempt to flee from the truth. So I repeated the question more explicitly, "Did that man pass through your life or not?"

"Amazing," you laughed. "Agatha Christie's novels contain more than sixty crimes, and other writers' novels have even more murders. Yet never does a reader raise their voice to call for these writers to be put on trial for these crimes. But a woman writer has only to write one love story to have many fingers of suspicion pointing at her, calling for a criminal investigator to find more than one piece of evidence that will indicate that it is her story. I believe critics should find a way of settling this matter once and for all. They should either admit that a woman's imagination goes beyond that of a man, or decide to put us all on trial!"

I laughed at your argument, but I also admired it, though I was not convinced.

"While waiting for critics to settle this matter," I said, "let me repeat a question you haven't answered yet. Was that man really a part of your life?"

"The important thing is that he died after this book," you said, continuing to play upon my nerves.

"Oh, is that because you think you are capable of killing the past with one stroke of the pen?"

"What past?" you said, continuing to evade the question. "We might also write to turn our dreams into monuments."

Deep inside me, I had a feeling that the story was personal and that this man had passed through your life. And probably your body too.

I could almost smell his tobacco between the lines. I could almost touch his stuff scattered among the pages of the book. In every paragraph there was something of him, of his tanned complexion, of the taste of his kiss, of his laugh, of his breath, and of your shameless desire for him.

I wonder if he really was that outstanding in his love for you. Or were you simply outstanding in describing him? Or was it just a womanly imagination that your rich vocabulary gave him such virility and so many dreams, and then produced a fine memorial of the same shape.

I wonder why I went on reading that book. Did I disguise myself as a lover wearing the uniform of a moral policeman? I found myself digging into the words between the commas, hoping to catch you red-handed with a kiss here or maybe to discover his initials there.

I thought long and hard. I remembered you telling me that you had been in Paris for four years, during which time you had been staying with your uncle from when he was appointed to his post, two years beforehand. So, I wondered, what did you do before that while you were all alone?

That novel of yours exhausted me. It was enjoyable and tiring, just like you. Later on, I admitted that my relationship with you had turned a corner after I had read it, and that I doubted my capacity to resist you anymore because I was ill-equipped to face words as a weapon. You simply said, as if you were not really concerned, "You shouldn't have read me then!"

"But I like reading you," I answered foolishly. "Besides, there's no other way to understand you."

"You're wrong," you replied. "You won't understand a thing that way. A writer is a human being living on the edge of truth, but not necessarily mastering it. That's the work of historians. In fact, a writer's job is to become an expert at dreams or some kind of polite lies. A successful novelist is either someone who lies with amazing honesty or a liar who speaks of real things.

"I suppose," you added after some thought, "the latter is truer."

Oh, you little liar! Your lying was so sweet, but also most painful. I decided not to probe further that day into your memory since you were not going to confess anything to me. Maybe because you were a woman specializing in playing games, and maybe because there was nothing to confess.

All you wanted was to convince me that you were no longer the baby I had known. In fact, you were vacuous and your lies were as vast as your vacuousness. Otherwise, what was the secret of your attachment to me? Why did you haunt my memory with questions, and lure me to talk about everything? Why all this thirst for knowledge? Why this desire to share my memory and all I had loved, or even hated? Was memory your hang-up?

* * *

My exhibition had to end in order for us to realize that we had only met two weeks earlier, and not months, as it seemed. How could we have exhausted memory in just a few days? How did we learn, in the few hours we spent together, to be sad and happy, and to dream at the same time?

How did we become a copy of each other? And how would we be able to leave a place that had become part of our memory? How could we do that? Somewhere that placed us for a few days beyond the boundaries of time and place, in an enormous gallery filled by silence and furnished with art and a quarter of a century of madness and suffering.

We were one painting among many other paintings.

We were a painting with moods and many colors, drawn once by chance and then continued by the hand of destiny. I was enjoying my novel situation as I changed from being the exhibitor to being no more than one of the exhibits.

Never before had I felt as sad as at that time. I took down those paintings hanging on the wall, one after the other, and packed them in crates to leave the gallery empty for another painter who would come along with his drawings, his sadness, his happiness, and his stories that bore no resemblance to mine.

I felt I was packing up my days with you.

My hand suddenly stopped as it was about to lift the painting I had left to the last. I looked closely at it and I felt something was missing in it. There was not much in it, simply a bridge crossing from one side to the other, hanging toward the upper side with ropes from both ends, like a swing of sadness.

Beneath that metal swing there was a steep rocky gorge–a sharp contrast to the mood of a provokingly calm blue sky.

I had never felt before then that this painting needed fresh details that would offset such contradictions, and clothe the nakedness of the basic two colors filling it.

Nostalgia was not just a painting. It was a statement, the stuff that dreams are made of, the result of events of years of nostalgia, not only by the passage of a quarter of a century.

I carried it under my arm, as if I was setting it apart from the others. I was suddenly in a hurry, wanting to sit down in front of it, after all these years, with a brush in my hand and with other colors, and breathe more life and noise into it. Finally, I wanted to move the stones of the Rope Bridge, one by one. But in my distraction, another obsession took over everything else. How would we meet again from now on, and where?

Your university vacation ended almost at the same time as my exhibition. We were now surrounded by all the impossibilities of time and place. We were pursued by all the eyes that could steal our secret and by all those people we did not know, though they knew us. What madness! What was my destiny with you? Why was my physical handicap the only one that was obvious? Why all these precautions? Why did it specifically have to be *you*? Merely the probability of encountering Si Sharif some day was enough for me to push the idea away from my head and suddenly feel the embarrassment of the situation, and that confusion that would inevitably expose me.

We agreed that you would phone me and we would arrange to meet. It was the only solution. There was no way I could visit you on the university campus as your cousin was following courses there too. God! Could we ever have found a more complicated situation?

The longest weekend I ever had was that weekend when I had to wait until Monday morning for your phone call.

On Sunday, the phone rang. I rushed to it, reckoning it was you, hoping that you had succeeded in snatching a few seconds to talk to me. It was Catherine on the line! I hid my disappointment from her and listened to her chatting away about her daily preoccupations and her forthcoming trip to London. After flitting from one subject to another she then asked about the exhibition.

"I read a nice piece on your exhibition in one of the weekly magazines," she said. "You must have seen it. It was by Roger Naccache. He seems to know you, or at least knows your work well."

"Yes," I said briefly. I did not feel like talking. "He's an old friend."

I gently got rid of her. I had no wish to see her that day. Maybe I had a wish to paint that overwhelmed any physical need. Maybe I was just obsessed by you.

I went back to my studio with heavy steps. I had already started to prepare some colors that I wanted to use for some new touches on that painting. But I was confused. Standing in front of that painting I became once more the beginner I had been twenty-five years before.

Was it the new relationship with you to which I added some muddled coloring? Or was I confused because I was confronting my past? Was I allowing memory, not my painting, to have some 'retouching'?

I felt as if I was on the brink of making some foolish move. I was aware, in spite of a determination that contradicted logic, that one does not have to play around with the past and that any attempt to beautify it would be only a distortion.

I was genuinely aware of that, but suddenly this painting began to annoy me. Everything in it was so simple, to the point of being naïve. So why did I not go on painting it that day? Why could I not deal with it using the logic of my art?

Didn't Chagall spend fifteen years working on just one of his paintings? He kept going back to it between working on other paintings, adding something here or a new face there. He insisted on putting into it all the things and all the faces he had loved since his childhood.

Don't I also have the right to go back to this painting? To put on that bridge the steps for pedestrians and to scatter at the side a few houses clinging to the rocks, and down below a part of the river that sliced through the city, sometimes tranquil and sometimes foaming? Shouldn't I add on the traces of my first memory that I was unable to add when I was just a beginner, an amateur?

I do not know how I remembered at that moment Roger Naccache, the friend of my childhood and of my exile. I recalled how fond he was of Constantine, how attached he was to its memory, even though he had left it with his parents in 1959 and never went back. They left with others in the Jewish community, wanting to build a secure future in another country.

Every time I visited him, he would insist on my listening to a new album by the Jewish singer, Simone Tamar, singing the *ma'luf* and the *muwashshah* of Constantine with her superb voice, giving an amazing performance. She wore the sophisticated Constantine dress that had been presented to her when she first came back here and used it for the record sleeve.

A few months ago, Roger told me that Simone had been murdered by her husband in a fit of jealousy. He had accused her of being in love with an Arab! I asked him if that was true.

"I don't know," he said, and then added bitterly, "what I know is she loved Constantine."

Roger also loved Constantine. His secret dream was to return there, if only once, or to have someone bring him just one fig from the fig tree that used to reach up to his window, a tree that had been in his garden for generations.

I used to listen to him with mixed feelings of happiness and embarrassment, telling me—in a cherished Constantine accent that survived a quarter of a century of exile and never lost any of its resonance—telling me how he missed that lethal city.

What Roger did to help me years ago, when I arrived in Paris and tried to settle down, added to my embarrassment. Though I never asked him to help me, he had friends and contacts that made it a lot easier for me to solve the kind of problems and to sort out all the arrangements that faced a man in my circumstances.

I asked him once why he had not once gone back to Constantine. "I don't understand your fears," I said. "People still know your parents in that neighborhood and have warm memories of them."

"What I'm afraid of is not people not knowing me, but of me not knowing that city, the alleys and the house that is no longer mine after so many years.

"Let me live the illusion," he went on, "that the tree is still there, producing figs every year, and that the window still looks over people I love, and that narrow alley still leads to places I used to know. The most difficult thing, you know, is to confront memory with incompatible reality."

A proud tear glistened in his eye and he added, jokingly, "If I happen to change my mind, I'll go back with you. I'm afraid to face memories on my own."

Today, after many years, I suddenly call his words to mind. He never opened that subject with me again and I wonder if he ever succeeded in tricking his memory. What if he was right? What if it is true that we should preserve our memory in its original frame, its original picture, and not seek to expose it to violent confrontation with reality? Because such a confrontation would cause an internal crash, like a glass shattering into a thousand fragments. The most important thing in these circumstances is to preserve the memory.

I was persuaded by this logic, and I felt that Catherine's call indirectly saved me from a folly I was about to commit. This painting will not have any historical value anymore if I add something here, or conceal something else there. It will become a fake painting for a phony memory. Does it matter then if it is more beautiful?

I looked at the palette of colors in my hand. I thought that I should do something with these colors anyway as I nervously held the brush that was anticipating—as I was—a moment of decisive creativity.

Suddenly, I found the solution in a very simple and logical idea that had not crossed my mind before. I took *Nostalgia* away from its wooden stand, and in its place I put another blank canvas where, without a great deal of thought, I started to paint another bridge with another sky, another valley, houses, and passersby.

This time, I was pausing at all the details, studying each and every part of it as an independent painting.

To my surprise I found myself running to those details and almost starting with them! It was as if, in the end, I was less concerned with the bridge than with the stones and rocks on which it stood and on those plants growing haphazardly below, benefiting from the humidity or rottenness deep down there, and those secret passages carved by the steps of man over the years, in the middle of rocky alleys from the days of the Roman Empire to the present. Meanwhile, the old bridge is unaware of all that is happening down below, unable in its pride to monitor what is happening at its feet, seven hundred meters below.

Is not getting across bridges the ultimate goal for all who are born among cliffs and mountaintops?

This idea, born just then by chance in my mind, amazed me. But what amazed me most were the details that preoccupied me all the time that day, especially since they had failed to attract my attention in all the years since I had painted the same bridge for the first time.

Was it because I was starting out? Bound by the broad outlines of things, like all beginners, my ambition at the time did not go beyond my wish to astound the doctor or perhaps myself. I rose to the challenge with just one hand.

Is it because today, and after all these years, I do not have to prove anything to anyone anymore?

All I want to do is to live my secret dream and to spend the rest of my time asking questions, the answers to which were in the past a luxury, available neither to the youth nor the handi-capped fighter that I then was.

Perhaps it was because it was not the time then for detail. We lived collectively and operated collectively.

It was a time of great causes, great slogans and great sacrifices. No one had the time or the desire to discuss marginal issues or to stop at small details. Was it the absurdity of youth or the absurdity of the revolution?

It took me all Sunday evening and a great part of the night to complete that painting, but I was thrilled to do it. The voice of Dr. Capotsky came back to my ears, saying, after all these years, "Paint something that you love the most."

Here I am obeying him and painting the same painting with the same confusion, but what I was painting this time was not a painting exercise but an exercise in love.

I felt as if I was painting you, just you. It was you with all your contradictions. I was painting another copy of you, more mature, yet more complex. Another copy for another painting that grew with you. I was painting with an amazing zest and perhaps with a secret lust. I wonder if it was then that lust for you slipped into my brush without my knowing it?

Your voice surprised me the next morning at exactly nine o'clock. It came like a cascade of joy, a jasmine tree, flowers tumbling onto my pillow. I was trying to discover your voice over the phone, lying on my bed after an exhausting night of work. Your voice opened wide the windows of my bedroom and gave me a morning kiss.

"Have I woken you up?" you asked.

"Not at all, because you didn't let me get to sleep last night."

"Why?" you said in an Algerian accent, joking but serious at the same time, "I hope to God there's nothing wrong."

"I was painting late."

"Why should I feel guilty about that?"

"It's not your fault. It's only the fault of the muse, and you are my muse."

"*Mais non*!" you suddenly shouted in French—as you always did when you lost your temper. "I wish you wouldn't paint me. It's a real disaster with you."

"What's so disastrous if I did?"

"Are you mad?" you went on nervously. "Do you want to turn me into a painting which you take around from one gallery to another, one city to another, foreveryone who knows me to look at?"

It was my wish that morning to tease you. Perhaps because I was so happy, perhaps because I was really crazy. I did not know how to be happy like other people.

"Didn't you say once," I said, "that our inspirations are only other people? We paused before them one day for one reason or another: ships that pass in the night. painting you means nothing at all except that I simply met you one day."

"Are you stupid?" you shouted back. "Do you want to convince my uncle and the others that you did a painting of me once on a sidewalk—standing perhaps before a red light? You only paint things that either excite you or that you love. That's no secret."

Were you luring me to a confession? Or just skirting round it? Or were you so dumb as to pretend to believe me when I pretended not to understand. Still, that morning I found an opportunity, and over that telephone line separating us, and yet bringing us closer, an opportunity to make a confession.

"Suppose I love you," I said.

I waited for your reaction, expecting more than one answer to these words. But your answer surprised me.

"And suppose," you said after a moment of silence, "I didn't hear you."

I was taken aback. I did not really understand whether you

found this declaration less or more than you had expected. Or were you as usual playing on words with utter delight, knowing you were also playing on my nerves, throwing me from one question to another.

"Where do we meet?"

That was a most important question that we decided to answer seriously. We discussed endlessly a safe place where we could drink coffee or have lunch together, but the whole of Paris was too small for us. You only knew places where students went, and I only knew the cafés in my own neighborhood. In the end, we made a rendezvous to meet at a café near my place that served lunch.

I committed a major blunder. I did not know then that I was choosing somewhere just next door that would allow memories to chase me later on.

I cannot remember now how that café became the permanent location for our folly, and how it gradually started to resemble us. Before, we used to find a new corner each time, a corner that suited our changing moods during two months of stolen happiness.

We would meet there at different times of the day, depending on your timetable and my working schedule.

You used to call me each morning at nine on your way to the university and we would arrange the program for the day, a program that only concerned us.

Day after day, I was rolling toward a cliff of love with you, bumping into stones and rocks and all sorts of impediments on the way. But I was in love with you, and paid no attention to the cuts on my feet or the offence to my conscience, a conscience that had been as unblemished as a crystal vase. I continued on my descent with you, fast and crazy toward a more distant phase of insane love.

I felt no guilt because of my love for you, at least not during the period I was satisfied with it, having persuaded myself that it could do no harm to anyone.

At the time I did not dare dream of more than that. A wave of emotion took me over and swept me away: that was enough for me, with its intensity of happiness sometimes and sadness at other times.

Love was one thing, but when did I become crazy for you? I look hard for when that happened and wonder. Was it the day · I saw you for the first time? Or when I was alone with you for the first time? Or when I read your work for the first time?

Was it the day you laughed or the day you cried?

When you spoke or when you were silent?

When you became my daughter, or when I imagined you to be my mother?

Which woman in you made me fall?

With you I was in a constant whirl. You were like that Russian wooden doll that hid another doll inside it, and then a smaller one until there would be seven dolls hidden neatly in only one.

Each time, I was surprised by another woman inside you. After a couple of days, you took on the features of all women, and I found myself surrounded by more than one woman, both when you were with me and when you were not. I fell in love with all of them. Was it possible for me then to love you in just one way?

You were not a woman. You were a city, a city teeming with diversely conflicting women, different in age and features, in dress and perfume, in timidity and boldness, women who ranged from before the days of my mother to your own days.

Women, all of them are you.

I knew that only when it was too late. After you had swallowed me up, as closed cities do to their children.

I was witnessing your gradual transformation into a city that had haunted me since time began. I was witnessing your sudden change as day by day you took on the features of Constantine, its elevations, its grottos and memories and secret caves, visiting its Muslim saints and wearing its incense for your perfume and a big brown velvet skirt the color of my mother's clothes.

I could almost hear the sound of your golden ankle bracelet ringing in the caves of my memory as you strolled to and fro on the bridges of Constantine.

I could almost spot the henna on your heels as you prepared for celebrations. I was regaining my old accent with you. I was pronouncing the letter *t* the Constantine way, as *ts* and I was calling you *yalla* flirtingly, like the men of Constantine who no longer use the word to summon their beloved women. I was calling you *Umaima*, the name that Constantine alone inherited ages ago from the Quraish, the tribe of the Prophet. And when your love removed my final weapon of defense, I would, in submission, confess to you the same way our lovers back home would confess. I used clipped words that meant, "I want you, I desire you," words that had been cut and made shorter to hide their original meaning and had become just another term of affection. Constantine was a two-faced city that would not acknowledge lust nor permit a lover's yearning. Yet it still took on everything quietly so as to preserve its reputation as ancient cities did. That is the reason it blesses adulterers and thieves along with its saints. But my problem was that I was neither a thief nor a saint, nor yet a shaykh who pretended to have all the blessings. And so Constantine did not give me her blessings.

I was simply a man in love, loving you with the madness of an artist, with the intensity and folly of a painter who had created you in the way that the pre-Islamic communities used to create gods with their own hands and then sit around to worship them and present their expensive offerings. Perhaps that is what you loved most about my love for you.

"I used to dream," you once said, "of being loved by an artist. I've read great stories about painters. They are the craziest of all creative artists. Their craziness is extreme, surprising, and scary. It's not the same with poets or musicians.

"I've read lives of van Gogh, Delacroix, Dalí, Cézanne, Picasso, and many others less famous. I never get tired of reading about painters' lives. It's not so much their fame as their extremism and their changing moods. I'm fascinated by that point between creativity and insanity, where they suddenly declare their rejection of and disdain for any logic. It's not just this point alone that deserves to be contemplated and marveled at. We are made to feel helpless. A painting, in the end, challenges us: in the end, it is nothing but the painter's own life.

"Some creative artists are content simply to pour out their genius into their creations, but others insist on branding their lives too with the same genius, leaving us with unique life stories that cannot be replicated or faked.

"I think this kind of insanity is exclusive to painters. I don't suppose any poet has reached the stage that Van Gogh got to, for example, when, in a moment of despair and disdain for the world, he cut off his ear and gave it to some girl. I don't suppose anyone could do what that artist—I can't remember his name—did when he hanged himself in front of the painting of the woman he loved. It was suspended from the ceiling and he had spent days painting it. He was united with her in his own way. He was adding his signature to both his life and his work at the same time."

"It seems to me," I commented, "that what you like about painters is their incredible capacity to torture themselves, right?"

"No, but there is some kind of curse that only stalks painters, and there is a kind of controversy that clings only to them. The price of their work goes up according to the degree of their suffering, hunger, and madness, and their death inflates the price of their work. It's as if they have to withdraw and let their works take their place."

I did not argue. I stood there listening to you repeating words I knew very well, but which still surprised me as they came from you.

I did not ask you that day if you loved me for my probable insanity or for some other reason. Nor did I ask myself if you subconsciously intended to turn me into an expensive painting, the price of which would be my own destruction.

Would my suffering really add to the value of any painting that I might paint anyway, regardless of whether my suffering was due to hunger or to madness?

I wondered only about two things. Where does art start and where does the sadism of others begin? This question had nothing to do with art or creation, it seemed to me, but rather with human nature.

We are by nature sadistic and enjoy hearing about the suffering of others. And out of selfishness we think the artist is another Messiah who has come to be crucified for our sakes. His suffering causes us joy and sorrow simultaneously. His story leads us to cry but will not make us lose any sleep. It will not press us to feed another artist who may be starving or dying of injustice right in front of us. Instead, we find it quite normal for the wounds of others to become the source of poetry and songs, or a painting that we may keep and trade with, for the same reason. But is madness exclusive only to painters? Is it not a common feature of creative people and all those haunted by this compulsion to create?

Logically, anyone who creates cannot be a normal person with normal moods and normal sorrows and joys, with normal standards of loss and gain, happiness and misery. He is a moody person, surprising in a way that nobody can understand, behaving in a way nobody can justify.

That was the first time I spoke to you about Ziad.

"I know a Palestinian poet who used to study in Algeria," I said. "He was happy with his loneliness and his sorrow, satisfied with a simple income as a teacher of Arabic literature, with his small room at the college and two published collections of his poetry. The day came when his financial situation improved and he bought an apartment. He was about to marry one of his students with whom he was madly in love and whose parents had finally agreed to let her marry him. Suddenly he decided to give everything up, go back to Beirut and join the resistance."

I tried in vain to convince him to stay. I could not understand his folly and his determination to leave just as he was about to realize his dreams.

"What dreams?" he would say ironically. "I don't want to kill that wandering Palestinian inside me because there won't be any value in anything I own."

He would blow out the cigarette smoke as if he was trying to disappear behind it and disclose a secret to me.

"And then," he would add, "I don't want to belong to a woman, or, if you like, I don't want to live with her. I'm afraid of happiness when it becomes a kind of house arrest. Some prisons weren't meant for poets."

The girl who was in love with him used to come and see me, begging me to persuade him to stay, saying he was mad and heading for certain death. I tried in vain, but could not find a single argument that would tempt him to stay because, in his sudden extremism, whatever I said became a further incentive to leave.

"There is some kind of greatness in leaving the stage," I remember him saying sardonically once, "when you are enjoying success. It's the difference between ordinary people and exceptional men."

I then asked you whether you thought a poet like that was less crazy than a painter who cut his own ear off.

Ziad replaced comfort with a misery into which he had not been forced. He replaced life with death into which he had not been pushed.

He wanted to go to his death with his head held high, without being pushed into it by defeat. It was his own way of overcoming in advance what had never been overcome before—death.

"Did he die?" you asked impatiently.

"No, he didn't . . . or at least, he was still alive at the date of the last card he sent me for the New Year, six months ago."

A heavy silence fell between us, as if the thoughts of both of us were with him.

"Did you know he was indirectly the reason for my leaving Algeria? With him I learned that you can't reconcile all the characters living inside us, and that we've got to sacrifice one of them to let another live. Only when we are confronted with this kind of choice can we discover what we are originally made of, because we become automatically biased to what we believe is more important—and that's ourselves."

"By the way," you interrupted, "I meant to ask you, why did you come to France?"

"My reasons may not convince you," I said with a deep sigh that opened up a heart that had been locked up by disappointment. "I'm like that friend of mine. I hate to sit on summits where you can easily fall off. I hate the idea that the chair I'm sitting on will turn me into someone else to whom I bear no resemblance.

"Immediately after independence, I avoided any political post I was offered when everyone else was running breathlessly after them.

"My only dream was a post in the shadows that would let me make some changes creating waves. When I was appointed head of press and publications in Algeria, I felt I was born for that post, because I'd spent the years of my time in Tunis studying the Arabic language deeply. I tried to get over my complex of being an Algerian with French as my first language. Within two years I was bilingual, and I wouldn't go to sleep without reading something from both languages.

"I lived by books to the extent that I almost switched from painting to writing, especially as painting was considered to be, by some at the time, a cultural perversion and a luxurious art that had nothing to do with the struggle for liberation.

"When I went back to Algiers afterward I was filled with words. And as words were not neutral, I was filled with ideals and values, with a great desire to change minds and start a revolution in the Algerian mind that had not been changed by historical earthquakes. But the time wasn't right for my big dream, which I don't want to call 'cultural revolution,' because later on those words, together or separated, would lose any meaning.

"Too many mistakes were being committed in good faith. There were changes in factories, farmers' villages, buildings, and big plantations, but human beings were being left to the last.

"How can one empty, miserable human being, preoccupied by trivial everyday problems, with a mentality that is ten years behind the modern world—how can such a person build a nation or start an industrial or agricultural revolution, or any other kind of revolution?

"All the industrial revolutions in the world started within human beings themselves, and for that same reason Japan and Europe have become what they are today. But Arabs went on building big buildings and calling the walls 'revolution.' They took the land from one person and gave it to another and called this act 'revolution.'

"Revolution is when we don't need to import even our food from abroad. Revolution is when a citizen gets to the level of the machine he is operating."

My voice was suddenly taking on a new tone, one that had so much bitterness and disappointment that had piled up over the years. You were looking at me with some surprise in your eyes and perhaps some silent admiration: I was discussing my political concerns with you for the first time.

"Is that why you came to France then?" you asked.

"No, but perhaps I came because of circumstances that were a result of such mistakes. Maybe because I made up my mind to quit a terribly bad situation. From reading the simple-minded books I had to read and publish in the name of literature and culture for a nation hungry for information.

"It made me feel like I was selling my people tins of food that were past their sell-by date. I felt somehow responsible for the corruption of their minds. I was feeding them lies, after being changed from an educated man to a wretched policeman, snooping on the spelling and punctuation of writings, taking away a word here, another there. I was held responsible for what others wrote. I felt ashamed to summon someone to my office and persuade them to remove from their book an idea or an opinion I agreed with.

"One day Ziad visited me, this Palestinian poet I told you about. I'd not met him before. I'd called him in to ask him to take away or change a few words in his anthology, words that seemed to me harsh against some regimes and particularly against some Arab rulers he had referred to, openly calling them all sorts of names. I could never forget the way he looked at me that day.

"His eyes stopped at my missing arm for a second, and then looked at me in a humiliating way. 'Don't amputate my poems, sir,' he said, 'Give me back my poems and I'll get them published in Beirut.'

"I felt my Algerian blood stirring in my veins and I almost got up and slapped him in the face. I calmed down and tried to ignore the provocation in his looks and his words.

"I wonder what made me then forgive him. Was it because he was a Palestinian, or was it his courage which no other writer had ever faced me with before? Or was it because his poems were poems of genius? His verses were the most magnificent words I had encountered in those terrible days, and I believed, deep down, that poets, like prophets, are always right.

"I received his words like a slap on the face that brought me back to reality; to my shame, they woke me up. That poet was right. How could I not have realized that all I had been doing for years was turning the texts I had dealt with into mutilated—amputated—versions, like myself? I wanted to meet his challenge. I looked again at his manuscript and said, 'I shall publish them as they are.'

"In that position I held, there was some manliness and courage that no other employee could afford without losing his job. In the end, an official—whatever position he held—exchanged his manhood for an office desk.

"The book caused trouble when it appeared, but I felt that there were some things I was required to do that I could no longer put up with. What prevents me, I asked myself, from exposing these foul and bloody political regimes, over whose crimes we keep silent in the name of unity and solidarity? Why do we have the right to criticize some regimes and not others, depending on what is broadcast and on the prejudices of our leaders? Bitterness and despair started gradually to take me over. Should I change my career and swap my problems for some other kind of problem? Should I become another player in another game this time? What would I do with my forty years, one amputated arm, and one other sound one?

"What would I do with that arrogant, stubborn man who concerned me and who refused to compromise his freedom? Did he have to live, and learn to sit on his principles and adapt to every shift in the wind?

"I had to choose in order to survive, and thus I chose.

"My meeting with Ziad was a turning point in my life. After that, I discovered that stories of close friendships were like stormy love stories: they often started with confrontation, provocation, and a trial of strength.

"It wasn't possible for two men with strong personalities, sharp wit, and extreme sensitivity, two men who had borne weapons at some stage of their lives, two men who had got used to the language of violence and confrontation, to meet without coming to blows.

"The mutual challenge in our first clash was inevitable. It revealed that we were made of the same mettle.

"In the course of time, Ziad became my only true friend with whom I was at ease. We used to meet several times a week, spend evenings together, drink together, and talk at length about politics and often about art. We would curse everybody and depart happily with our insanity.

"It was the year 1973. He was only thirty years old and had had two collections published, approximately sixty poems, and a similar number of scattered dreams.

"My age was: a few paintings, a little bit of happiness, many disappointments, and two or three jobs since independence. I enjoyed some luxury, a car and a driver, and an obscure taste of bitterness.

"One day two or three months after the October 1973 war, Ziad left. He went back to Beirut to join the Popular Front for the Liberation of Palestine, of which he had been a member before coming to Algeria.

"He left me all his favorite books, the ones he used to carry from one country to another. He also left me his philosophy of life, some memories, and a girlfriend who used to visit me from time to time to ask about him, that same girlfriend to whom he refused to write and who refused to forget him."

You emerged from a long silence. "Why didn't he write to her?" you said.

"Maybe because he hated to stir up the past. Maybe he wanted her to forget him and get married quickly. He wanted another destiny for her, different from his."

"And did she get married?"

"I don't know. I lost track of her years ago. She probably got married. She was very attractive, but I don't think she ever forgot him. It's very hard for a woman who has known someone like Ziad to forget him."

I felt you were going far away in your thoughts. Were you already fantasizing him? Had I started that day with the first of my blunders, following it up with others by answering your many questions about him with words that aroused your curiosity as both a woman and a writer? I told you a lot about his poems and about his last collection, in which he wrote poems the way people shoot into the air at the wedding or the funeral of a relative or a loved one. He was burying an old friend called poetry, swearing that he would only write after that with a weapon. In fact, Ziad was not writing. He was only firing his gun, loaded with anger and revolution in the face of words. He was firing at everything around him. Afterward he did not trust anything anymore. Oh, what an amazing man he was!

Today, I must admit he really was amazing, and I was a fool. Did I have to talk to you about him, imagining that mountains do not meet? Why did I tell you about him with all that enthusiasm and romanticism? Did I want to get close to you through him and to convince you—through him—that I had been previously connected with writers and poets and would therefore have greater value in your eyes? Or was I describing to you his most attractive features because, until then, I thought I looked like him? And I thought I was only describing myself to you. Perhaps it was all true, but I wanted you also to discover the Arab feeling in exceptional men to whom our nation has never before given birth. Such men as Ziad were born in different Arab cities, belonged to different generations and different political ideologies, but all were somehow related to your father, to his steadfastness, his pride, and his Arab feeling. They all died or were to die for the Arab nation.

I did not want you to close yourself up in the shell of one small country and become an archaeologist, excavating memories in the space of one city.

Every Arab city is called Constantine. And every Arab left everything behind him and went on to die for a cause. His name might have been Si Tahir, or they could have been related to him. I wanted you to fill your novels with heroes more realistic than those with whom you left behind your political and emotional naïveté.

"If you had known men like Ziad," I foolishly told you, "you wouldn't love Zorba anymore, and you wouldn't need to create illusory heroes. Among Arabs there are already heroes who go beyond the imagination of writers."

I did not expect then for things to happen as they did. I did not anticipate that I would one day become the archaeologist digging between your lines for echoes of Ziad, asking myself which of us you loved more and for which of us you erected your last mausoleum, your last novel.

One day as we were getting ready to leave you suddenly planted a kiss on my cheek. "Khalid," you said in your Algerian accent. "I love you."

Everything around me stopped at that second. My life stopped at your lips. I could have held you then, or kissed you, or answered you with a thousand 'I love yous' and then another thousand.

Instead I remained seated and asked the waiter for another cup of coffee. Then I said the first words that came to my mind, "Why today in particular?"

"Because today I respect you more," you replied quietly. "It's the first time in three months that you've spoken about yourself. I've discovered some astonishing things today. I didn't imagine you'd come to Paris for these reasons; usually artists come here just looking for fame or fortune. I didn't expect that you could have given up everything there to start here from scratch."

"I didn't start from nothing," I corrected you. "We never start from zero when we follow a new path. We start from ourselves and I started from my convictions."

I felt that day we were embarking on a new stage in our relationship. I felt that you were like a piece of putty suddenly taking the shape of my convictions, the shape of my ambitions and future dreams.

I remembered a sentence I had read in a book by an art critic: "A painter does not present to us a picture of himself through his paintings. All he gives is a project about himself, uncovering the outlines of his forthcoming features." And you were my next project; you were my forthcoming features, my city of the future. I wanted you to be the most beautiful, the most fascinating. I wanted you to have another face, not mine exactly, another heart, but not the same as mine, other fingerprints, but not those that time had left on my body and soul. That day after some hesitation, I suggested you consider visiting my studio so I could show you my latest work. I was very happy when you accepted my invitation at once and without apprehension. It meant a lot to me that you did not misunderstand me. I had decided to abandon the invitation if I felt you were in any way annoyed. You completely surprised me when you cried delightedly like a child who had just been offered a trip to a fun fair, "Oh, great! I'd love to visit your studio."

Next day you phoned to say you had two hours at lunchtime when you could come. I put the phone down and fantasized, running ahead of time. Were you actually coming to my place? Was it really going to happen? You were going to ring my doorbell, sit on my couch, and walk ahead into the room? You, at last . . . you?

Will I sit next to you at last instead of in front of you? Will we finally sit there, without a waitress chasing us with orders and services, and not be followed by the eyes of people in the café or passersby?

Will we finally actually be able to talk to each other, be sad and happy, without others witnessing the changes in our moods?

In my happiness, I went and opened the door wide in advance, unaware that I was opening my heart wide to emotions and hurricanes.

What madness was it to bring you here and to open my other private world, and let you become part of my home? That home became my paradise as I awaited your arrival, and that same house became my hell.

Was I aware of all that? Or was I happy and foolish like any lover who did not see beyond his next date? I wondered if all I had wanted was really to show you my latest painting and my private garden of insanity!

I remembered Catherine and that painting I had done of her just to apologize for the time I was unable to paint anything but her face when others were racing to paint her naked body, to be exhibited for inspiration, in fine art galleries. I recalled the time I had invited her to visit me to see that same painting. I did not expect an innocent painting to be the trigger for an un-innocent affair that lasted two years.

Wasn't there in my invitation to you some lack of forethought or a subconscious desire to create the right circumstances for other things?

Was I actually doing that? I recalled what Catherine said when she surrendered to me in that studio, in the middle of the chaos of unfinished paintings and blank canvasses. She leaned against the wall and said, full of meaning, "This place inspires love!"

"I didn't know that before," I had replied in a detached manner.

Did my studio really inspire love? Or was there something that encouraged recklessness in every place of creation? But I knew, in spite of everything, that you were not and never would be Catherine, because no recklessness would break down the barriers between us.

Today, six years after that visit, I recall the day and relive it with all its changing emotional upheavals.

There you are, arriving in a white dress (why white?), your perfume preceding you, at the tenth floor. My heart runs ahead of you to the elevator and ambles up to you.

The words stammer as they welcome you in French (why French?).

Here I am almost placing a kiss on your cheek, but instead I find myself shaking your hand (why shaking your hand?).

I asked if you had had any difficulty finding the flat and the words came out in French (again why French?). Was I looking for greater freedom or more courage inside that language, a language more foreign to my traditions and psychological restraints?

You sat on that couch and looked round the living room. "I didn't imagine your place to be like this," you said. "It's beautiful, and furnished with a lot of taste."

"How did you imagine it then?"

"Chaotic . . . and with more things."

"I don't have to live in a dusty apartment with things scattered all around to be an artist," I laughed. "That's another mistaken impression people have about painters. I may be possessed by chaos but I don't necessarily live it. In fact, it's the only way of putting some order inside me. I chose this high apartment because it was furnished with light, and that's all a painter needs. Because a painting is a space furnished not with chaos but with light and the play of colors and shadows."

I opened the big glass window and invited you out onto the balcony. "Look at this window. It is the bridge that links me to this city. It's from here, from my balcony, that I deal with the changing sky of Paris. Every day, good old Paris presents me with a psychological forecast. On this balcony, I watch it shifting from one stage to another.

"It often happens that I work in front of this window, and it also happens that I sit outside just to watch the Seine, changing into a vase filled with the tears of a city that is expert at shedding tears. But what I enjoy most is sitting here when it is raining, close to it but yet sheltered from it at the same time. Watching the rain arouses extreme emotions."

You looked up at the sky as if praying for rain. "Rain inspires me to write," you said in Arabic. "What about you?"

"It inspires me to make love," I almost said.

I looked up at the sky for a long time. It was clear blue, like a June sky. That blue suddenly irritated me. Perhaps it was because I was used to seeing it gray or perhaps because I wished in my heart that it would rain and that the rain would conspire with me to pull you to my chest, like a little wet bird.

Not a word of this did I disclose to you. I looked away from the sky and into your eyes.

It was the first time I was seeing them in daylight, and I felt I was getting to know them. I felt confused before you, just like the first time. Your eyes were brighter than usual, prettier than usual. There was in them profundity and serenity at the same time. Some innocence and some kind of love complicity.

It seemed as if I was looking at you for a long time.

"Why are you looking at me like that?" you asked as if you already knew the answer.

Your voice in Arabic came to me like music played by a solo player and I found the answer in a poem, the first two lines of which I had memorized:

Your eyes are two palm trees at the hour of dawn
Or two verandas to which the moon has taken a detour.

"You also know the poetry of al-Sayyab? It's really wonderful!" you said in amazement.

"I know 'The Song of the Rain,'" I answered ambiguously.

I felt that you loved me at that moment in particular, as if in your eyes I had become al-Sayyab. As always happened when I surprised you with a poem or an Arabic saying, you asked, "When did you read that?"

"All I ever did, my dear," I answered this time, "was read. Paper currency determines the wealth of others, but book titles measure mine. I am a wealthy man as you can see. I read everything I can get hold of just as they have stolen everything they could lay their hands on."

You continued to stare at the stony, old, gray bridge under which the exceptionally blue water of the Seine was running. "You are lucky to have this view," you said. "It's nice to see the Seine from your balcony, but what is the name of this bridge?"

"It's the Mirabeau Bridge. I found out recently that Apollinaire immortalized this bridge in some of his poems. A couple of days ago I came across some of them in one of his collections. He seemed to adore it. You know, poets are like painters. They have this irresistible habit of linking with love every place they have lived in or passed through. Some have immortalized an unknown village, others a café where they had once written, or a city they had crossed by chance and found themselves falling in love with forever."

"Did you paint this bridge too?"

I took a deep breath. "No, I didn't," I said, and that's because we don't necessarily paint what we see. Instead we paint what we have once seen and fear not to see again. That is why Delacroix spent a lifetime painting Moroccan cities where he only lived for a few days, and Atlan spent his life painting the one city of Constantine.

"I didn't realize this until I stood in this room two months ago, in front of that very window, and painting with unusual intensity my latest painting.

"My eyes were focused on the Mirabeau Bridge and the Seine, but my hand was painting another bridge and another valley in another city. When I was through I had simply painted *The Arches of Sidi Rashid* and *The Canyon of Sand*. Only then did I realize that in the end we don't paint what we live in, but what lives in us."

"Can I see this painting?" you asked impatiently.

"Of course," I said and led you into my studio.

You stood in that vast room filled with paintings. You looked at the walls and the paintings stacked up on the floor, with the expression of a child in a magic city, and after a while you said with astonishment, "This is all so superb. You know, I've never visited a studio before."

I wanted to tell you that no woman had visited it before you. But the painting of Catherine leaning against the wall reminded me of another woman who had passed by there. My thoughts drifted to her for a while and then you suddenly said, "Where's the painting you told me about?"

I took you to the other side of the studio. The painting was still on its easel. As if in that position it was canceling out all the others scattered around. There is always an intimacy between any painter and his latest work. There is a silent emotional conspiracy that can be broken only when another virgin canvas comes into the frame. I wonder how I could have resisted for two months the challenge of the color white and the temptation of all the paintings that had thrust their whiteness in my face. Why did I refuse to paint anything after that painting? I preferred to keep it that way on that same easel as testimony that she was my lady and the lady of all the paintings around me. It seemed as though I was refusing to put her in a corner or on a wall, refusing to cast her aside like a one-night stand.

How could I do that when it had given me some kind of thrill that no woman had given me before? Perhaps because I had never made love with my homeland through painting. You gazed at it.

"It's very like your first painting, *Nostalgia*," you said, "but it's different in many details, especially in the rough earthy colors you use. They give it a greater maturity, more life."

I moved my eyes from the painting and fixed them on you. "You've put life into it," I said. "It's you."

"Me?"

"Do you remember the day I told you over the phone that I'd stayed up all the previous night completing your portrait? That day, you'd accused me of being crazy and you were scared I'd revealed your features. Don't worry. I'll never paint you, and nobody will ever know that you've crossed over into my life. You know, brushes also have their dignity.

"You are a city, not a woman," I added. "And every time I paint Constantine, I paint you, and only you will know."

"What about her?" you asked all of a sudden as your eyes switched to the painting of Catherine. In the tone of your question there was some of the stubbornness of children and some of the jealousy of women. I lifted that painting off the floor.

"Does this painting really upset you?" I said.

"No," you lied.

At that moment I felt capable of committing any act of folly. "I'll destroy it in front of your eyes if you wish," I said.

"No!" you yelled. "Are you mad?"

"I'm not mad," I said very quietly. "This painting doesn't mean a thing to me. This woman was a one-night stand in a city of one-night stands."

You looked at her very closely and smiled in a confused way. "She's your other city, isn't she?" you said.

Where did you get that bullet from to fire at that painting?

"No, she is not my other city," I said, adding ambiguously, "She is my other pillow, just my other bed."

I sensed a blush coming to your cheeks and that there were conflicting emotions affecting you, one after the other. "It doesn't matter," you mumbled quietly, as if speaking to yourself.

I held your arm. "Don't be jealous of this painting," I said. "there is only one woman in this house worth being jealous of, and that's you."

You looked where I was pointing. On the floor there was the statue of a woman, life size. "Why this?" you said in surprise.

"Because she's the only woman with whom up to now I've felt at ease. She shared most of my tears away from home. In the past, I had a small copy but two years ago I decided to give myself a present and have a bigger statue made. That was in a fit of madness but I have never regretted it. She looked so much like me. I've got one arm and she hasn't any. We lost our limbs at different times and for different reasons, but we held onto each other, and our handicaps don't get in the way of immortality."

You made no comment. It seemed to me that you did not believe a word of what I had said. For a man to live with a statue of a woman is crazy, isn't it? Even if the man is a painter and the woman is Venus.

The problem with you was that you were taken with a genius that touched madness, but you were not smart enough to discover it. That is why every time I wanted to give you a proof of my madness you would not really believe me. You were trying, with feminine foolishness, to steal a glance at the painting of Catherine as if it was the only thing that was of any concern to you, and I was trying to understand you. What was it about the painting that annoyed you? Was it its unspeaking presence at that moment between us that reminded you of another woman who had passed through my life? Or was it because she was a blonde and had that provocative temptation of lips with eyes hiding behind a lock of chaotic hair?

Were you jealous of the painting or of her? How could you blame me for one single painting of a woman when I had no right to hold you to account for all you had written before you knew me, or to question the existence of that man because of whom you made me suffer? I still did not know whether it was a lie or not.

Your eyes turned back to my last painting. You looked at it for a while and then said, "So this is me?"

"It might not be you but it's the way I see you. You've got some of the crooked lines of this city, the shape of its bridges, its pride, its dangers, its caves, and that foaming river that divides its body, its femininity, its dizziness, and latent seductiveness."

"You're dreaming," you said, interrupting me with a smile. "How can you make a comparison between me and that bridge? How could an idea like that cross your mind? You know the only bridges I love are the little wooden ones we see on New Year's cards, sprayed with snow and silver, with fancy carriages traveling over them. Constantine's metal bridges suspending in the air are sad and scary. I can't remember ever going across them on foot, or even trying to look down from them without feeling dizzy and frightened."

"But dizziness is love," I said. "It's standing on the edge of an irresistible fall. It's looking at the world from a pinnacle of fear. It's the charge of conflicting feelings and emotions, pulling you in different directions at the same time, because falling is always easier than standing on frightened legs. To paint you as a high bridge like this one is to confess to you that you are my dizziness. No man has ever said that to you before. I don't understand how you can love Constantine and hate bridges, how you can search for creativity and yet be afraid of getting dizzy. If it weren't for the bridges, the city wouldn't have existed, and without a sigh of dizziness, no one would have ever loved or created anything."

You were listening to me and discovering something that had never attracted your attention before in spite of its simplicity.

"You might be right in the end," you said nonetheless, "but I would have preferred you to paint me and not this bridge. Any woman who meets a painter has a secret dream that he will make her immortal, that he will paint her, not that he will paint her city. It's the same as when a man who meets a woman who is a writer hopes she will write something about him, not about someone else who has no kind of relationship with him. This may be narcissism or arrogance or even something else that we cannot explain."

I was taken aback at your admission, and I felt some disappointment. Had I then painted a fake copy of you? Was it true that there was no relationship between you and that bridge? Was that painting really a photocopy of my memory when what you wanted was, in the end, just to become another copy of Catherine, to become an ordinary painting with an obvious mood, and a face with lots of makeup that looked like her face? Have we not got over all that?

"If that's what you want," I said with some desperation, "then I'll paint your portrait."

"I must admit," you answered bashfully, "that my dream, right from the beginning, was to have you paint my portrait, so I could keep it as a souvenir, on the condition that you didn't sign it—if that's possible."

I wanted to laugh—or to grieve. I was unearthing the strange illogic of things. It was my right then to sign symbols and paintings that would bear no resemblance to you, but I could not put my name at the bottom of your portrait. You were the only woman I have ever loved, and my name would not be linked to yours, not even at the bottom of a painting. Some people bought only my signature and not my paintings, and here are you, wanting my painting without my signature. But I am headstrong and mad, refusing this new logic for things, and refusing, in love's name, to turn you into an orphan, a parentless painting that any artist, any brush, could claim as his own.

My silence confused you.

"Does it really upset you to paint me?" you said, half in apology.

"No, I was only rediscovering that you are the copy of some country, a country whose features I had once painted although others put their signatures at the bottom of my victories. You know there are always signatures ready for such occasions because from the beginning of time there have always been those who write history and others who sign it. That's why I hate unsigned paintings: their authorship can easily be filched."

I wondered if you understood anything I was saying. Suddenly I had started to doubt your political awareness because, at the end of the day, all you cared about was your portrait.

"You know," you said as we were leaving the studio, "we won't be seeing each other for two months. I'm leaving for Algiers next week."

"What are you saying?" I cried, stopping you in the hallway. "Is that true?"

"Of course, I always spend the summer vacation with Mother in Algiers, and I've got to go next week with my uncle and his family. None of them will stay here in Paris."

I stood there in the middle of the hall, stupefied. I took your arm as if I was trying to stop you leaving. "And what about me?" I asked sadly.

"You? I'll miss you enormously. I think we'll suffer a bit. It's our first separation, we'll be smart and get over it and time will pass quickly.

"Don't be sad," you added like someone who either wanted to solve a problem or to get rid of it quickly. "You can write to me or call me. We'll stay in touch."

I was on the point of bursting into tears like a child whose mother has just told him she was leaving without him. What amazed me most was the heartless way you gave me the news. It was as if my suffering appealed to you in some way. Should I hold on to your dress like a child and sob? Or should I talk to you for hours, and try to convince you that I would be unable to live without you? Should I tell you that I had become obsessed by you?

How do I convince you that I had become enslaved to your voice as it floated over the phone? I had become enslaved to your laugh, to your looks, to your delightful feminine presence, to your spontaneous contrariness in all things and at all times. I have become enslaved to a city that has become you, to a memory that has become you, to everything you have ever touched or to any place you have ever visited.

All of a sudden, I was invaded with sadness as I stood in that hallway examining you with the amazement of someone who cannot believe what is happening. You were so close to me, almost touching me, as never before, and I was looking into your face for some sign that would reveal your emotions, but I could make no sense of anything. Was it your perfume that was searing through my feelings and paralyzing my mind, making me incapable of carrying on my search? The only thing I was aware of was that in a few moments you would be as far away from me as you were then close to me.

You raised your face to me and I wanted to say something that I could not remember any more. But before I could say a word, my lips shot ahead and I started devouring yours in a sudden feverish kiss, while my one arm embraced you like a belt and with one grip you became a part of me. You shuddered like a fish that had just come out of the sea and then gave up. Your long dark hair flowed all over your shoulders like a gypsy's black scarf, arousing an old desire to seize it with the roughness of forbidden love. Meanwhile, my lips were looking for a way to implant my signature on your lips, that were already drawn for love. This was inevitable. You who put shadow on your eyes and fever on your lips instead of lipstick. Was it possible for me to resist for long the face of your femininity? Here are my fifty years devouring your lips and here is the fever transferring itself to me. Here I am finally melting in a kiss that was Constantinian in taste and Algerian in confusion.

There was nothing more beautiful than your passion. If only you knew how cold are the kisses of exile, how cold the lips with too much lipstick and too little warmth, and how cold the bed that had no memory. Let me stock up enough of you to face the years of cold. Let me hide my head in your neck, let me hide in your lap like a child in distress. Let me steal from the fleeting years one moment, and one dream that all these burning spaces are mine. Burn me in love, Constantine. Your lips were delicious, like mulberries that had slowly ripened. The perfume of your body was like a jasmine tree that had quickly blossomed.

I was hungry for you. A lifetime of thirst and waiting, a lifetime of complexes, obstacles, and contradictions, a lifetime of desire and caution, of inherited values, suppressed desires, a lifetime of confusion and hypocrisy. I was picking up the fragments of my life on your lips. In one kiss, I gathered all the opposites, all the contradictions; and inside me woke the man I had killed long ago for the sake of another who was once your father's comrade.

This man could have been your father.

On your lips I was born and killed at the same time. I killed one man and gave life to another.

Did time stop at that instant? Did it finally bring us to the same age, and did it cast aside our memory for a while? I do not know.

All I knew was that you were mine, and I wanted to shout out, at that moment, a saying of Goethe's Faust: *Oh, Time, stop! How beautiful you are!*

But time did not stop. It was lying in wait and conspiring against me as usual. And you were then looking at your watch in an attempt to conceal your embarrassment, reminding me that you had to go back to the college. I offered you a cup of coffee in a last attempt to keep you, but you stood in front of the mirror rearranging your looks and your hair.

"I'd prefer something cold if possible," you said.

I left you in the room and went to the kitchen, but I deliberately took my time, feeling suddenly ashamed of the effects of my kisses on your lips. When I returned you were standing in front of the bookcase looking at the titles. You were turning over the pages of some of the books. You pulled one small volume out and looked at the cover.

"Isn't this the collection of your poet friend, the one you told me about?"

"Yes," I answered, happily for I had found a subject that took me away from my confusion. "And there's another one by him too on the same shelf."

"Is his name Ziad al-Khalil? I know the name."

You turned the book over and I saw you gazing for a long time at his picture on the cover and reading a few lines.

"May I borrow these two books? I'd like to take my time reading them over the summer. I've nothing to read."

"Of course, it's a very good idea," I answered with excitement— or foolishness. "I'm sure these books will have an impact on your writing. You'll find some fantastic lines, especially in the last book, *Projects for the Love to Come.* It's the best Ziad has ever written."

You put the two books into your handbag, as happy as a child going home with his favorite toys. Of course, I did not realize then that I was going to be your other toy and that these two volumes would leave their mark on the course of our story. You were gradually regaining your natural features as if the hurricane of my love had not passed over you. Now I wonder whether that was merely acting, or for real. I tried to forget my disappointment with you in front of that painting, the reason for your visit in the first place. I also tried to lighten your disappointment.

"I'll paint you. Painting you will be my amusement for the summer," I said, and then added without any ulterior motive, "You'll have to come again and pose for me. Or you can give me a photo and I'll work on that, transferring your features onto the canvas."

"I've not got much time to come back to you in the next couple of days," you answered quickly, as if it was all ready. "And I haven't got a photo on me. You'll have to use the one on the cover of my book until I get back."

I admit that I did not understand then whether your answer bore any hint that you would not be coming back to my place, or whether you were just answering spontaneously in your innocent way. Was it not you who had insisted that I paint you? Then why did you turn the painting into a personal matter that concerned only me? I did not argue much. I knew that I would paint you anyway. Maybe it was because I did not know how to refuse you anything. Maybe it was because I did not know how to spend the summer without your ghost appearing before me, albeit through painting.

That day you left after placing a couple of kisses on my cheek and promising to see me again. After that kiss, it was impossible to shake hands anymore. I realized that something in our relationship had changed. The genie that arose so suddenly from inside us could not return so easily to the bottle where we had kept him confined for weeks on end. I knew that I was moving in an instant from love to passion, from innocent feelings to lust. It was going to be very difficult from now on to forget the taste of your kiss and the warmth of your body that has been glued to mine for just a few seconds.

How long did that kiss last? Two minutes? Three? Or five minutes of madness, no more? And I wonder whether those minutes were the cause of all that happened to me afterward. Is it possible that five minutes could wipe away fifty years of my life? How could I not have felt any regrets afterward and not an iota of shame toward the memory of Si Tahir when I committed the highest sort of moral treason that day? But no, in my heart there was only love. I was filled with passion, lust, and madness. I was finally happy. Why should I spoil my happiness with regrets and questions that would plunge me into misery? I cannot remember who said, "Regret is the next mistake that we commit."

In my heart there was not even a small crack through which anything other than love could sneak in. How could I have allowed myself to be so happy, knowing that all I had ever had of you in the end was a few moments of stolen joy and that I still had a lifetime of suffering ahead.

FOUR

YOUR DEPARTURE had the taste of original sin, and loneliness turned me in days into a painting, the only one hanging on the wall. Then my thoughts slid back to the opening sentence of a novel by Malek Haddad that I loved: "How great God is! He is as great as I am lonely! I look at the writer and he seems to me like a painting."

In my isolation and loneliness, I was writer and painting at the same time. And how big and cold was that universe on whose wall I hung waiting for you. With you being away I was sliding down slopes of simultaneous psychological and emotional disappointment. I was living through that mysterious anxiety that always haunted me before and after every exhibition. I automatically reviewed the inventory of my happy moments and my disappointments. My exhibition was over, and only one French magazine and a few immigrant Arab magazines had written about it. I can say that it had enough press coverage. Everyone who wrote about it described it as an artistic Arab event in Paris. Only the Algerian press ignored it, out of incompetence as usual. Only one newspaper and one weekly magazine wrote about it very briefly, as if they suffered from a lack of space rather than a lack of material. Moreover, that journalist friend of mine never came, even though he had promised to come to Paris and have a long interview with me for the occasion and for other personal matters.

I do not enjoy being in the spotlight, sitting and talking to a journalist for hours about myself. But I had wanted to do that interview so I could finally talk at length to the only person who really mattered to me, the Algerian reader.

'Abd al-Qadir called to tell me that he had to stay in Algiers to cover one of those festivals that were successful and booming those days for mysterious reasons that only God—and others—knew. I found no fault with him. There was no comparison between a festival or an official gathering that took a lot of time and hard currency to prepare and any art exhibition, no matter who the artist was or however many years it took him to complete his paintings. In the end, I could find no fault with the Algerian press: what kind of entertainment could an art exhibition offer to the Algerian citizen who lived on the brink of explosion or suicide? They had no time to meditate or to enjoy art, and they preferred a festival of popular music where they could dance and scream and sing until dawn. They would spend not only all the money they had in their pockets on these folk songs, but also their frustrated libidos. It is the only wealth that we really had in our youth, and it is like those banknotes that they do not know where to spend except in the black markets of misery.

Some realized this before others. In 1969, in the middle of the cultural emptiness and wretchedness that the country was going through, someone created within the space of a few days the biggest festival that Algeria—and Africa—had ever witnessed. It was called the First African Festival. The whole continent, all the tribes of Africa, were invited to sing and dance, naked sometimes, in the streets of Algiers for a whole week in honor of the revolution. Millions spent their time on a festival of joy that was to be both the first and the last. But its greatest achievement was that it eclipsed the trial of the historic leader that was taking place at the same time. He had been interrogated and tortured with his men in the name of that same revolution.

Even though I had no ties of friendship with that leader who also happened to have the name of Tahir, and no particular animosity toward the ruler who had once been a leader and a fighter, I became aware of the game our regime was playing and of the greed of the rulers. Later I felt more skeptical about regimes that organized too many festivals and conferences. They always had something to hide.

Was it coincidence that my problems started then and that the first taste of bitterness was born in my throat that day? When I met the same friend a few months later, he apologized with an honest regret and promised not to miss my next exhibition. I patted his shoulder. "It doesn't matter," I laughed. "A few days later and no one will remember the name of that festival, but history will inevitably mention mine in a century's time."

"You know, you are arrogant," he replied half seriously, half in jest.

"I'm arrogant so as not to be despised. We have no choice, my friend. We belong to a nation that has no respect for its creative citizens, and if we lose our arrogance we will be trampled underfoot by the illiterate and the ignorant."

I often wondered afterwards if I really was arrogant. Then, after some thought, I discovered that it was only true at the moment when I was in front of a blank canvas, with a brush in my hand. At that instant, I needed all the arrogance I could muster to conquer its blankness and deflower it. I had to overcome my doubts with macho feelings and with the pride of my brush.

But as soon as I had completed a canvas I would wipe the sticky colors off my hand and throw myself onto a couch nearby. I would gaze at the painting in complete amazement, realizing that I was the only one sweating and shedding blood, while it was an Arab female receiving my turbulence with a scary hereditary coolness.

Once, when I collapsed with one of my greatest disappointments, it happened that I ripped a canvas up and threw the shreds into a wastepaper basket because the mere existence of the painting irritated me.

Some paintings are so cold and naïve that they arouse in the artist not only a feeling of genius, but also a complex about manhood. Despite all that, no one will know any of this. Maybe no one will ever suspect my weakness and private defeats. Others will see only triumphs hanging the walls, elegantly framed. Except for the wastepaper baskets, they will always be in a corner of my studio and in my heart, away from the lights because anyone who stands before a blank canvas and creates something must be a god: otherwise he would change his profession.

Could I be a god? I am the one whom your love turned into a Greek city, with nothing in it standing except lofty crumbling columns.

What use is my arrogance when the salt of your love dismantles my inner organs every day?

Two months—and nothing but an impossible phone number and a few words that you left with me.

Silence was beginning to become my favorite color.

I was conscious of your dialectic attitude towards art and literature. You rid yourself of things every time you wrote about them, as if you killed problems with words. And I became filled with them every time I painted, as if I was bringing to life their forgotten details, and I was finding myself increasingly attached to them as I hung them on the wall of memory.

If I paint you does that not mean that I am lodging you in the rooms of my house, as well as in my heart?

It was an absurdity that I had decided not to commit from the beginning, but then I discovered night after night the vanity of that decision.

Why was the night my defeat?

Was it because every time I retreated into myself I was with you? Or was it because art had the rituals of secret lust that often erupted at night, outside time and outside the law? Or was it on the edge separating reason and madness, on that line between the possible and the impossible, yet erased by darkness?

The big mistake I was committing was you.

With my lips I was painting the outline of your body.

With my masculinity I was painting the outline of your femininity.

With my fingers I was painting all that the brush could not reach. With my one hand I was possessing you, planting you, harvesting you, dressing and undressing you, and changing the curves of your body to make them fit mine.

Woman! You became my homeland.

Give me another chance to be a hero. Let me, with one hand, change your concept of measuring masculinity, love, pleasure. Oh, how many arms held you with no warmth? How many of those hands left the traces of their fingernails on your neck and their signature on you? They loved you in error and hurt you in error.

Thieves and pirates loved you. Bandits too. But they did not lose an arm. Only those who loved for nothing became handicapped.

They have everything and all I have is you. You are mine tonight. You are mine tonight and every night. Who will take your shadow away from me? Who will remove your body from my bed? Who will steal your perfume away from me? And who will stop me from getting you back with my other hand?

You are my secret pleasure, my secret folly, and my secret attempt to overthrow all reason.

Your defenses collapse in my hands every night, and surrender to me. You come to me in your nightgown to stretch out at my side. I pass my hand through your long black hair, spread out on my pillow. You shiver like a wet bird, but, in time, your body responds to mine.

How did it happen? What was it that led me to this folly?

Did I become addicted to your voice? A voice that came to me like a cascade of love and music, and rolled over me, as if they were cascades of pleasure.

Your love is a telephone asking, "How are you?"

Your voice covers me at night with a blanket of kisses, and leaves its eyes by my side like a lantern of lust when the lights go out. It worries about me in the darkness, in my loneliness, in my old age. It takes me back to my childhood without consulting me. It tells me stories that only children believe and sings lullabies to me.

Was it lying to me? Do mothers lie, too?

Children do not believe that.

But what led me to my madness? Was it your kiss stolen from the impossible? Could kisses do all that? I remembered reading about kisses that changed lives, but could not believe it.

How could Nietzsche, the philosopher of force, who long

contemplated superiority and force, how could he have fallen for one kiss? A kiss he had stolen on a visit to a temple with Lou, a woman adored by more than one writer, more than one poet of her age. One of them was Apollinaire, who courted her at length and mourned her at that same time. He found a link between her name and the French word *loup*, 'wolf,' proof of his destiny with her.

Did he not say, "When you call on a woman, do not forget to bring along a stick"?

But before her he was a broken, weak, and helpless man, and that caused his mother once to say, "This left my son with only three choices: marry her, kill himself, or go mad."

This is how Nietzsche was when he fell in love. Should I then be ashamed of my weakness with you when I am neither a philosopher of force, nor a Samson who lost his hair and legendary strength because of a kiss? Should I be ashamed of kissing you? Should I regret it when I began to live at your lips?

I do not know how Nietzsche was cured of a woman he never married. Did he put an end to his life or did he go mad?

All I know is that I spent two months struggling with conflicting emotions. I was on the verge of something like insanity, a state you used to admire in me when you flirted with me. And you considered it as the sole proof for the genius of an artist.

So be it. Today, after all these years, I admit to you that I have reached with you that fearful level of unreason.

Was it only passion? Or was it because unconsciously I wanted to give you the toy you had not received yet, the crazy man you had been dreaming of?

Often at that time I would review the drama of my time with you, scene by scene. I would come to different conclusions each time. Your love would sometimes seem to me a mythical tale larger than both of us. Something preordained centuries ago, when Constantine was a city called Cirta. But I would sometimes wonder if I was a man to whose memory you were attracted and whose folly gave you the idea of a story.

What if I was no more than the victim of some literary crime that you had been dreaming of committing in a forthcoming book?

Then suddenly your childlike side overwhelms the criminal side in you, and I remember that I also was an image of your father, and because of one stupid kiss I blew up forever that secret bridge that once brought us together.

I decided then to apologize to you. I decided to get up and go straight to my studio and sit there for a long time in front of a blank canvas and say to myself, "Where do I start?"

I contemplate for ages the picture of you on the cover of your book, the novel you gave me without signing it for me. I realize that your face has no connection with the picture. "How can I set an age to the new face I know and the old one on the cover at the same time?" I wondered. "How can I copy you and not cheat on you?"

In the middle of my perplexity, I think of Leonardo da Vinci, that genius who was capable of drawing with his right hand and his left hand with equal perfection. Which hand did he use, I wonder, to paint the Mona Lisa to give it fame and immortality? What hand shall I use to paint you? What if you are a woman who can only be painted by the left hand, the one that is no longer mine?

It once occurred to me that I should paint you upside down and just sit there looking at you. I would finally discover your secret, and perhaps that was the only way to understand you. I even thought I should put the painting on display and call it *You*. Many would stop and look at it and might like it, even though no one would recognize you.

Was that not what you wanted in the end?

More than a week went by, and more than one weather forecast, before your voice came to my ears one morning and without any ceremony you said, "How are you?"

My heart was surprised as it was not expecting such a morning treat. Words stumbled in my mouth. "Where are you?" I asked.

"Guess," you said with a crooked kind of laugh, your voice seemingly so close—or thus I imagined it.

"Are you back in Paris?" I asked as if I was dreaming.

"Paris?" you laughed. "I'm in Constantine. I came here a week ago to attend a family wedding, and I felt I had to call you from here. Tell me about yourself. What have you been doing all summer? Are you traveling anywhere?"

"I'm tired, very tired," I said, summing up all my suffering in a few words. "What took you so long to call?"

Like a doctor about to give a prescription or a holy man who has been asked for a charm, you replied, "I'll write to you. I swear I will very soon. You must excuse me. You don't really know how difficult and tiresome life is here. You don't have a moment to yourself in this city. Even using the phone is an adventure here."

"And what are you doing there?"

"Nothing in particular. I'm moving from one house to another, from one party to another. I haven't even had a chance to walk round the city. I've only crossed it by car."

Then, as if you had remembered something very important, you added, "You know, you're right, the most beautiful things in Constantine are the bridges. You are in my mind whenever I cross one of them."

I wanted at that moment to ask you, "Do you love me?" but instead I stupidly said, "Do you love them?"

It took you a while to answer, as if I had asked you a question needing some reflection, "Maybe I have started to love them."

"Thank you."

"You fool," you laughed, ending the conversation. "You'll never change."

"You open the window to look outside. You open your eyes to look inside. Looking is merely climbing the wall separating us from our freedom," wrote Malek Haddad.

I lit a morning cigarette—exceptionally that morning—and sat on my balcony with a cup of coffee, watching the Seine flowing slowly under the Mirabeau Bridge.

It was a beautiful summer and its clear blue stirred me that morning for no particular reason. It reminded me suddenly of the blue eyes I never loved. Was it because there was no river in Constantine that I declared my hostility to the Seine?

I got up without finishing my cigarette. I was suddenly in a hurry.

So be it. Forgive me, river of civilization. Forgive me, bridge of history. Forgive me, friend Apollinaire, because this time I shall paint another bridge, not this one.

I was obsessed by you this time, your voice coming from there to arouse once more that city sleeping within me.

The last time I handled the brush was three months ago. Something inside me was about to explode one way or another. All these feelings and conflicting emotions that I had lived through before and after your departure were building up and ticking away inside me like a time bomb.

I simply had to paint for relief.

To paint with my full complement of hands and all my fingers. To paint with my existing hand and the missing one. To paint with all my changing moods, my contradictions, my madness. To paint with my memories and with my oblivion. It was the only way for me not to die of despair that summer in a city that had been abandoned by all except tourists and doves.

That morning I started a new painting, *The Arches of Sidi Rashid*, but I did not expect as I started on it that I was embarking on the weirdest painting experience of my life, that it would be the first of a series of ten others that I would finish during a period of unremitting toil that would last six weeks. The only time I would stop was to snatch a few hours sleep, after which I would often wake up seized with a crazy appetite for more work.

The colors suddenly started to take on the color of my memory and became a gaping wound very difficult to stop. As soon as I finished one painting another took shape in my consciousness. As soon as I had finished one neighborhood another would be aroused. As soon as I had finished one bridge another would spring to mind.

I wanted to give satisfaction to Constantine, stone by stone, bridge by bridge, and neighborhood by neighborhood, like a love who gives satisfaction to the body of a woman who is no longer his.

I was going back and forth with my brush as if with my lips. I was kissing its soil, its stones, its trees, its valleys. Distributing my passion over the space with colored kisses, nostalgia, madness, and a sweating love. I was happy to see that my shirt was clinging to my body after an hour of devotion to the city.

Beads of sweat are the tears of the body. In loving, just as in painting, we do not mourn with our bodies for any woman, nor for any painting. The body chooses for whom it sweats.

I was happy that Constantine would be the painting my body would weep over.

I still expected in that last month of the summer a letter from you, one that would give me some of the strength and anxiety I had missed during the two months of your absence. Then a letter from Ziad took me by surprise. His letters from Beirut always surprised me, even before I opened them. Every time I wondered how that letter got here. From what camp or front did it come? Under what falling roof might he have written it? In what box did he post it, and how many postmen handled it before it reached my mailbox in this sixth arrondissement of Paris?

I always treated his letters with special affection. They reminded me of the times during the war of liberation when we used to smuggle letters under our clothes to send to our families. Many of them never arrived and died with the people who had written them. And many arrived when it was too late. There are stories about such letters that could fill more than one book on the subject.

The last letter from Ziad had arrived more than a year earlier. He often wrote to me for no special occasion, long letters sometimes, short letters other times. He called them 'a declaration of life.'

At the beginning I laughed at that description that meant he wanted to tell me that he was still alive, but afterward I became alarmed at his long silences and the break in the flow of his letters, because for me it bore apprehensions of something else.

This time he wrote to tell me that he might be coming to Paris at the beginning of September. He expected me to give him a quick answer to make sure I would be around then.

His letter surprised me. I was happy and astonished at the same time. My thoughts flew to you and I said to myself, "Long live this man because as soon as I mentioned his name to you, he's turning up."

I then wondered whether you had read his poetry. Did you like it? What would your reaction be if I told you he was coming to Paris? Especially if you were afraid he might be dead and wanted to know more about him.

Summer was in slow decline and I was slowly recovering my equilibrium. Paintings saved me from collapsing. I had to paint them in order to get away from that rocky journey that I embarked on when I was with you.

I lost a lot of weight but I did not care. Or at least I did not pay much attention at the time. I was looking at my paintings all the time and forgetting to look in the mirror.

I thought the weight I had lost in a few days was an eternal glory gained, and I enjoyed looking at my insanity hanging in front of me: eleven paintings that occupied all the spaces on the walls of my house.

My attachment to these paintings probably came, too, from the fact that I knew well, after the last stroke of the brush on a painting, that several months could pass before I felt a burning desire to paint again.

I was done with memory. I emptied myself and I was feeling better.

It was the beginning of September and I was happy. Or at least in a state of anticipated happiness. You were finally coming back, and I was waiting for the autumn as never before. The winter fashions on display in shop windows declared your return. The wind, the orange sky, the changing climate, all carried your suitcases.

You will be back with the autumn breeze, with the reddish trees and the school satchels.

You will be back with the children returning to school, with the traffic, with the strikes and with bustle and din restored to Paris. And with mysterious melancholy, the rain, the onset of winter, and the end of madness.

You will be back with me. My winter coat, the serenity of my exhausted life, and the fuel of my icy nights.

Was I dreaming then? And how could I have forgotten that beautiful saying of André Gide, "Do not prepare your joys!" How could I have forgotten advice like that?

In fact, you were a whirlwind of a woman who came and left amidst hurricanes and destruction. You were a coat for someone else and a cold for me.

You were the fuel that devoured me instead of keeping me warm.

You were you.

And so, I was waiting for September.

I was waiting for your return so we could finally talk with absolute honesty. What was it that you precisely wanted from me, and who was I to you? And what was our story called?

I made a second mistake.

It was not the time for questions or answers. It was the time for another madness. I was waiting for security, and you arrived as a whirlwind colliding with another whirlwind called Ziad.

And what storms there were!

Ziad had not changed since the last time I saw him in Paris five years earlier. Maybe he was a little stouter, more of a man of his age than when he visited me for the first time in my office in Algiers in 1972. He was then younger and slimmer and maybe had fewer worries.

His hair was arranged with chaotic politeness. His rebellious shirt that never got used to wearing a tie always had the top two buttons unfastened. His distinctive voice, sad and warm, makes you think he is reading a poem. Even when he says ordinary things, he seems like a poet who has lost his way and is there by chance.

In every city in which I had met him, I would feel he had not arrived at his final destination and that he would shortly be on the move. Even when he was sitting on a chair he seemed to be sitting on a suitcase. He was never at ease where he was, as if cities were only railway stations where he was waiting for a train.

There he was, just as I had left him, surrounded by his stuff, weighed down by his memories and wearing the same old jeans as if they were part of his identity.

Ziad looked like the cities he had passed through. There was something in him of Gaza, Amman, Beirut, Moscow, Algiers, and Athens. He looked like all the ones he had loved. There was something in him of Pushkin, al-Sayyab, al-Hallaj, Ghasan Kanafani, Lorca, and Theodorakis.

Sharing so many of his memories made me unconsciously love everything he loved. I needed him then. I felt as I met him that I had missed him during all those years, but I was not aware of that. After him, I never met a single person I could call a friend.

That was Ziad. Time and distance had separated us and only our old convictions brought us together.

Ziad still had first place in my heart because he never lost my respect, for one reason or another, during all those years. Is that not rare nowadays?

Ziad arrived, and the house that had been closed for three months to everybody, including Catherine, now woke up. He filled it with his presence, with his clutter and chaos, with his high-pitched laughter sometimes, with his indefinable presence always. I almost thanked him just for opening wide the windows of the house and occupying one of the rooms, or maybe all of them.

We automatically resumed the old habits we had been used to five years earlier when he had visited me for the first time.

We went back to the same restaurants and discussed almost the same subjects. Nothing had really changed since then. None of the Arab regimes that Ziad had reckoned would fall had actually fallen since we had met. Not one political earthquake had occurred to change the map of a nation. Only Lebanon had become the home of earthquakes and quicksand, and who could it swallow up in the end?

That was the question we tried to address with more than one answer. Discussion always ended on Palestine, the conflicts among the various factions, the battles fought in Lebanon among their partisans and the settling of accounts that had led to the death of more than one Palestinian abroad.

Ziad's discussions always ended as usual, by cursing those regimes that purchased their glory with Palestinian blood and under fake names and with talismanic words like defiance, resistance, and confrontation. In fury, he would call them all kinds of awful names, some of which I was hearing for the first time. I had to laugh.

I also learned that different factions had their own vocabulary that had emerged through their revolution and their distinctive experiences. With nostalgia I would recall the special vocabulary of other times and of another revolution.

The week I spent with Ziad was probably the best time I had ever had with him. For many years afterwards I tried not to remember anything but that week. I did that to push away the bitterness and remorse, justified or not, over what I went through later. All the pain, the jealousy, and the shocks I exposed myself to by bringing the two of you together without any introduction or explanation.

"We're lunching tomorrow with a friend of mine, a woman writer," I told him. "You have to meet her."

He showed no special interest in what I had said. He went on reading his newspaper.

"I hate women when they try to practice literature as a compensation for other practices," he said in his own characteristic manner. "I hope this friend of yours isn't some menopausal spinster. I have no patience with such women!"

I made no reply. I smiled and went on contemplating the idea.

I told you over the phone, "Let's have lunch tomorrow at the usual restaurant. I have a surprise for you."

"It's the painting you've done of me, isn't it?" you asked.

I hesitated for a moment.

"No," I said, "it's a poet."

So you have met.

This time I can also say that those who say only mountains do not meet are wrong. And those who build bridges between them so they can shake hands without having to bend their heads do not understand a thing about the laws of nature. Mountains only meet during major earthquakes but they do not shake hands then. They turn into one common heap of dust.

So you have met. And you were both volcanoes. What was so strange about me being the victim that time too?

I still remember that day. You were a bit late. Ziad and I had already ordered drinks and were waiting for you. You came in.

Ziad was telling me something and suddenly he went silent. His eyes stopped for a moment to follow you as you entered the restaurant. I too turned my eyes to the entrance and saw you approaching where we were. You were wearing a green dress, elegant and seductive as never before. Ziad stood up as you came closer, while I remained seated out of astonishment. It was clear that he did not expect you to be the way you were.

There you were at last. Something glued me to my chair. It seemed as if the exhaustion of the past weeks and all the suffering during your absence had suddenly fallen on me, preventing my legs from moving.

There you were at last. Was it really you?

Before realizing that I should introduce you to each other, you had already introduced yourself to Ziad. He was about to tell you who he was when you interrupted him, "Let me guess, aren't you Ziad al-Khalil?"

He paused in amazement. "How did you know that?" he asked.

You turned to me as if you were suddenly aware of my presence. You placed two kisses on my cheek.

"You have a first-class promotional manager in this man," you said to him. Then you examined my face. "You've changed somehow," you said. "What's happened to you during the summer?"

"He's done eleven paintings in six weeks," Ziad interrupted with irony. "That's all he's done, nothing else. He forgot to eat or to sleep. I believe that if I hadn't shown up in Paris, he'd have died of starvation or exhaustion in the middle of his paintings. But artists don't do that anymore."

"What did he paint?" you asked him—not me—in a quavering voice, anxious in case I had made eleven copies of you.

"Constantine," he smiled, looking at me. "Nothing but Constantine and lots of bridges."

You pulled up a chair. "No," you shouted. "Please do not mention the name of that city to me. I've just got back from there. I can't stand the place: it's designed for suicide or insanity."

You then turned to me, "When will you ever get that city out of your system?"

Had we been alone I could have answered, "When I get you out of my system." But Ziad answered you, perhaps on my behalf, "We never get our memories out of our systems, my lady. That is why we paint. That is why we write. And that is why some of us die, too."

Ziad was really amazing. He was a poet in every sense. He would come out effortlessly with poetry. He could love and hate effortlessly and seduce effortlessly.

"Are you Algerian?" he asked. I was looking at him as he talked to you but I was not listening to what you were saying. It seemed to me at that moment that the conversation was just between the two of you. I had not said a single word since you arrived. I was merely a spectator to this strange encounter with destiny. I was looking at you, searching in your details for an explanation for what was happening to me.

I remember asking you once, "What is the prettiest thing in you?"

You cast a mysterious smile at me and made no answer. You were not the prettiest, you were the most delicious, and I wondered whether there was an explanation for desire. Perhaps Ziad was like you. I realized this in time as I observed you both chatting away. He also had some obscure charisma, an attraction that had nothing to do with beauty. It was this resemblance that annoyed me from the first moment. I was even more annoyed when you noted how pale and unhealthy I looked. Watching both of you, so radiant and healthy, made me envious.

Was it at that moment that jealousy entered into my heart? I realized I was nothing but a shadow sitting between the two of you. I felt that my face was a jarring addition to your joint canvas.

You did not notice what was going on inside me. So you made no apology. Worse still, you were saying a few words to me and speaking much more to him.

"I loved your last collection, *Projects for the Love to Come*. It helped me somehow to tolerate this miserable summer break. There are parts I read so often that I know them by heart."

You started reciting them to Ziad's astonishment.

Melancholy is invading me, don't leave me to the sorrow of the
  night
I am leaving my lady . . .
Open wide your door today before weeping.
Those exiles seduce me to stay
And these airports are harlots
Awaiting the final departure.

I was listening to you recite poetry for the first time. Your
voice had music coming from a machine that had not yet been
created. A melody I was discovering for the first time in the
melancholy of your tone, created for joy in the first place. But
here it was playing a different tune.

Ziad was rapt listening to you. Suddenly he seemed to be sitting
outside time and outside memory. He looked as if he had decided
to sit on something other than his suitcases and just listen to you.
When you stopped, he continued the poem as if he was simply
reading his destiny to you:

No homeland for me, but you
A ticket for the earth . . .
A bullet of love with the color of a coffin . . .
Nothing else have I, but you,
Projects of love . . . for a short life.

At that moment I felt a charge of electrified sadness, and
maybe electrified love too, that passed by us and penetrated the
three of us.

I loved Ziad and admired him. I felt he was stealing the sad
words from me, the words for my country and even words for
love too.

He was my tongue and I was his hand, as he was pleased to
put it, but I felt then that you had become our heart, the two of
us at the same time.

I should have anticipated all that went on between you both, but
how could I have stopped in the way of you being swept away?

I was like a scientist who has created a monster that he can no longer control. I was discovering in my folly that I had written your story with my own hand, chapter by chapter, with utter stupidity. I could not even control my heroes. How could I have put before you a man who was twelve years younger than me? He was one who would be better than me in presence and in the wiles of seduction, and I tried to match myself with him before you.

How could I untie the bond of words that was bringing you together in agreement? Could I have stopped a writer from loving a poet whose lines she has memorized?

Could I have persuaded him not to love you, when he was not cured of his old Algerian love? Here you were, stirring up his memories and opening wide the windows of oblivion.

How did it happen? How did it happen? How did I bring you face to face with your destiny that was also mine?

"She's gorgeous," he said to me that evening. "I don't remember reading anything by her. Maybe she started writing after I left Algiers, but I know her name. I remember reading it somewhere. It's not new to me."

"You didn't read her name. You only heard it. It's the name of a street in Algiers named after her father, Tahir 'Abd al-Mawla. He was a martyr in the revolution."

Ziad put his newspaper down and looked at me without saying a word. He was plunging deep into his thoughts. Was he beginning to uncover the exciting details of meeting you in those circumstances and all the surprising details towards which he could not be neutral? I needed to talk about you. I almost told him about Si Tahir.

I almost told him you were the daughter of my friend and commander. I almost told him the extraordinary story of my connection with you. You, who could have been my own daughter a quarter of a century ago, had suddenly become my beloved.

I almost told him the story of my first painting, *Nostalgia*, its coincidence with your birth, the story of my latest painting, its relationship with you and the reason for my most recent folly and for the decline in my health. I almost explained to him the secret of Constantine.

Did I remain silent so as to keep your secret to myself, the way we keep a big secret that we enjoy carrying alone? Did love for you have the tang of a secret deed, a lethal pleasure? Or was I ashamed to admit to him that you were the one I loved? He used to be the one I was never ashamed to open my heart to and with whom I shared everything.

Or was it because you were a love that could not be shared, and I had decided from the beginning that you would belong to only one of us?

Was it out of friendship or out of total folly that I wanted to give him the chance of loving you, knowing that you might be his last love, who would give him a few days of joy, stolen from probable death that awaited him at any second, in every city.

Why did Ziad come to Paris? It was obvious that it was not a tourist trip. Could it be to meet some people, to build up private networks, or maybe to gather or transmit intelligence? I do not know. He was worried. He avoided making appointments over the phone and rarely left the apartment by himself.

I never asked him why he was in Paris. Some habits of the life of struggle still remained with me, making me respect the privacy of others when it had to do with a good cause.

I respected his privacy, and he appreciated my silence. We transferred this mutual confidence to the story we shared with you.

I wondered whether he had, with his excessive sensitivity, detected something between you and me. Or did my apparent indifference deceive him into an unawareness of the love that raged inside me?

How could he have expected that when I was gradually with-drawing on tiptoe so as to give him more space?

I let him answer the phone for me, talk to you, and invite you to the apartment on my behalf. You would come, and I would never try to ask myself which of us you had come to see. For whom did you make yourself attractive?

The first time you came to see us, after that lunch, was proba-bly the most painful. If Ziad had not told you about my paintings you would not have noticed them. You moved from one room to the next just as if you had been at home. That corridor did not mean anything to you, nor did you remember the kiss that had turned my life upside down. Was that moment the most painful? Or was it when you opened a door by mistake and I said, "That's Ziad's room." You stood in front of that half-opened door for moments that seemed longer than any time you had ever spent in front of all my paintings. Coming back to the living room to sit on a sofa, you said, "I don't understand why you have painted all those bridges. It's crazy. One or two would have been enough."

Was it conviction or courtesy that made Ziad answer for me? He noticed the impact of your words on me and the disappointment that made me lose my tongue. "You didn't really look at these paintings properly. You made a judgment at one glance. Paintings are never the same, even if they look the same. There are private codes that unlock the mystery of each one, and we're bound to search for those codes so we can grasp the artist's message. If you had looked just as quickly at the famous picture, *Card Players*, you would have seen just two men sitting at a table with white cards hidden from each other. Cézanne's message was not of a scene of card playing, but was of a fraud: one of the players was older than the other."

"How do you know all this?" you interrupted. "Are you an expert in art as well? Or is what Khalid has contagious?"

He laughed and came closer to you. "It's not my area of expertise at all," he said. "This is a luxury not within the grasp of a man like me; on the contrary, you will be surprised by my ignorance about art. I know only a very few artists, whose work I have discovered by chance, and from specialist books. But I love some modern schools that have raised questions through their works.

"Art for art's sake," he went on, "doesn't convince me, and the famed Mona Lisa doesn't move me either. I like art that puts me face up to my own existence. This is why I admire Khalid's last paintings. He's really amazed me this time. He has become part of that bridge, in one canvas after another, first in joy and then descending into an anguish that reaches the darkness. It is as if he may have lived one day or a whole lifetime. In the last painting, the only clear thing about the bridge is a distant ghost beneath a thread of light. Everything around it has disappeared under the fog and the bridge shines out, a question mark hanging in the sky, nothing supporting its columns below, nothing limiting it to the right or the left. It's as if it has suddenly lost its primary function as a bridge!

"Is it dawn or dusk? Is he agonizing or being reborn with the threads of dawn? This is the question that is left hanging like the bridge in painting after painting, pursuing a constant game of light and shadow, with unending death and rebirth, because whatever hangs between earth and sky carries its own death within itself."

I was listening to him in amazement. I felt I was discovering other dimensions that had not occurred to me when I was painting those pictures. Was what he said true? Certainly Ziad could talk about my work better than I could. He was like all the critics who offer amazing explanations about works of art we have produced without awareness of any philosophical baggage.

Such analyses make the simple and honest artist laugh. They amuse him because he does not care about symbols or complex art theories. On the other hand, they may fill another artist with arrogance and upset his balance if he is one of those many people who take themselves too seriously and start preaching and promoting a new school of art.

In that analysis offered by Ziad, there was one point I had not noticed before.

As I painted those bridges, I thought I was painting you. But in fact, I was only painting myself. The bridge was simply an expression of my situation that is forever in suspense. I was unconsciously reflecting onto it my worries, my fears, my turmoil.

That may be the reason why the first thing I painted after I lost my arm was that bridge. But I then kept asking myself, "Do all these bridges mean that nothing in my life has changed since then?"

It could be the right explanation, but that was not everything. Ziad might have theorized about the symbol of the bridge in more than one way, but he would not surely go beyond the common symbols. Symbols take their dimensions only from our own lives, and in the end Ziad did not know what was inside my memory.

He had never visited that city, the city that knew the secret of bridges. It all reminded me of a modern Japanese artist. I once read that he spent many years of his life painting only grass. When he was asked why, he said, "Painting the grass makes me understand the field, and when I understand the field I become aware of the secrets of the world."

He was right. Each one of us has his own key that opens to him the mysteries of the world.

Hemingway was able to understand the world the day he understood the sea. Alberto Moravia the day he understood desire. Al-Hallaj the day he understood God. Henry Miller the day he understood sex. And Baudelaire the day he understood sin and damnation. And what about Van Gogh? Did he really know how sadistic and vile the world was when he sat with a bandage on his head, in front of that window through which all he could see were the enormous fields of sunflowers. His extension would only give him the choice of painting more than one canvas of the same view. His feverish hand could only paint those simple and silly flowers. But he went on doing it, not to earn a living, but to take it out on them even a century later. Did he not say to his brother what turned out to be an accurate prophesy after the painting *Sunflowers* had broken all the sales records, "The day will come when the price of my paintings will be more than the price of my life."

Taking this idea I then asked myself, Are artists also prophets? And I linked this idea to what Ziad had said, "All that is in suspense carries its own death within itself."

But still, I wonder, what prophecy was carried within the paintings I had produced in an advanced state of unconscious frenzy? Was it the death or the rebirth of that city? Or was it the resistance of its bridges that have been suspended there for centuries in the face of all the winds? Or maybe its fall in a sudden destruction, at a moment when the only thread separating night and day was a very thin one; it was like an error, an error of history.

I was still under the influence of that disturbing prophecy when your voice pulled me out of my preoccupations.

"You know, Khalid," you said, "You are lucky not to have

been to Constantine for many years. If you had it wouldn't have inspired you to paint so many beautiful things. The day you want to be healed, all you have to do is to visit it, and you will stop dreaming!"

Of course, I did not know then that you would one day take on the task of killing those dreams, luring me there against my will.

Ziad broke in again with another prophecy, gently blaming you, "Why do you insist on killing this man's dream? There are dreams we die for. Let him be happy even in his illusions."

You did not comment. It was as if my dreams were no longer of major interest to you.

"What about you?" you asked him. "What is your dream?"

"Also another city probably."

"Is it Hebron/al-Khalil?"

"No," he smiled. "We don't always carry the names of our dreams. We don't belong to them. My name is al-Khalil and the name of my city is Gaza."

"When were you last there?"

"Not since the June War, fifteen years ago." Then, he went on, "What's happening to Khalid today amuses me. He tried to persuade me years ago in Algiers to marry and settle down there. He didn't understand then how that city was pursuing me, to the extent that it plucked me out of all other cities. Now he's going through the same process and is haunted and pursued by a city."

What I find strange is that he never spoke to me about this, as if he was not concerned by it before. Some things are like happiness. We do not realize they are there until after they have been lost.

This was probably what had happened to me. I was slowly becoming aware that I had been actually very happy with you before the summer break, before Ziad dropped in and before our love changed from a violent passion—on both sides—into a triangular affair: an equilateral triangle. It was transformed from a game of chess, played by two players in which love filled the black and white spaces, and passion ruled the board with the ebb and flow of love, into another game in which the three of us sat around with our open cards and hidden sorrows. We gazed at each other with our different heartbeats and our common memories, trying to create a new set of rules for love. We were forging the papers of which we all had copies. We were trying to outsmart logic, not so that one of us could win the round, but rather in order to avoid any of us losing at all. This way the end would be less painful than the beginning.

It was clear that Ziad somehow felt how I loved you but he was unaware of the roots or the extent of that love. He let himself be carried away in loving you without much thought or any sense of guilt.

None of us was fully conscious enough to realize that passion had only two dimensions and that there was no place for a third party. We had turned it into a triangle that swallowed us up just as the Bermuda Triangle would swallow everything that crossed its path.

How did we reach this point? What kind of wind was it that carried us to a strange land and to different rituals? What destiny scattered us and then gathered us together, with our different ages and history, our distant dreams and battles? What kind of wind was it that joined us, different parties in a conflict, in which we were unconsciously in harmony and in discord?

Many months later, I read in Ziad's papers a thought that amazed me in its similarity to these feelings of mine. "Our passion is another lost round in the times of lost battles," he wrote. "Which of the defeats then is the most painful?"

All that had happened was written. We were two people for one land and two prophets for one city. And there we were, two hearts for one woman.

Everything was designed for pain. There we were sharing our pride, a round loaf of Arab bread along with our wounds. A round-headed bullet, shot at a red square while destiny practiced shooting at black squares that would gradually and dizzily get smaller and smaller until the merciless bullets hit the center where they do not miss, where one of our hearts would be.

In those winter evenings, Ziad often stayed in his room to write. I saw that as a sure sign. He had not written anything for many years, and going back to write with such appetite meant only one thing: he was in love.

I used to smile sometimes, as the sound of soft music came out of his room until late at night. He wanted to fill his lungs with life, as though he did not completely trust it, and was afraid that if he slept, something would be taken away from him. He would listen to the same tapes—I do not know where he got them from—tapes I was not so fond of, such as the classical music of Vivaldi, or another of Theodorakis.

I used sometimes to spend the whole evening alone in front of the television, thinking that he too was living out his insanity. There is one madness for the summer and another for the winter. Mine has ended and his is just starting.

But how could I assess the degree of his madness? Where could I get a seismograph in order to learn exactly what was going on deep inside him? How was that possible, when his fits were private thoughts committed only to paper, while my madnesses hung on the wall, eleven witnesses that expressed me and bore witness against me?

And, I wondered, was I cured of my own madness?

No, I was not. It only became repressed, divorced from creativity. It became a flow of sick emotions that I frittered away on desperation and jealousy. If Ziad changed his clothes I would imagine that you would be coming over. If he sat down to write, he would be writing to you, and if he went out, it would be to see you.

In my cloud of jealousy I even forgot why he was in Paris and about his other concerns and contacts. Then came that trip I had almost forgotten about. It was probably the most painful experience ever. I had to leave you together for ten whole days in the same city and often in the same house—mine—because it was difficult for you to meet anywhere else.

I left Paris trying to convince myself that it was an opportunity for all of us to put some order into our relationship. I felt that one of us had to withdraw to sort out finally this mysterious dilemma we were in.

Of course I was not convinced by this logic, or rather by the stubbornness of fate that had selected me. It was obvious that fate was on your side. That hurt me so much. But what hurt me most was that you were with another man. And that that man was my friend Ziad. And that I was being betrayed in my own home, in rooms where I myself had not found joy with you.

How far would you go with him? And how far would he go along with you? Will our shared memory stop him? What about all the values that bound us together?

I had told you so much about Ziad, but not the most important thing. He was once one of my secret cell, possessing the secret papers of my enrollment. He represented my glory and my defeat, my convictions and my excuses. He was the secret lifeline for another lifetime. Would he betray me?

I started to blame him and perhaps hate him. I forgot in my mad jealousy that all I did with you was the same as what he was doing. I had also betrayed Si Tahir, my commander and friend, the man who once entrusted you to me and gave his life to the cause.

Whose betrayal was then the greater?

Ziad who might fulfill his dreams and desires, or myself who did not have the chance to do so?

Was it me who had been sleeping and waking up with you, even raping you, for months in my sleep? Or was it him to whom you would give yourself voluntarily?

Some cities are like women: their names defeat you in advance, they seduce you and confuse you. They fill you, they empty you. Memory of them strips you of all projects, so that love becomes the center of all your concerns.

Some cities are not made so you can visit them alone—wander around, go to sleep, and wake up alone to have breakfast by yourself.

Some cities are as beautiful as a memory, as close as a tear, and as painful as remorse. Some cities are so much like you. So how can I forget you in a city called Granada?

Love for you would come to me with the low white houses and their red roofs, with the vine trellises and heavy jasmine trees and the streams crossing Granada, with the water, the sun, the Arabian memories. Love for you would come to me in the scents, in voices and faces, with the dark brown skin of Andalusian women with their dark hair.

It would come with the happy dresses and a feverish guitar like your body, with the poetry of Lorca whom you love, and the sorrow of Abu Firas al-Hamadani whom I love.

I felt you were a part of that city as well. Were you all Arab cities and was every Arab memory you?

Time passed and you were still like the waters of Granada, transparent like nostalgia, with a distinctive taste that had nothing to do with the water that comes out of pipes and taps.

Time passed and your voice came to me like the echo of fountains in magical times in the memory of the abandoned Arab castles, when the evening falls suddenly on Granada, a city that was suddenly aware that it was in thrall to an Arab king who had just left her. His name was Abu Abdullah and he was the last Arab lover that kissed her.

Was I that king who did not know how to preserve his throne?

Did I lose you by the same folly of that Arab king, and was I going to cry over you some day, just as he had done?

As Granada was falling as a result of his own negligence, the king's mother said to him, "Cry like a woman over a lost kingdom that you failed to keep like a man."

Did I fail to hold on to you in the way I should have done? Against whom should I be declaring war? I ask you, who are both my memory and my beloved, against whom?

Against whom am I declaring war, when you are my city, my citadel?

So why the shame? Is there one Arab king, one Arab ruler who has not cried over some city since the time of Abu Abdullah?

Fall, Constantine. It is the age of the speedy fall.

Did you really fall that day? This I will never know. What I do know is the date of your last and final fall, the one I witnessed afterwards.

What madness it was, when distance made my love for you stronger and you took on the features of that city too. Here I am, a madman sitting every night, writing letters to you out of jealousy, desire, and bewilderment. I would tell you the details of my day and my impressions of a city that amazingly looked like you.

"I want to love you here," I once wrote to you, "in a house that is like your body, drawn in the Andalusian style. I want to flee with you away from canned cities and dwell within your love in a home that resembles your Arab femininity, a home where my first memory can disappear behind the arches, the round shapes, and the beautiful engravings. I want to live with you in a house with a garden shaded by an immense citrus tree, like the one Arabs plant in their Andalusian gardens. I want to sit by your side and admire you, just the way I am sitting here by a small pool in which red fish are swimming.

"I want to smell your body, in the way I sniff at the unripe citrus. You are a forbidden fruit. I desire you every time I pass by a fruit tree."

How many letters did I write to you! Can a writer resist words?

I wanted to surround you with letters, to get you back with them. I wanted to enter—with you and Ziad—your circle of words that excluded me in the name of art. I rejoiced to create words for letters never written before to a woman, letters that suddenly exploded in my mind after fifty years of silence.

Had I unconsciously started writing this book then, after my love for you had shifted to this language in which I was writing letters for the first time?

Before you, I wrote letters to women who had crossed my life in my youth but I had never put so much effort into searching for the right words. French seemed to seduce me effortlessly with its freedom to say things without complexes, without restraint.

With you I was discovering Arabic, learning to exploit its awesomeness, to locate its hidden charms and inspiration. I fell for its letters that were like you, dots on letters like the dimples on your body.

Are languages feminine too? Are there languages to whom we become committed, learning to cry, laugh, and love in their way, even feeling cold and orphaned once they leave us?

Did you read those letters? Did you feel the complexity of my desolation and my fear of life in the cold?

Were you surprised or did they come at a wrong time? I had to write to you before Ziad could have his way with you and become your language. But what is the good of love letters when they arrive when love has gone?

Did Dalí and Éluard not love the same woman? And Paul Éluard wrote to her, in vain, the most beautiful letter, the most magnificent verses to win her back from Salvador Dalí who had run off with her.

She preferred the unknown madness of Dalí to the verses of Éluard. She remained committed to the brush of Dalí until the day she died. He married her more than once, according to more than one rite, and all his life she was the only woman he painted.

The fact is, love does not repeat itself every time.

Artists do not always beat poets. Even when they try to disguise themselves in the garb of words they put on.

There was a pain in my throat when I returned to Paris, a pain that had been with me throughout my days in Spain and that had prevented me from enjoying the success of my exhibition and the lively and useful people I had met during those days. There was an internal bleeding that would not stop. For me, a new feeling of hatred and jealousy would not leave me, reminding me every second that something was happening there.

Ziad welcomed me very warmly, but was he really happy to see me back? He gave me the mail that had come while I was away and a record of phone calls that I did not even look at. I knew I would not find your name.

He kept asking me about the exhibition and the trip, telling me about the latest political developments with some anxiety. I attributed this to confusion on his part for some reason or another. I listened to him and checked the flat with my senses, like in the story of the ogre who use to sniff his lair every time he returned, looking for a human being who might have sneaked in.

I sensed you had been in the flat. Some obscure feeling made me sure of that but I had no evidence whatsoever to prove it. Who needed evidence anyway? Where would you meet but here? And if so, would you just sit and talk? You were a powder keg and Ziad was a crazed lover who adored flames.

Men dream of burning in your fire, even if it was only illusory. How long could he have resisted that kind of fire?

I was scanning Ziad's face for some kind of happiness, a happiness that I could use as a pretext to prove that you had been here. Nothing, absolutely nothing on Ziad's face but anxiety and concern.

Suddenly he spoke about you, "I've asked her to come tomorrow and have her last lunch with both of us."

"Why last?" I asked in some surprise.

"Because I'm leaving on Sunday."

"Why Sunday?" I asked, feeling a mixture of sorrow and joy.

"I've got to get back. I was only waiting for you to return. I wasn't supposed to stay here for more than a fortnight. I've already been here a whole month, and I've got to get back.

"Before," he added ironically, "I get used to the Paris way of life."

Was it you, the Paris way of life, he was afraid of getting used to? Was he again running away from another love, or had his mission finally ended and did he really have to leave?

Saturday went by amid the chores of my return. Ziad was getting things together for his departure. I tried to avoid sitting with him that evening, but Sunday was waiting for us just round the corner, putting us finally face to face in that last definitive lunch. You greeted me with an unexpected warmth that I said to myself was out of guilt or perhaps gratitude. Did I not offer you love on a poet's plate . . . in my flat?

Then you thanked me for the letters, admiring my writing style, like a teacher returning a pupil's homework. Thanking me in front of him irritated me. I sensed that you had spoken to him about my letters. Maybe you had shown them to him.

I meant to say something, but you went on, "I wish I'd been there with you. Is Granada so pretty? Did you really go to Lorca's house in Fuente Vaqueros? Is this the name of his village as you said? Tell me about him."

The way you started speaking to me from the margins, as it were, shocked me and also made me think. Was that all you had to say after the turmoil we had gone through? After the ten days of hell I had spent by myself?

I do not know how a scene from Lorca crossed my mind.

"Do you know how Lorca died?" I asked.

"He was executed."

"No. He was placed in a wide valley and ordered to walk. He did, and they shot him in the back. He fell without really understanding what was happening."

That was the saddest part of his death. Lorca was never afraid of death. He expected it and often went to it the way we go to meet a friend, but he would have hated to have received a bullet in his back.

Ziad received my words like a bullet in the chest, I felt. He raised his eyes to me. I thought he was about to say something, but he did not.

We understood each other without much talk.

Later on I regretted the intended hurt that I had caused him. His pain meant more to me than yours. But that was the least I could do after all the suffering he had caused me. Perhaps it was also the most.

Our lunch turned into a meal of awkward silence, interrupted by some artificial talk you made up to relieve the heavy silence. You used your feminine intuition and perhaps you argued a bit, but it was all in vain.

Something had snapped between us, and there was no way it could be put together again.

"Will you come with me and Ziad to the airport?" I asked you later.

"No, there's no way I could go to the airport. I might bump into my uncle there. Sometimes he's at the Algerian Airways office. I also hate airports and hate saying goodbye there. We don't say goodbye to the ones we love because we're never really away from them. Goodbyes are for strangers, not for lovers."

That was one of your astonishing ways of putting things, just like something you said once before, "We only inscribe books to strangers. Those we love are part of the book and they don't need a signature on page one."

Why another goodbye?

Was a second goodbye necessary?

I watched you devouring him with your eyes all through that meal. Your eyes were bidding farewell to his body, piece by piece. Eventually they stopped at every part of him as if you were storing up a collection of pictures of him for times when you would have nothing else.

He avoided your eyes, perhaps out of consideration for me, or because my painful words made him lose any appetite for love, or food either. His eyes were sad, looking inside him and also beyond the time of his return.

My sorrow was no less than yours, but it was unique and singular, like my disappointment. It was mysterious and complex, like the way I felt about the strange story of the two of you.

My tension was all the greater because of your refusal to come with me to the airport. I had hoped to be alone with you on the way back without too many questions and to try and learn how far you would be able to erase those days from your memory and come back to me without any injuries or even scratches.

I was certain that your heart was committed to him. And maybe your body too, but I trusted the logic of time. I thought that in the end you would return to me because there was nobody else and because I was your first memory and your first yearning for a father figure. I represented that.

So I had a bet with myself that things would run their logical way, and I waited for you.

Ziad had gone and I was gradually regaining the life and habits that I had before he had turned up.

I was happy albeit with a sense of bitterness. I had got used to having him around. He had left me to my winter loneliness, to gray days and long evenings.

Ziad was gone and the flat became as empty as it had been full when he had been there.

The only thing left was a suitcase that alone bore witness to the fact that he had passed by. He had left it in a cupboard and it was full of papers. It hinted at a possible return, for which you may be the one reason.

I had to admit though, that I was more happy than sad. I felt as if I had got you back by getting back my own flat with Ziad out of it. I felt that your presence would in some way fill the place, and I would be alone with you every time I was there by myself.

I would bring you back to it gradually. Didn't you admit many times that you liked it, you liked the way it was furnished with the lights in it and the view overlooking the Seine? Or was it only Ziad you loved? His presence, that clothed everything, making it look prettier. At first I was waiting for your phone call. So I clung to the telephone seeking comfort in it but your voice started gradually withdrawing. Your call came once a week, then once every two weeks, then rarely and then finally it stopped altogether.

It came in small doses like medicine. Sometimes I felt you were only calling out of politeness, only because you were bored, or to glean some news of Ziad from me. During all this time, I wondered if he was writing directly to your home address because you never asked me about him. Or perhaps he had already told you he would not be writing to you as usual. Did he tell you that you should learn to forget, as he had? And you were applying that sentence on me too.

Ziad hated all half-measures. He was an extremist like any man holding a rifle. He also hated what he called 'half-pleasures' or 'half-punishments.' He was decisive. To him it was a matter of either to love you and give up everything so he could be with the object of his love, or to dump you because what awaited him there was more important. There was therefore no justification for tormenting the soul with either desire or memory.

For a long time I wondered what his choice had been. Had he behaved with you as he had behaved with that girl in Algiers years ago when he had been on the point of marrying her?

Did he change with age or with you? Because what happened between you was not an ordinary story between two ordinary people. I tried to make you talk about him sometimes, hoping to learn something that could help define the new rules of the game and adapt. You would prevaricate as usual. It was obvious how much you wanted me to talk about him, but you revealed nothing to me.

You contradicted yourself all the time, mixing jokes and seriousness, truth and lies, in an attempt to run away from something.

Your words were white lies to my brush, and I colored them with colors that fitted what I knew about you. I covered what you said and the worries surrounding all the things you said with purple, blue, and gray. I gathered together all the things you used to say and formed a dialogue in my mind.

I got used to recollecting what you had said to me and made a continuous dialogue on paper, putting in suitable comments of another dialogue and words you had not spoken.

I suppose that I then gradually discovered the mysterious relationship that bound you—along with the color white—to my mind. Your lies were not the only white thing about you. You were a woman with an incredible power to bring about that color in all its manifestations and contradictions.

Perhaps it was also then that I started, without my realizing it, to push that color completely away from my paintings in a daft attempt to do without you, to wipe you out.

There was some sort of conspiracy between you and the color that had started the day I saw you crawling while your white baby clothes were drying on the stove. The first hint of a sign from a destiny that was being prepared for me, for you, more than just a white dress.

It was a color like you and had to be mixed into the composition of all colors and everything else. So how much did I have to destroy before I could get rid of it? And how many paintings did I have to abandon if I decided to do without the color white?

I tried in every way (and with every color) to get rid of you but I just became more involved in loving you. Did I not tell you once, in a moment of despair, "You know, your love has become like quicksand. I no longer know where to stand."

"Stay where you are," you said, painfully mocking me. "Don't move, because every attempt to escape will pull you down deeper and deeper. That's the advice people of the desert give to anyone caught in quicksand. How is it you don't know that?"

You certainly upset me, but I laughed, maybe because I loved your sharp humor even when it hurt, and rarely do we meet an intelligent woman who torments us. Maybe you were preparing me to meet my probable death. It seemed as beautiful as it was inevitable. I remembered a popular saying. It had not before caught my attention, *A free bird cannot be ruled; but if it is, it can never be beaten.*

That was how I felt then, just like that proud bird that came from a line of eagles and could not easily be caught. If it was, it would surrender with pride and dignity, not like a little bird that would jump and kick around trying to escape from a trap.

When one day I answered something you said with this saying, you cried out, "That's lovely. I've never heard it before."

"That's because you've never known real men," I said with a sigh. "It's no longer the age of eagles, it's the age of birds in cages at the zoo."

That was six years ago. Today I recall by chance the same conversation and your final advice, *Stay where you are. Don't move.*

How could I have believed in your concern for me over the hurricanes, the whirlwinds, and the quicksand? You left me in pain for years while storms howled round me, and quicksand shifted beneath my feet, yet I did not move.

For years, I stood there foolishly at the threshold of your heart. I did not know that you were swallowing me in silence. You were manipulating the ground from under my feet and I was sinking into the depths. I did not know that you would keep coming back to me like a whirlwind. You haunted me even after years of absence.

Today, after all the violent turmoil, your book comes back to trigger inside me a mixture of extreme and conflicting emotions.

The Corner of Oblivion, your book is called. Where does oblivion come from, I ask myself.

I remember the February day when the voice of Si Sharif came on the phone, "You're invited to dinner, at my house."

I was so surprised at the invitation that I forgot to ask what the occasion was. All I knew was that he had invited others and that I would not be alone. Delight was tempered with confusion. I was embarrassed. I had only called him once since our last meeting to wish him a happy holiday, although he had pressed me to drop into his office for a coffee.

That led me to make one sudden, foolish decision, to offer him one of my paintings. Had he not just offered me an unexpected pleasure? I had to prove to him that my paintings were paid for by the heart and not by suspect money. Then I had another bright idea. I would at last be in the house you lived in, albeit in the form of a painting on the wall.

Next day I went to dinner, carrying my painting. My heart shot ahead of me, as I looked for the building in that rich neighborhood. I cannot remember now who first found your house: my eyes or my heart. I detected your perfume the moment I entered the hallway, and also in the elevator. It was everywhere, leading me on. At the door, Si Sharif greeted me with a warm embrace. Then it became even warmer when he saw the big painting that I had difficulty carrying. It seemed to me, for a second, that he did not really believe it was a present for him. He hesitated to take it, so I said, "It's one of my paintings, a present for you."

His face lit up and he began tearing the paper away impatiently, as if he had just won the lottery. He then cried out loud as he saw the arches hanging in the sky in the middle of the fog.

"This is the Rope Bridge," I said.

I did not get to say anything as he embraced me again. "God bless you, thank you."

I had never been embraced with such warmth. He had given me something. He might never realize how precious that was to me.

Si Sharif escorted me to the living room, holding my arm with one hand and the painting with the other. He introduced me to his guests, expressing his gratitude, or probably wanting them to witness his gratitude to me and perhaps our friendship, a relationship that I was known to grant only to a few. He gave many names to many faces that I did not recognize. I greeted them, wondering who most of them were. I knew only one or two of them, and the rest I considered to be like hangers-on or parasites, emerging from nowhere, stretching their tentacles rapidly and doubling their leaves and branches until they soon covered the whole area. I do not know why, but I had always been able to smell out such creatures. Probably because they all look alike, whatever job they had.

There was a meretriciousness in their newly acquired wealth and their latest fashions, and they used a vocabulary that made you think they were a lot more important than you had expected.

It took me one quick look around and a couple of exchanges to realize what kind of 'high' society had gathered: it contained the overseas Algerian elite, experts in saying the right thing and wheeling and dealing. I felt an alien in their midst.

In showing off the painting to his guests, there was pride and affection in his voice, "You know, Khalid, today you've made a fond wish come true. I've always wanted to have something of your work in my home. After all, you're a friend from childhood. You remember where we grew up?"

There was some of Constantine's presence in Si Sharif's character, some of the old Algeria and its memories, some of the tone and bearing of Si Tahir, and I liked him for that. Deep in him there was still something pure and uncorrupt in spite of everything: but for how much longer?

I felt he was surrounded by drones and the dregs of society and it worried me a lot that in time this would rot his inner core. I feared for him, but mostly for the sullying of a great name he bore, a legacy from Si Tahir. Were these feelings just a guess, or a logical deduction from the painful sight of those around him? Would you escape the contagion? What choice would he make? Would he swim against the current? The small fry have no life in a pool run by sharks. The answer was ahead of me that evening. He had chosen his polluted pool and that was that.

From behind a Cuban cigar, one of the guests spoke to me, "I've always admired your work. I gave instructions to contact you so you could take part in some of our projects, but I can't recall seeing any of your paintings at our . . ."

I had no idea who he was or what projects he was talking about. But talking about himself in the plural was enough for me to understand that he was a high-ranking somebody. Si Sharif cut in, noticing that I had failed to recognize the man. "Mr. X is an art lover. He is in charge of major projects that will change Algeria's cultural profile."

Then he seemed to notice something else. "But you haven't been to Algeria for many years," he added. "You haven't seen the new cultural and commercial complexes. You must do so."

I made no reply. I was watching him descend the ladder of values into stupidity and complicity. I shut up, keeping to myself what I had heard about those complexes and other national sites built stone by stone on deals and commissions exchanged by crooks big and small. I thought of the martyrs whose misfortune it was that their memorials were facing these betrayals.

That was Mr. X.

He looked honest and simple, except for his very elegant suit. But his continuous conversation about projects in the near and distant future, all linked to suspicious foreign names and to Paris, sounded shameful from a former army man.

There he was, a cultural phenomenon in the military world. Or was it the other way around? Or was it that this unnatural marriage had become natural since the plague of jobbery had spread in more than one Arab military headquarters? Everybody was being so nice and polite to him, hoping to lick off some of the honey dripping from his hands in the form of hard currency at a time of national drought and hardship. All evening I was asking myself what I was doing there among this strange crowd.

I had expected to be among the family, or at least to have a rare date with my homeland where Si Sharif and I could share old memories. My homeland was absent that evening. Its wounds and its ugly new face were there instead. It was a French evening. We spoke in French about foreign-interest projects financed by Algeria. Had we really gained our independence?

The evening ended at around midnight. Mr. X was tired and had commitments in the morning, or that night as well perhaps. Money quickly acquired soon awakens appetites for more than one pleasure.

It may be that I was happy that evening. I had become an object of general interest for reasons I do not want to go into.

Indeed, I may have been the second star of the evening, along with Mr. X, in whose honor I understand the party had been held. I was invited along because he loved to be surrounded at parties by artists. It showed he loved creativity, and had more than military taste.

In fact, he was pleasant and courteous. He gave me his views on various artistic issues. He spoke of his love for some specific Algerian painters. Indeed, he joked that he envied Si Sharif for being the owner of that painting of mine, and that if I took a painting with me he would invite me to his house next time I was in Algiers.

I laughed at his bonhomie.

But I was also so utterly distressed that I was on the brink of tears.

I wondered, that night, when I was alone in bed, what madness had taken me to that house, a house I expected to be your house. I had entered it and left it without having the chance of a glimpse of the hem of your dress crossing that corridor separating me from your world.

Next morning, the phone woke me up. I expected it to be you. It was Catherine.

"Morning kisses and best wishes!"

Before I could ask what the occasion was, she added, "It's Valentine's Day. I'm calling you instead of sending a card. What are your wishes this lovers' day?"

She surprised me and I was hesitant.

"Wish for something, you fool," she said in the ironic tone I love, "for all wishes come true on this day."

I laughed and almost said I wished for some oblivion, but said something else, "I wish to retire from emotion. Would you tell your saint that?"

"Are you mad? I hope he can't hear you, or he'll hold back his blessings for good. What is it with you? Was our last date so exhausting?"

I laughed about that day with Catherine. Then I put the phone down to weep with you. I was experiencing the pain of Valentine's Day for the first time.

Not one phone call came from you. Not even to thank me for the painting, or the visit, or about the time you stood me up.

So, it is a day of love.

It was a day for me of humiliation, my love and hate, my memory and my oblivion. Every celebration that passed would remind me of all these. Love has its holiday when lovers exchange wishes, but when will there be a day for oblivion, my lady?

Three hundred sixty-five days for three hundred sixty-five saints. Why was there not a day to celebrate forgetfulness, when all the postmen can go on strike, when phone lines go dead, radios ban love songs, and we give up writing love poems? Was not splitting up the other side of love? And disillusion the other side of passion?

Nearly two centuries ago Victor Hugo wrote, "How impotent love is! It repeats only one phrase, *I love you,* and how fertile it is at the same time because there are a thousand ways of expressing it."

Let me astonish you on this lovers' day and try to tell you how much I love you in a thousand ways. Let me take the thousand roads that lead to you, let me adore you with a thousand conflicting emotions, forget and remember you with the extremes of memory and oblivion.

I want to submit to you and to deny you, with the utmost freedom and the utmost enslavement, with contrasting passions of love and hatred.

On this lovers' day, let me hate you with some love.

Was it that day that I began to hate you? When exactly was the birth of that feeling that was to blossom so quickly that it became as violent as love? Was it the effect of my repeated disappointments with you? After all these missed opportunities, including our first meeting? Or was it that mysterious tension haunting me, that constant hunger for you making me lust after no woman but you?

I wanted only you. I tried in vain to deceive my body by offering it someone else, a woman other than you, but no! You were the only thing it wanted.

Perhaps the greatest pain was, when in a moment of affection, my fingers touched her short blonde hair. I suddenly lost any desire to make love and I recalled your long, black gypsy hair that used to cover my bed.

Her skinny body reminded me how comely you were. The flat straight lines of her body reminded me of your curves. Your perfume would come to me, even when it was absent, and fill my senses and displace her perfume. The child in me told me that it was not my mother's perfume.

Every day you sneaked into my body and threw her out of my bed. Grievous pain for you woke in me the longing for you, and a suppressed desire accumulated in my body night after night, like a time bomb. Tell me, does one's manhood wake up early, or does desire never sleep?

Tell me, woman, sleeping deeply every night, are men the only sleepless ones? And tell me, why am I so confused, almost bursting into tears on her breast, almost confessing to her my passion for another woman. I am impotent with her because I am no longer in control of my manhood. It only takes orders now from you.

When did my hatred of you begin? Was it the day Catherine rushed into her clothes, politely faking an appointment, leaving me alone in that bed that no longer satisfied her desires. I discovered as I shed a manly tear that masculinity loses itself. My virility refused to play that game or the logic of male pride. We are not in control of our bodies as we suppose. I wondered sardonically whether St. Valentine had responded so quickly and turned me into a retired lover.

I remember I cursed you and hated you and felt some bitterness and was close to tears. I had not cried when they amputated my arm, but I did so when you stole the last thing I possessed, my manhood.

One day I asked you, "Do you love me?"

"I don't know. My love grows and declines like faith."

Today I can say that my hatred for you grows and declines like faith.

"Are you a believer?" I asked with a lover's innocence.

"Of course I am. I carry out all the obligations required by Islam."

"Do you fast?"

"Of course I fast. It's my way of defying this city. My way of communicating with my homeland and my past."

I was surprised. I do not know why I had not expected you to be like that. You seemed to be free of all that baggage.

You said, "How can you describe religion as baggage? It's conviction and like all convictions is a matter that concerns ourselves alone. Don't trust appearances. Faith is like love, a private emotion that we live through in our constant inner privacy. It is our secret shield, our serenity. It's the place to which we retreat to renew our energy."

Those who show an excess of faith would often have emptied their inner feelings to display to all for reasons that have nothing to do with God. How beautiful your words were that day. They released memories and roused the Constantine morning call to prayer inside me.

Your prayers came to me with the prayers, the chants, and the voice of that muezzin in the old Constantine Qur'an schools. I drifted back to that old mat I sat on as a confused child, repeating with other children verses we did not then understand, but just copied onto our slates. We memorized each and every verse out of fear of a long stick that would beat our feet till they bled at the first mistake we made.

Your words came to reconcile me with God. Me, who had not fasted for years. They reconciled me to home, and set me up against this crazy city that was robbing me of a small part of my faith and past every day.

You were the woman who roused angels and devils within me, and then you went and watched me, having turned me into the field of battle between good and evil. You were pitiless.

Angels won that year. Influenced by you, I decided to fast. But I was also fleeing from you to God. As you said, "Worship is our secret shield." I took refuge in faith from your darts. I tried to forget you and the likes of you, to forget that you and I lived in the same city. I spent long days in religious unconsciousness, training my body to be hungry just as if I was in training for being without you. I wanted to regain control over my senses, where you had infiltrated, senses that had taken orders from you alone. I wanted to bring back the man I was before you, his self-respect, his principles, his values on which you had declared war. I must admit I was to some extent successful in that, but I did not succeed in forgetting about you.

How could I have lured myself into another trap and love you? Going through that suffering, I realized I lived through it according to your timetable.

I sat and broke the Ramadan fast with you. Fasted with you. Had my first and last meal with you, having the same Ramadan food you would have. I did nothing without being at one with you in everything, without my realizing it.

You were, in the end, nothing but my homeland. All roads led to you.

Just as my love for the homeland was unending, so was my love for you. Even against silence and strong resistance. Love for you was present in my faith and thoughts. Does worship go on and on?

Ramadan was over. Suddenly I switched off my passing spirituality for another June. The month had more than one reason for me to be pessimistic.

In addition to June 1967, that month brought other painful memories. The most recent was of June 1971, when I was in prison, being interrogated and tortured. I was with those who had not yet learned to hold their tongues. The first painful June, I was in the al-Kudya prison, which I had entered with hundreds of other men. We had been rounded up during the May 1945 demonstrations and stood trial before a military tribunal at the beginning of June.

Which June was the more oppressive? Which experience was the most painful? I had avoided raising these questions; the answers had made me pack my bags and leave for 'home,' a home that became a big prison with no identifying addresses on the cell-doors and no specific charges against the prisoners. To that prison I was taken at dawn, surrounded by strangers, and blindfolded. It was an honor not available to our major criminals.

A quarter of a century earlier would I, a keen, proud young man, cherishing wild dreams, have expected to see a day when an Algerian would strip someone like me and take away my watch and everything else and then throw me into a cell (a solitary cell this time) in the name of the revolution?

The very revolution that had already stripped me of my arm!

More than one reason, more than one memory had made me shun the month of June that had already snatched much of my happiness over the years. But that June came with an avalanche of disasters to respond to all my pessimism. Was there some law of disasters that decreed that they all came at once? It did not rain, it poured! Volcanoes did not smolder, they erupted. It was an absurdity of life. It took one coincidence, as slight as a hair, to bring unexpected happiness, love, and good fortune. But when that hair is snipped, the flow of events to which I was linked was also no longer there.

That 'hair' has managed, six years later, to destroy the last pillar of my home and has brought the roof down on me. I had thought in June 1982 that I had suffered enough and that fate would forget me for some time. It may be that I feared a collapse.

I was ignorant of the first clause in the law of life.

The course of man's life is merely the sum of a series of blind linkages—nothing more.

The beginning of the summer of 1982 had a strangely bitter taste. For what could be more bitter than swallowing one's personal and national disappointments in one gulp? I was living between your persistent silence and the Arab defeats.

Destiny lurked for me this time in another corner. The sudden Israeli assault on Beirut and their occupation over several weeks took place under the eyes of more than one Arab ruler and under the noses of millions of Arabs. All this pushed me down the ladder of depression.

I remember one news item setting me apart and drowning out all other news: Khalil Hawi, the Lebanese poet, killed himself with a bullet to protest against the Israeli invasion of the south of Lebanon. He refused to share 'his south' with them.

I had never heard of this man before, but his death had a distinctive taste of pain, a unique bitterness. When a poet could only protest through his death, finding no paper but his body on which to write, he would be shooting us as well.

My heart went out to Ziad. He used to say, "Poets are like butterflies. They die in the summer."

At that time he was fond of the Japanese novelist, Mishima, who also committed suicide in protest against another disappointment. I wondered whether when he made that comment he was aware of the title of one of Mishima's works—*Death in Summer*. Or was it some earlier idea he defended by citing the names of poets who had chosen this season to die. I would listen but laugh at his superstitious 'summer theory,' fearing it could be contagious. I would tease him and say, "I could give you the names of twenty poets who did not die in the summer."

"Of course, some die between two summers."

"Pig-headed poets," I could only reply.

My thoughts went to him and I wondered where he could be. In what city? What front? What street? All the streets were surrounded and all the cities were graveyards waiting for the dead.

Eight months had passed since he left, and only one short letter had come thanking me for my hospitality. And what could he be doing since then? Until now, I was never worried about him. He had always lived in the heart of battles and ambushes and shellings. I guess death feared or respected him and did not want to get him with the others.

Nevertheless, a strange emotion awakened fears within me. I became gloomy when I recalled his summer theory, the suicide of the other poet. What if they imitated each other in death too? What if they were only butterflies? Had they been like great whales they may have opted for a collective death in that season, casting themselves up on the beaches. I remembered that Hemingway had killed himself in the summer of 1961, leaving behind the manuscript of his last novel. What linked the summer with all those other novelists and poets who did not accept this logic? No doubt I was getting deep into this idea. It was as if I was countenancing fate, or defying it, simply by inviting it to give me a slap, from which I have not yet recovered.

Ziad died.

His name leapt out from a small announcement in a newspaper, his name leapt out to my eyes, to my heart. Time stood still.

The words caused a lump in my throat. I did not cry out. Nor weep. I was paralyzed and thunderstruck. How did it happen? How could I not have anticipated it when his eyes had held more than just a goodbye.

His suitcase was still here in the cupboard in his room. I kept coming across it when searching for my own things. Did he know that he would not be needing any luggage on that final trip? Or was he thinking of coming back and moving in with you, as I used to jealously fancy? I had never asked him about his plans. You were always around in those last days. I avoided sitting with him, unwilling to listen to a confession I feared or a decision I expected.

He carried only one bag and left. He said, "May I leave my suitcase here? You know what airports are like these days. I don't like carting my stuff from one airport to another."

Then he added cynically, "Especially as nothing is waiting for me at the last airport."

His instinct was right. Only a fatal bullet awaited him. I remember him saying once, "We have a graveyard in every country. We die at everybody's hand, in the name of all the revolutions and all the dogmas."

It was not his convictions that killed him that time, just his identity.

I drank that evening to his laugh and to his distinctive tone of voice that was unlike any other. I drank too to his proud distress, that was unlike any other sorrow. I drank to his beautiful departure, the final farewell.

I wept that night. A proud, painful weeping, surreptitious from a sense of manliness. I asked myself which man I was crying over and why.

He did it his way; he died as a poet during the summer, a fighter in some battlefield, the way he always wanted.

He beat me even by his death.

I remember a remarkable saying of Jean Cocteau, the poet and artist, who once wrote a film scenario in which he imagined his own death. He turned to Picasso and his handful of friends who came to mourn. "Don't mourn," he said with that bitter sarcasm in which he excelled. "Just pretend to mourn. Poets don't die, they only pretend to be dead."

What if Ziad was only pretending to be dead, out of perverse obstinacy? Just to demonstrate to me that poets do go in the summer and come back with all seasons.

And what about you?

Did you know?

Did you hear about his death? Or would he come to you one day with another story and with other heroes?

How would you take it?

Would you cry, or sit down and build him a shrine of words and bury him in a book, as you were accustomed to bury me and all those you had loved and decided to kill one day?

How would you commemorate him? In what language? He hated tributes as much as he hated ties and smart suits.

In actual fact, he defeated you. He put you face to face with that dividing line between the game of death and death itself. Not all heroes can be put to death on paper.

Some choose their own way to go, and you could not finish them off just by writing a novel. He was false, like a hero ripe to be put into a novel.

He was a proud man, and used to claim that Palestine was his only mother. Sometimes after a few drinks he would acknowledge that his mother had no grave of her own. She was buried in a mass grave after the first massacre at Tell al-Za'tar. "They took souvenir pictures standing in their big boots on dead bodies and giving victory signs. She could have been among those bodies."

It was only then that I saw him cry.

So why cry over you, Ziad?

You had a death in every battle, an unknown grave in every massacre. With your death you are simply perpetuating the logic of it all.

Nothing ever waited for you but the railway train of death.

Some took the train of Sabra and Shatila, others the train of Tell al-Za'tar or Beirut, 1982.

Others here and there still wait for the last trip in some camp, in the ruins of houses or even in some Arab country.

But between one train and the next train . . . there is another.

Between one death and the next death . . . there is another.

Happy were those who took the first train, my friend, how happy they were and how forsaken we were when we were confronted with an item of news. After that, there were many booking offices for train journeys in different Arab states. Home was a railway station, with a railway journey in prospect for every soul. It was wretched to stay put, and wretched too to take that train journey.

Ziad was gone then and all I could see was a black suitcase in the corner of the cupboard, forgotten now for many a month. But now it suddenly dominated everything in the house, and became the only thing in it. It was as if I had eyes for nothing else.

When I came home I felt it was waiting for me, that I had an appointment with it. When I left the flat I felt I was running away from it and that it was pressing down on me, without my fully realizing it.

But how could I run away from it while it was lying there waiting for me every evening? And when I turned the television off, sat down alone and lit a cigarette before going to bed, then the agony began. I went back to the questions: what was inside the bag? What do I do with it?

I tried to work out what people usually did with the property of the dead, their clothes and their personal things.

The memory of Mother came back and the painful days before and after her death.

I remembered her clothes, her personal possessions, and her favorite dress even though it was not the most beautiful of dresses. I used to see her wearing it on special occasions. It carried her perfume and her personal scent, the fragrance of old jasmine and a blend of natural aromas, for me the scent of motherhood.

I asked about that dress some days after she was gone, and I was told with some surprise that it had been given with other things to the poor women who had prepared the food that day.

"It's mine," I cried. "I wanted it."

"Things of the dead," said my eldest aunt, "must leave the house before they do, except for precious items that may be kept as mementos or for luck."

What about Mother? That bracelet that never left her wrist for a single day, as if she had been born wearing it. What, I wondered, had they done with that? I did not dare ask.

My brother Hassan then was no more than ten years old and was unaware of what was going on around him except that his mother had died and was gone forever.

I was surrounded by a bunch of women who were deciding everything, as if the house suddenly belonged to them.

What about Mother's jewelry? Probably her jewelry had become the property of one of the aunts, or perhaps Father had taken possession of it with the rest of her gold which he could give as a present to his new bride.

Each time I went back to these memories in detail, my relationship to this suitcase became even more complex. Some things had a value that meant nothing to others. What do I do with the suitcase left behind by its owner eight months earlier without any clear instructions? And now he was dead.

Should I give it as charity to the poor, since that is where the property of the dead should go? Or should I keep it as the memento of a friend, since we only keep things of value?

Was the suitcase a burden? Or a trust?

If it was a burden, why had I taken it unquestioningly? Why had I not persuaded him to take it with him, on the grounds that I might be leaving Paris, for example?

If it was a trust, then didn't the situation change with his death? Didn't it become a legacy? Do we treat the legacy of martyrs as things for charity? Do we put them at the front door as a gift for the first person who passes by?

I know that during those days I became obsessed with that trust, and I made up my mind that only its contents would decide by their value and nature what I should do with them. I then suddenly got scared after having given it no previous thought. Was it Ziad's death that had given it that stamp of anxiety? Or was I afraid that it might carry a secret about you, something I was afraid to learn?

I had to open the bag in order to close the door on my suspicions.

I took the decision one Saturday night, a week after hearing of Ziad's death.

I had another thought that was a bit stupid. Perhaps I should have taken it to the PLO headquarters and handed it over for them to send on to Ziad's relatives in Lebanon or wherever. But I abandoned this naïve idea, calling to mind that he didn't have any relatives in Lebanon anymore. Who would they have given it to then? To some tribe or faction or to some Abu Something. There was more than one such candidate who thought of himself as the only representative of the Palestinian cause and the only legitimate heir of the martyrs, and that all the rest were traitors.

And at whose hand had Ziad died? A criminal 'brother' or a criminal 'foe'? Didn't he always say, "They turned the cause into causes, so they can kill us with some other name."

By whose bullet had Ziad fallen? The cream of the Palestinian youth had fallen to a Palestinian bullet, or to an Arab one.

That evening my hand trembled as I tried to unlock the suitcase, an operation that reminded me that I had only one hand. It was not locked. It was as if he had left it open on purpose, just as a door unlocked was a tacit invitation to come in. That thought made me feel a bit more comfortable. At some time he had granted me permission to enter his private world without embarrassment. Or did he do this because he hated locks? They were like doors that were opened with force. His hatred for them was like his hatred for the secret police and soldiers' footsteps. All these ideas did not stop a shiver going down my spine.

Another thought passed through my mind.

He already knew he was going to his death. This suitcase had been prepared for me from the beginning. I could have opened it months ago. It no longer existed as far as he was concerned from the moment he had left the flat. It was his way of severing the train of memories—as usual.

I opened up the suitcase after putting it on the bed, and I glanced at its contents. I felt consumed with life and death as I looked at his clothes. I handled the gray pullover and the black leather jacket he was always wearing.

There was a smell of his presence, his death, and his life being released from his clothes.

There was I with him again, and without him, and with what was left of him.

Clothes . . . clothes, the dust jacket of a human book. The cloth exterior of a brittle being.

The being was broken, but the externals remained.

Another memory unfolded in the case. Why did he leave it for me?

Among the clothes was a sky-blue silk shirt, still in its shiny wrapping, unopened. I guessed that it was a gift from you.

Then there were three music cassettes. One was of Theodorakis, another, some classical pieces. These I put to one side, recalling that whenever he moved on, Ziad used to leave his cassettes for me. There were books. And more clothes. And also a love that was left hanging.

But this was the first time he had left things together in a suit-case, packed carefully as if he had done it himself in preparation for some trip. It was as if he wanted to take it with him wherever he was going, and wear his favorite black jacket and listen to the music of Theodorakis.

Suddenly my hand fell on your book at the bottom of it all. A first shock. My hand trembled. It paused for just a moment and then I grabbed it. I sat on the edge of the bed and opened it. It was as if I was opening a mail bomb. I flipped through the book as if I did not know it. Then I remembered something. I raced to the title page looking for a dedication.

Only a blank page and not a single word, no signature, no dedication. A pang of distress paralyzed my hand and I felt like crying.

Which of us had the fake copy, when we both had copies without dedication?

Which of us did you persuade was inside the book, as he was inside your heart and so no need for a dedication?

Did he believe you as well?

Did Ziad make you believe that he had decided to take the novel to reread wherever he was going?

That blank page was enough to convict you. It said, with

unwritten words, more than you could ever have written. So was it of any importance whether I found any letters of yours in that suitcase or not? You were a woman, an expert in writing on blank pages. I was the only one to know that.

Apart from your novel I found a black medium-sized diary at the bottom of the suitcase, like some deep secret. As I picked it up an orange Metro season ticket fell out. It expired at the end of October, the last month he used it to travel.

I glanced at the ticket, but I really only wanted to examine the diary, but I stopped and looked at the picture on the ticket. Pictures of the dead are confusing. And more confusing are the pictures of martyrs. Confusing, and more painful.

Suddenly, they become sadder and more mysterious.

Suddenly, they become more enigmatically beautiful, and we become uglier than they.

Suddenly, we are afraid to look for long at their eyes.

Suddenly, we are afraid of our future pictures as we look at them.

How gallant was that man Ziad. That hidden, mysterious, inexplicable charm. Even that snapshot taken and developed within three minutes, with five prints, was able to make him a man apart.

Even after his death he was compelling, with that strange mocking sadness. It was as if he was already mocking a moment such as this.

I understood once more that you loved him. Before you, I loved him in another way, as we love someone we like and who is, for some reason, a role model.

Many times we sat with him, went out in his company, and were seen with him. It was as if, deep down, we believed that the beauty and obsessiveness, the talent and all the qualities in him we cherished might be infectious and be transferred to us simply by our all living together with him.

What a daft thought! I did not discover whether that was a cause for my misfortunes until recently, when I read a remarkable article by a French writer—who was also a painter: *Don't look for beauty, because when you have found it, you may have corrupted yourself.*

And I may have done just that.

I put the picture away and began turning the pages of his diary.

I felt that something might surprise me, or might upset me and open the gates of another late-season hurricane. What did he write in this diary?

I knew that the truth always starts in a small way. I sensed that the truth here was very small, in the form of this pocket notebook. I was frightened. There were pages and pages of poetry, with marginal notes scattered all over the page. Some poems took up two or three pages. Then there were short thoughts of a few lines written in the middle of the page, always in red. It was as if he wanted to distinguish them from the rest of what he had written. Perhaps it was because it was not poetry. Perhaps it was more important than poetry.

Where do I start? How do I find you hidden in the secret recesses of Ziad? If only I could discover that.

The titles of the poems held me. I began by reading one poem and then tried to unravel the codes and symbols, and sometimes the more revelatory details.

I left those and turned breathlessly to another page, searching for more details, more proofs, for words that would tell me, unequivocally, what happened between the two of you.

But I was in such an emotional state of conflicting feelings that my mind was almost numbed. It made me incapable of distinguishing between what I was reading and what I imagined.

I looked at myself in the midst of Ziad's things and his open suitcase, holding his little black notebook and I felt ashamed. Opening that suitcase was nothing but a dissection of Ziad's corpse, embodied in these relics. I was trying to dig out his heart.

A heart that was beating for you continued, even after death, to beat in my hands. I felt the impact of his words, bitter, sad, and lustful.

On my body pass your lips
Where only swords have passed.
Woman of fire, light me up
Love brings us together one time

And death pulls us apart another
And a handful of soil rules us always . . .
Lust brings us together
Then one day
Pain pulls us apart when it becomes as big as a body
I become one in you
Woman of soil and marble
I watered you, then wept for you and said . . .
Princess of my love
Princess of my death
Come!

Many times I read this passage, with new emotions and new doubts each time, trying with the helplessness of one who is not a poet. Where was that frontier between symbol and reality?

Each verse cancelled the previous one, and the female was more and more a body united with the earth, and it was impossible to separate one from the other.

But reality was unmistakable in words of lust and desire:

Pass your lips on my body . . .
Woman of fire, light me up . . .
Lust brings us together . . .
I become one in you . . .

Was the revolution then just a word to Ziad? Did he only use it to justify himself? Did he prefer to be defeated by death and not by a woman? The problem of pride. Personal prevarication. Princess of my death, come.

Now death came in the end. Did you come that day? Were you really alone with him? Did you really pass your lips over his body? Did you light him up and become one with him?

That probably happened. The date of the verses corresponds to the time I was in Spain.

My heart filled with strange emotions, unlinked to jealousy. We are not jealous of the dead. But we cannot change the taste of bitterness in these circumstances. How could I stop the tears as my eyes read this thought written in red ink?

There is not much time left
You who are standing at the crossroads of contradictions
I know
You will be my last mistake.
I ask you
How long will I still be your first mistake?
You have plenty of time for more than a start
But all endings are short.
I now end up with you
Who gives to life another life that is good for more than one
* ending?*

Some words held me and baffled me:

Red ink suddenly takes on a color similar to pink blood shyly
* dripping on a page.*
Let it be the color of your first mistake.

I closed the diary quickly, fearing to reach the core of these
pages and be shocked at some unexpected turn. I recalled something Ziad said a long time ago, "The reason I admire Adam is
because the day he decided to taste the apple, he ate it all and
not just a bite. Even then, he knew there weren't half-sins or
half-pleasures. There is no third place between heaven and hell,
and we should deserve to enter either place."

I admired his philosophy of life, and I did not know why it
hurt me to have agreed with him on such matters.

Was it because he stole the apple from my secret garden this
time?

Or was it because he was having it before my eyes, with relish
and comfort?

Trees don't choose . . .
They also make love standing up.
Palm of my passion . . . Stand!
Alone, I mourned the woods they have burned
To bring the trees to their knees,
But trees die standing.

Come, stand with me
I want to show you the man in me
All the way to this final burial place.

I began suddenly to feel the folly of having opened this diary.

My personal examination and interpretation of each word exhausted me. I began to feel remorse. After all, I did not want to hate Ziad then. I was just unable to. Death had granted him an immunity from hatred and jealousy on my part. I felt diminished before him, before his death. Moreover, I had nothing to charge him with, except words for which there was more than one interpretation.

So why did I insist on the most unfavorable interpretation?

I was pursuing him with suspicions, when I knew he was a poet who specialized in linguistic rape. It was his way of avenging a world that failed to measure up to him.

He was born outstanding. His only destiny was the destiny of trees. Was I to call him to account even for the manner of his death, or for the way he loved?

I remember his silence. And then his look that was focused for some time on my amputated arm. Then he said something that led to a change in the course of my life. That first time he came to my office I made some comments on his poetry and I suggested that he drop some verses.

"Don't amputate my poems, sir," he said. "Give me back my poems and I'll get them published in Beirut."

Why did I accept his contempt then, without offering any reply? Why did I not slap him with my other, unamputated hand, and throw his manuscript back at him?

Maybe it was because I admired in him the steadfastness and loneliness of trees, at a time when pens were like reeds that bend with the wind.

I got to know him as I stood there, and so he left me with a manuscript as he had done on that first occasion, but without any explanation this time.

The remains of a former career stirred in me. I was examining the notebook, counting the pages with the eye of a publisher. A sudden excitement filled my heart, overwhelming all other emotions. A crazy idea took hold.

I would publish these writings, these last thoughts of Ziad, and call the volume *The Trees* or *The Jottings of a Man who Loved You*, or any other title I might stumble on along the way. In this way I would give him another life, a life without summers. That was how poets avenged a destiny that pursued them as the summer pursues butterflies.

They would be transformed into poetry, and who is able to kill words?

I would spend long hours transcribing one poem, or finding a title for another. I was organizing the chaos of these thoughts and also the scattered paragraphs to make them suitable for publication.

It gave me great pleasure to do this, but I also felt some bitterness. Pleasure for my bias for butterflies and pleasure for breathing life into words that only I could have either buried with the notebook or immortalized in the form of a book.

And bitterness, bitterness for rummaging through the papers of a dead poet and wandering around in possession of the circulation of his blood, feeling his pulse, his sorrow and his ecstasy, and entering his closed secret world without permission. Then acting on his behalf, selecting, editing, and omitting. All this made me ask myself whether I had the right to do so. Who could claim he had authority for such a task? But then, who would presume to sentence other people's words to death? Who would decide to take possession of them?

Deep inside me, I knew that poets' and writers' deaths had an extra taste of sorrow that set them apart from other people. The only consolation was probably that after they died they left on their desks the beginnings of dreams and incomplete scribblings. And so their passing caused us embarrassment as much as grief.

Ordinary people show their dreams and cares and their feelings about the world. They dress each day with a smile or a look of despair, a laugh or a chat, and their secrets die with them.

Ziad's secret embarrassed me at first, but then his words started creating inside me an irresistible urge to write, an urge that grew every time I felt that his words did not plumb the depths of my wound.

Perhaps he did not know my side of the story. The one only I knew.

When was the idea of this book born? Was it during that time I spent surrounded by Ziad's poetic legacy? When I unexpectedly encountered the literature and the manuscripts from which I had been separated ever since I left my job several years ago in Algiers?

Or was it during that last unexpected encounter with a city where that same destiny had arranged for me a late appointment? Was it possible that I would find myself face to face with Constantine without warning, making me explode into torrents of yearning, nostalgia, and disillusion.

So the words swept me away to where I am.

FIVE

I WELL remember that extraordinary Saturday evening when the phone rang as I was watching the news. It was Si Sharif on the line, with an eager warmth that at first made me happy and took me out of my evening routine of silent loneliness.

His voice was a cause for celebration. It was my only link to you after all the other approaches had been blocked. I felt optimistic. He always had the means of access to you in one way or another. But this time it was more than that.

Si Sharif apologized first for not making contact since our last evening together. He told me about his busy life, and endless visits of senior colleagues to Paris.

"I've not forgotten you all this time," he added. "I've put your picture up in my living room, and so I'm sharing my house with you, you know! Your views have had a great impact on me and have made more than one person envious of me. I then have to explain that the relationship, our friendship, goes back to our teens."

I listened to him, but my heart raced to you.

It was enough for me to know that the phone call came from a house you were in. I had become a naïve lover, filled with enthusiasm and folly. His voice brought me back to reality.

"Do you know why I called you this evening?" he asked. "I've made up my mind to take you with me to Constantine. You've

175

given me a painting of Constantine and I'll give you a journey there."

"Constantine? Why Constantine?" I cried out.

"We're going there," he said, as if he was imparting good news, "to attend the wedding of the daughter of my brother, Si Tahir."

Pause.

"Maybe you remember her," he went on. "She came to the opening of your exhibition months ago with my daughter, Nadia."

I suddenly felt my voice was separated from my body. I was unable to make any answer.

Can words floor a person like a thunderbolt in this way?

Because of one word, could I hold on to the phone?

At such moments I am reminded that I have only one arm. With my foot, I dragged a chair over and sat down.

Perhaps Si Sharif noticed my silence. "What upsets you about such a trip, my friend?" he said, breaking into my astonishment. "Your name came up a few days ago at a meeting of some friends in security. They assured me that there is nothing against you, and you can visit Algeria whenever you wish. Things have changed a lot since you came here. You should go back to Algeria even if only for a quick visit. I'm taking on the responsibility of your trip and pay for your expenses. So, what's worrying you so much?"

I tried to find some way out of my own tenseness. "The fact is," I answered, "I'm not psychologically ready for such a trip. I'd prefer it to be in different circumstances."

"There'll be no better conditions to return now. I'm sure if I don't drag you by the arm this time, it'll be years before you get back. Are you going to spend your whole life painting Constantine? And aren't you happy to attend the marriage of Si Tahir's daughter? She's your daughter as well. You knew her when she was little and should attend her wedding as a blessing. Do it for Si Tahir's sake. You must stand at my side on that day in the place of Si Tahir."

Si Sharif knew my weak spot, he knew what Si Tahir meant to me. He kept playing on the loyalty left in me to our past and to our shared memories.

I was standing on the line dividing reason and unreason, between laughter and tears.

"You knew her as a baby . . ."

No, my friend. I also knew her as a woman and that was the problem.

"She's your daughter as well . . ."

No, she was not. She could have been, but she might have been my lover too, my wife as well. She could have been mine.

"Who's the lucky man?" I asked.

"I've engaged her to Si X. He was there that evening when you came to my house. I don't know what you think of him, but he's a good man in spite of all that's said of him."

The last sentence was in reply to a comment he had expected.

A good man. . . . Was that really what distinguished him?

I happen to know more than one good man who could have become her husband.

But Si X was a lot more than that. He was the man of secret deals, the man in the front row, a man of hard currency and hard tasks. He was a military man, a man of the future. With all that, did it matter anymore if he was *good* or not?

More than one lump gathered in my throat preventing me from expressing my real opinion of that person, or asking Si Sharif if he really thought that a man without any scruples could be *good.* I kept silent because I began to make no distinction between the two men. Besides, how clean was he to give away his 'daughter' to such a tainted person?

I lost any will to say anything. I was struck dumb by the succession of shocks in that one telephone conversation.

"Congratulations!" was all I could say. It could be interpreted in more than one way.

"Thank you! God bless you!" he answered conventionally.

"We'll see you there then," he added with the happiness of someone who has passed an exam. "We're looking forward to the wedding. It'll be on July 15. We leave in ten days. Call me and we'll sort out the details."

The call was over. A new phase of my life started. A new lifetime began on that day, with you officially out of it, but were you really out of it? I was the only one left on the chessboard. All the squares on the board were white. All the pieces had become one piece which I grasped with my one hand. Was I winner or loser? How could I know? The chessboard shrunk and with it space (or hope or anticipation). Another party had made a decision and we were all, as we had been from the beginning, at the beck and call of . . . destiny.

I often hated that destiny but yielded to it most of the time without offering any resistance. I surrendered with a mysterious enjoyment and with the curiosity of a man who always wishes to know how far destiny will take him. How ridiculous could it be? How unfair could life get?

Life was a disgrace if it only gave itself away to those who got rich quick and who behaved badly, people who would abuse that life.

At that moment I found a rare pleasure in comparing myself with the frivolity of others. In my actual setbacks I found evidence of triumphs that were beyond the reach of others. Was it at such a crazy moment that I agreed to witness your wedding, my funeral? Was it a humiliation that could be faced without embarrassment? Or was I a supreme masochist, insisting on living out my absolute misery in the absence of absolute happiness? Would I go with you to the end, torturing myself, searing my heart to cure myself of you?

That day I hated you more intensely than ever before.

My feelings switched into new feelings, a mixture of jealousy, bitterness, hatred, and probably disdain as well. What had gotten into you? Are women really like nations, forever being feebly seduced by military uniforms, even ones that were fading? I still wonder to this day why I consented to go to Constantine for your wedding. I already realized that the invitation was not just a friendly gesture from a man to whom I was bound by more than one tie. Above all, he was abusing Si Tahir's memory and using one of the few names still untarnished at a time when corruption was rife.

Si Sharif knew he was doing a deal, selling, with this marriage, the name of his brother, one of our greatest martyrs, in exchange for some big position and other fixes. He was acting in his name, in a way he would not have accepted had he been alive. He needed the blessing of the only friend and comrade-in-arms of Si Tahir. He needed me and nobody else to bless your rape. I was the last of the scattered sacred band surviving from those times. He needed my blessing to silence his own conscience.

Did he believe that Si Tahir would forgive him, after he had lived off his name all that time? Why did I agree to play along with this game? And why did I leave you to their fangs?

Was it because I knew that my blessing would be a pure formality? It would neither advance nor delay anything. If he was not marrying you off to this *Si*, then you would fall to another *Si*, one of the new ones. And in the end, did it matter whose of the forty thieves' names you bore?

Why did I agree to travel? Was it for those reasons, or was it because I had surrendered to the lure of Constantine, to its secret summons that had been chasing me forever, just as the sirens of the enchanted isles called to those sailors on whose boats fell the curse of the gods?

Besides, I was unable to miss out on a single appointment with you, even if it was your wedding. There were other contradictory considerations, so how was it possible for me to explain, outside logic, the decision I took?

I was like a mad scientist, trying to mix two explosive substances at the same time: you and Constantine, like two destructive formulas created by my own hand out of passion, nostalgia, and madness. I wanted to test them together as one might test a nuclear device in the desert. I would experience one inner explosion, go through it alone and be destroyed alone, and leave the explosion scene in pieces: a new man or the remains of a man. Did you not once say that deep inside each of us lived 'the lust of flames'?

After that, I discovered a similar feeling within my soul toward you and toward that city. Both of you had an inextinguishable flame and a supernatural power to start fires. But together, you pretended to be declaring war on the spirits. It was the superficiality of ancient and respected cities and the hypocrisy of women of good families, was it not?

Your voice came on Monday. There were no preliminaries. There was no hint of joy or sadness, not the slightest embarrassment.

You started talking to me as if you were carrying on a conversation we had begun the day before. You did not sound like one who had not spoken to me on that telephone line for six months. How strange is the connection between you and time! And how odd is your memory!

"Hi there, Khalid! Have I woken you up?"

I may have said no, but more probably I said yes. But I was speaking as one emerging from infatuation.

"It's you!" I cried.

You laughed, that childlike laugh that once used to delight me. "I thought it was me. Have you forgotten my voice?"

In response to my silence, you added, "How are you?"

"I'm trying to put up with it."

"Put up with what?"

"Time."

You paused and, as if you were feeling guilty, you said, "We all try to do that."

"Did my news upset you?" you added.

Strange was your question. As strange as your memory, just like your relationship with one you love.

"Your news is just one of those things."

"I thought you'd take the news of my wedding differently," you said with dissembling innocence. "I heard my uncle talking to you yesterday and I was happy to learn that you agreed without any argument or hesitation to come to Constantine. I decided you should be asked. I realized you were no longer a burden to me. I want you to come to this wedding. You've got to come."

I don't know why your words brought back the earlier talk with Si Sharif when he persuaded me that you were 'my daughter.' I felt once again that I was on that dividing line between sense and nonsense, laughter and tears.

"I wish I could understand why you all insist so much on my coming," I said with a mocking bitterness.

"My uncle's motives are of no concern to me at all, but I'd be very unhappy if you don't come."

"Is sadism, then, your latest hobby?"

"I fell in love with this city because of you," you said, surprising me.

"I fell in love with you when I read your book," I replied in the same way.

"You shouldn't have read it then."

"You shouldn't have loved this city then."

What you said next sent shockwaves through my body.

"But I loved you."

For a whole year I had waited in vain for those words. Should I show gratitude or should I weep? Or ask you why now? Why do you continue to torment me?

"What about him?"

"It is my destiny," you answered as if you spoke of something that was not your concern.

"We get the destiny we deserve," I broke in. "I had expected another destiny for you. How can you agree to be bound to *him*?"

"I don't. I'm only running away to him, from memories that have become uninhabitable. I have fed on impossible dreams and repeated disappointments."

"Why him? How can you drag your father's name into the mud like that? You are not just a woman, you are the nation. Aren't you concerned about what history will one day write?"

"You're the only person," you said, bitterly for the first time, "who thinks history sits like some recording angel registering our little victories, our books, our defeats. History doesn't write anymore, my friend. It erases."

I did not ask you what you meant, nor did I argue about your mistaken notion of values.

"What is it exactly you want from me?" I asked.

"I want you . . . ," you said like a child wanting a sweet.

I was so confused and I wondered whether you were the kind of woman incapable of loving one man, and had to have two men in tow at the same time. First it was me and Ziad, now it is me and him.

Your voice became sweet music again.

"Khalid, do you know how much I have loved you? I've wanted

you and desired you like crazy. Something in you made me lose my mind for awhile, but I decided to get you out of my system. Our relationship was sick. You said so yourself."

"Then why have you come back to me now?"

"Only to persuade you to come to Constantine. I want this city to give us its blessing even if only once, even if it is a lie. It conspired with us and gradually led us to our madness. I know we can't meet up there. We might not talk to each other or even shake hands. But I will be yours as long as we are there together. It will be the only one to know that I am offering you my first night. Would that please you?"

How many first nights have you had? How many illusions have you offered? Like the unsigned copies of your book that you offered to Ziad and to me.

Whose will you be after all these illusions? With whom will you start your first lie? I was then like the hungry Ethiopian to whom they read out a list of delicious dishes he will never taste; and then later they ask him how he found the meal and whether he had enjoyed it. I did not laugh.

"It would," I said with the stupidity of a lover.

I did not realize that you were offering me an illusion that I had immediately to give up to another man who would benefit from it for real.

But did it really matter? Giving something away I'd never had anyway?

That, my dear, is history. That is the past. We call on it to make up for the deficiencies of the present. We play tricks with memory. We toss a bone to it to play with, while the table is laid for others.

That is the way with people as well. We shower them with dreams, heaps of processed dreams of transient happiness. We turn away from the banquets to which we will never be summoned.

But I only became aware of that later. After the table was cleared away and everybody had gone I was left by myself, face to face with my memory.

"I want to see you," I said.

"No, it's not possible any longer," you cried. "And it's probably better that way. We must find a less painful end to our story. Let Constantine be our union and our separation. No need for more suffering."

You made up your mind then. You decided to kill me by the book, with a stroke of the knife back and forth, in one ceremony of encounter and farewell. How kind of you, how stupid of me.

More than one question was still left suspended, more than one accusation and more than one wish, but your call ended the way it began—somehow out of time. I was half asleep, stretched out on my bed in a daze, until later I wondered, "Did you really call? Or was I only dreaming?"

There we were again, like children.

Wiping the chalk from the floor to devise a new set of rules for the new game.

Playing smart to win, clothes getting dirty, scratching ourselves while hopping from one impossible square to another.

Every square was a trap set for us, where we left behind some of our dreams.

But then, we had to admit that we were past jumping on one foot and living in imaginary squares. We were wrong, my dear. Nations were not drawn with chalk, love was not written with tracings in the sand. We were wrong. History is not written on the blackboard, chalk in one hand, the eraser in the other. Life is not a swing that goes from the possible to the impossible.

Stop the game! Stop a moment! Let us stop running around in all directions. We have forgotten who was the cat, who the mouse. Who was going to devour the other?

Remember that they will devour us together.

There is not much time for us to lie. There was nothing ahead but that last curve, nothing below but destruction.

So let us admit having been crushed together.

You are not my love. You are my love project for years to come, the project for my next story, my next joy, another lifetime.

Meanwhile, love as many men as you wish and write as many stories as you want. Only I know the story that will never be written.

Only I know your forgotten heroes and the ones you made out of paper. Only I know the strange way you love and the unique way you kill your lovers to fill your novel. You killed me for several mysterious reasons, and I loved you for other mysterious reasons.

I turned you from a woman into a city, and you turned me from gems to rubble.

Do not spend so much time destroying me.

The time for earthquakes is not over. Still in the heart of this nation lie stones that volcanoes have not yet loosened.

Let us stop playing for a moment. All those repeated lies have been enough for you.

I know today that you will never belong to me.

Let me therefore be with you where you are to be with your other half.

Woman with the contours of our country!

Does it matter whether we remain together after today?

Just a small suitcase to take with me to my homeland. Nothing but a dark suit for your wedding, two bottles of whisky, a couple of shirts and some razor blades. Some nations produce all kinds of excuses for death, and forget to produce razor blades. With all my wounds I return home. No excess personal luggage, only the burden of a memory I bore alone, of no interest to anyone else.

No personal baggage. No extra weight, no extra expense.

The ticket was the heaviest thing to carry.

Walking on my last wound, I hastened back to Algeria.

An unexpected return after a decade of exile. I had expected another kind of reunion.

I could have reserved a first-class seat. It happens that those with such tickets are not allowed to sit at the back. But it does not matter. Those front seats are already reserved by those who have taken the nation's front seats. So I went home the way I left, on a seat at the rear, a seat of sorrow.

When we leave home, we carry what we have stuffed in the cupboards of our lives, pictures of those we love, treasured books, the memory of the faces of loved ones, letters, and other things we have written.

A final glance at the old woman next door who we may never see again. A kiss on a little cheek that will grow after we leave. A tear for our nation, to which we may not return.

We take the homeland as furniture for our exile. We forget when the homeland puts us down at its door, when, unaffected by our tears, it closes its heart against us without so much as a nod at our suitcases. We forget to ask who will take our place after we go.

Coming back, we bring only suitcases full of nostalgia, a bundle of dreams, rose-tinted, for such dreams cannot be bought at a cheap Algerian store.

It is not right to buy and sell the homeland on the black market. There are humiliations that are tougher for the veterans than a thousand tough assignments.

So here I am with a small bag in the middle of nowhere, some point between earth and heaven, fleeing from one memory into the arms of another.

I sit in an economy-class seat, a refuge of oblivion. I fly over the peaks of your love. The altitude is so high that I cannot see or forget.

In spite of the passing of time, I wondered whether I was committing some final act of folly by throwing myself back home in order to escape from you. I was trying to cure myself of you by returning, by seeking comfort in you from my homeland.

We are traveling together at last. I have a wedding present, one of my paintings. It occupies the empty seat at my side. We take the same plane for the last time, but heading in different directions.

Constantine! Two more hours for the heart to go back a lifetime. A flight attendant opens the door, unaware of the heart she has just forced open. Who can stop the hemorrhage of memory now?

Who will be able to close the window to nostalgia now? Who can face the wind that will raise the veil from the city's face and look her in the eye without shedding a tear?

Here is Constantine . . .

Here I am, carrying in my one hand a small bag and a painting on its last trip with me, after twenty-five years.

Here is *Nostalgia*, my inadequate representation of Constantine encountering its original in a nocturnal rendezvous. Like me, it almost collapsed on the steps, exhausted, astonished, and confused.

Cold eyes tossed us both. Imperious orders. Closed faces. All these pale gray walls. Is this *home*?

Constantine, how are you, Mother dear? Open your arms and hold me. Painful is exile and painful too is this return. So cold is your airport that I can no longer remember, and so cold is your mountain night that can no longer remember me.

Cover me, lady of warmth and of cold. Drop the cold and leave the disillusion to later. I come to you after years of cold and disillusion. Do not abandon me to my raw wounds.

Signs in Arabic, some official pictures and those faces, brown like mine, made me realize that I was face to face with my homeland.

They give a sense of estrangement that is unique to airports in the Arab world. Only Hassan's face filled me with sudden warmth and melted the ice of that first impression in the airport.

He hugged me and took my hand luggage. As we proceeded he said in a curious Algerian accent, "You haven't changed, sir! Still carrying paintings."

He then added, "This is a blessed day. Who'd have thought we'd ever see you again here?"

I felt as if Constantine was assuming his features and had finally come to welcome me. Hassan was no different from the city itself, its stones, its plasterwork, its bridges and its schools, its alleyways and its memories. He had been born and raised here, had studied here, and had become a teacher. He had left the city only for short trips to Tunis or Paris. He would come and see me from year to year and get a few things for his children. His small family was growing so fast that it was as if he had taken, all by himself, responsibility for the name of a big family. He had given up trying to persuade me to get married and knew that the only sons and daughters I would ever have would be my paintings. They alone would bear my name.

Today I discovered that the good man who always spoke with

stubborn enthusiasm and with the repetitiveness of teachers was only my brother. He still talked as if he was addressing his pupils.

In that extraordinary day of pain, disappointment, and joy, I felt as if my relationship with him was the only solid ground where I could stand with all my internal turmoil. His was the only chest on which, but for my pride, I could have cried at that moment.

Ten years had gone by, during which I had often waited for him at Orly International Airport. The roles were now reversed. Usually, he was the visitor, I was meeting him. I felt then that I was performing a family duty, not a ceremony, a duty I had chosen. It was one of the rare opportunities to take on the role of older brother, with all its responsibilities and obligations. I had always been away from my brother and it hurt because I knew how much he was attached to me and how he needed my affection after we lost Mother at an early age.

That was probably why he married so young and surrounded himself with a large family, a family he had never known as a child. I had been unable to make it up to him because I only appeared whenever I was moving from one exile to another. Today, it is the other way around: Hassan is reversing all the earlier roles. In spite of the age difference and in spite of six kids, he is making me feel that I was the younger brother and that he was seven or more years older than me. Was it because he was carrying my bag, walking ahead of me and asking me about the journey? Or was it that airport? It was a challenge to my manly pride and stripped me of the dignity of age. I let Hassan deal with all the formalities on my behalf. With his experience of living in this city of changing moods, he seemed older.

Or was it you, Constantine, the mother of extreme emotions? Love and hatred, tenderness and roughness? Stepping foot on your soil I became the shy and confused young man I was thirty years ago.

I looked at the city through the windows of the car that took me from the airport to the house, and wondered, Do you recognize me, Constantine? You welcome spies and men with broad shoulders and dirty hands in VIP lounges, while I stand in line like a traveling salesman and the unprivileged? Do you recognize me, Constantine, as you scan my passport but fail to look at me?

I was once asked, "Which of your children would be dearest to you?"

"Until he returns," I replied, "the absent one. Until he is better, the one who is sick. Until he grows up, the little one."

But Constantine was unaware of this notion. I did not blame the city. I blamed the books of Arab heritage I had read.

I did not sleep that night.

'Atiqa, Hassan's wife, had prepared a feast of dishes that I had not tasted for many years, and I had a great appetite. That had been one reason for my sleepless night. But it may also have been the shock of this latest emotional homecoming to the house of my birth and childhood. On the walls, stairs, and windows, in the rooms and corridors, memories were piled up inside me. They overwhelmed me and suddenly they wiped all else away. Here I was, living in my memories in the house. How could anyone else sleep amid these pillows of memories? Those who had moved on flitted through these rooms in my mind's eye.

I could almost see the long trail of Mother's blue skirt going back and forth in this room, a hidden presence of motherhood. I could almost hear Father's voice asking for water or yelling from the bottom of the stairs, "Make way . . . make way," warning the women of the household to hide themselves in a room because a man was paying a visit.

My eyes searched the new white walls for the nail on which Father hung my primary school certificate some forty years ago. A few years later, he hung another one, but after that nothing.

His interest in me made way for other interests and other plans that ended with Mother's death and his remarriage and the redecoration of this room.

I could almost see Mother's body being carried out through the narrow door, followed by a group of Qur'an readers and a group of weeping women.

I could almost see, just a few weeks later, another procession this time bringing in a young bride, with another group of chanting women.

One night I kissed Hassan farewell and set off to join the battlefront. He did not ask me where I was going. He was fifteen years old, but emotionally older than his years. Like me, being an orphan had taught him early to be an adult and to keep questions to himself.

But he did ask, "What about me?"

"You're still young, Hassan," I replied with a similar anxiety. "Wait for me."

"Look after yourself, Khalid," he said with the tones of an anxious mother. Then he burst into tears.

This was the nation I had one day substituted for my mother.

Today, a lifetime later, and after more than one shock and more than one wound, I realize that you can be orphaned by your nation. Some countries exercise humiliation, harshness and oppression, tyranny and selfishness. Some countries lack the idea of motherhood. They are only like fathers.

I did not get to sleep until the early hours.

There was a taste of bitterness that first night. I was dozing and woke up to the cries of Hassan's youngest child asking for mother's warm bosom and his breakfast. I envied him for his innocence, for his infant courage, and his capacity to speak up without saying a word.

That morning, in my first encounter with the city, I was lost for words. I felt that Constantine had beaten me, and that it had only brought me there to make me admit my defeat. I had no wish to resist fate. Others before me had been defeated at that city's hand. It made graveyards out of their madness.

And I was the last of its lovers. I was that handicapped lover, the alternative hunchback of Notre Dame, the last idiot of Constantine. What lured me into that idiocy? What made me spend a lifetime hanging around?

The city was like you. It had two names and more than one date of birth. Now, emerging from its past, it had one official name and one name for memory. Its other name was Cirta. The invincible. It was like a female city. And there were men with the arrogance of the military. From here they set out for Sfax, Masinissa, and Jugurta. Others had preceded them.

In its caves they had left their memories and carved out their love, their fear, and their gods. They left their statues behind, their tools, gold coins, triumphal arches, and Roman bridges.

Only one bridge was holding on, and the city now had only one name, Constantine, a name given it by the Emperor Constantine sixteen centuries ago. I pitied that arrogant Roman emperor for whom Constantine was not his favorite city. He was linked to it only for chance historical reasons.

I myself gave you a name that was not my name.

Perhaps for that reason I reflected this law of stupidity. I called the city Cirta, to return it to its first legitimate status.

Exactly. Just as I called you Hayat, life.

Like all invaders, the Emperor Constantine was mistaken.

Like its women, it was the illusion of victory and no one learned a lesson from the graveyard. There were Roman graves, Vandal, Byzantine, Fatimid, Hafisid, and Ottoman graves, and the graves of the forty-one beys who ruled the city before it fell into the hands of the French.

One could see where the French army stood for seven years before the city's gate. France, which entered Algiers in 1830, did not conquer this city perched on a rock until 1837, and there they left half their army and Constantine its best men. Since then, more than one bridge found its way to the city, and more than one road led to it.

The French followed a passage through the mountains to get there because they knew there was nothing below but a big drop. It was a city that was waiting forevery invader. It wrapped itself up in its black cloak and hid its secrets from tourists. Deep gorges protected it on every side. Secret caves and more than one saint protected it, their graves scattered on the slopes below the bridges. There was The Arches, the nearest bridge to my home and to my memory. In my drowsiness and confused memory I would walk across it as automatically as if I was drawing it. It seemed as if I was living my life through it.

Everything seemed so fast on the bridge: cars, pedestrians, and even birds, as if something was waiting for them on the other side. It may be that some of them did not know that they had left behind whatever they were looking for. In reality, there was no difference between the two sides of the bridge, the only difference being what was above and what was below. That frightful gorge that was on the other side of the metal barrier: nobody ever stopped there to look down. Man, perhaps out of nature, does not stare at the face of death. Not much. But I stopped to look down. Was it because I had some idea? Or did I wish just to be alone with this city on a bridge?

There are follies that should not be committed, as if you are arranging a date with your memory on a bridge. Especially when you suddenly remember the story of an ancestor who threw himself off a bridge: it could have been this one. I had forgotten about it for years.

It happened after the bey had threatened him with death, when news reached him of a treacherous conspiracy my ancestor and other notables were involved in to depose him. He had been a special messenger, a man of trust.

My forebear in those days was too weak to stand alone in the face of that awful death sentence. It was more than a matter of being led to stand in humiliation before that bey. So when the bey sent someone to fetch him, my forebear was a corpse in a deep gorge such as this, the deepest of valleys. He had refused to give the bey the honor of killing him.

I heard this story once from my father when I asked him what the story behind our name was.

It seems he used to not enjoy telling the story. Suicide was a disgrace, an irreligious act among the God-fearing community of Constantine. Because of this our family migrated to the west of Algeria, exchanging an unknown name for their earlier name. They did not return to Constantine until after a generation or more with a name taken from that other city.

What was I doing on this bridge looking into 170 meters filled only with the wheeling of crows? Had I come for the remains of some forebear called Ahmad? He was said to be handsome, with money and a lot of learning, and that one day he threw everything away here. So he left his sorrows and wounds as an inheritance to his family.

This was Constantine.

A city to which others give only a glance. A city concerned with its reputation and fearful of the tittle-tattle people are so good at, a city that purchases its honor sometimes with blood, sometimes with exile.

Has it changed, I wonder?

I remember in my youth hearing about a family that left Constantine suddenly for another city after a popular song about one of their girls had been written by a member of the family.

Was I here for a rendezvous with my memory or with my painting?

I was here without brush or paints, without the intimidation of a great blank canvas.

I was not creative at that moment, neither artist nor inventor. I was a part of the city, and I could become a part of its contours and details. I could cross that metal barrier just as I crossed into the frame and entered it forever. I could roll down into the rocky deep valley, a human drop for some color on an immortal painting, for a scene I wished to paint. Instead it painted me.

Would this not be a magnificent ending for an artist? To be merged into a landscape painting!

Looking down into the gorges and at the tunnels in the rocks above the foaming river, I knew that vertigo was summoning me to a sensuous death that could be my last chance of being united with Constantine, and with an ancestor with whom I felt some strange rapport.

The yearning to jump and to be destroyed was one that made me feel dizzy as I stood alone on that bridge.

I am sorry if I felt a sudden embarrassment about this city. Only outsiders should have a fear of heights. When exactly did Constantine place me among those who were disloyal?

In spite of all this, I confess I was not ready to die. Not that I was so attached to life, but the deep melancholy that had imbued me from the moment of my arrival in Constantine gave me another strange extreme sensation. With my bitterness and disappointments, I yet achieved an utter serenity, an inexplicable happiness. I learned to laugh at what provoked me and to face up to memories with a black sense of humor. Was it not just mad to be there? Was that not chasing after insanity in a city that recognized it? I was therefore enjoying that painful game, living the shocks to the full, in an intentionally masochistic manner.

After all, my disillusions with the city could become the crazy source of future genius.

But despite all this, I decided to flee from the bridge that I adored and that had been for a long time the focus of my life and memories. It was the source of all madness and inspiration. I had surrounded myself with copies of it. My eyes went back to the foot of the mountain that was so wonderfully sprinkled with wild flowers and daffodils, where the people of Constantine used to celebrate the arrival of spring, carrying their food and desserts and coffee. Everything looked sad and gloomy now. It was as if the flowers had disappeared for some reason.

The site of the shrine of Sidi Muhammad al-Ghurab from afar reminded me of a history book I had recently read and a shiver went down my spine.

What if I was unwittingly carrying the curse that befell Salih Bey, one of the biggest beys of Constantine? He wanted to complete his building program and various improvements to the city, such as repairing the bridge of arches, linking that tongue of land that was Constantine to the outside world. It was the only Roman bridge to have survived. Since then, more than one bridge found its place around the city and more than one road leading to it. The popular story has it that this bridge was one of the causes of the terrible destruction of Salih Bey.

He had killed there Sidi Muhammad, a saint with a great popular following. When the holy man's head fell to the ground, his body turned into a crow, *ghurab* in Arabic, and flew off to Salih Bey's house in the country. The crow cursed him and swore that he would meet an end no less horrible than that of the holy man. Salih Bey then left his house and lands forever, fleeing from that crow. He remained in his house in the city.

And so people called this spot Sidi Muhammad al-Ghurab. It was still, after two centuries, a pilgrimage site for the Muslims and Jews of Constantine. They came at weekends and spent whole weeks on holiday there. They would wear pink gowns and performed rituals inherited from generations back. They offered him pigeons and bathed in the warm water of the rocky pools where turtles used to live. They lived on spirits and surrendered themselves to primitive dances in circles out in the open to rhythms of popular music.

But Constantine held no grudge against the bey who had given it so much wealth. In a crazy way, Constantine treated the killer and the victim equally. It made the pilgrimage site of Sidi Muhammad al-Ghurab the most famous site in Constantine. Every street bore the name of some saint. It immortalized the name of Salih Bey, more recognized than the other forty-one governors it had known.

The saint was immortalized through songs that chanted of his tragic end and beautiful poetry was recited in his honor. To this day, women of the city mourn him with their black cloaks—though they may not realize it. This is Constantine.

There was division between its curse and its mercy, no barrier between love and hatred, and no known measures for its logic. It eternalized those it wanted and punished those it wanted.

Whoever accuses it of being a crazy place, or adopts some attitude towards it—either of love or hatred—in guilt or innocence, has to acknowledge that it is always itself and its opposite.

With every passing day, I became more and more involved with the memory of that city. I was seeking, during my long evenings with Hassan, in chats that sometimes went on until the early hours, some other way to forget.

I was searching in that family environment that I had long missed, I was searching for tranquility. I came back to that house every night because we were unexpectedly drawn together: I knew the house and the house knew me. It was as if I was climbing up to the purlieus of a faraway childhood and returning to the womb. I was hiding in the womb of an illusory mother, a womb that had been empty for thirty years.

One night I remembered Ziad. I would recall the times he stayed with me for a few months in Algiers, when his landlord refused to renew the lease. I had gotten used to giving him the bed and sleeping on a mattress on the floor in the other room. Ziad was not happy about this and showed embarrassment and thought I was being too polite. He could not believe I was enjoying the situation because it reminded me of my childhood, when I used to sleep next to my mother for many years. I still remember how comfortable it was. I miss that blue quilt. I remember those days when Mother set aside each autumn for washing and restoring the woolen mattresses: they were the only furniture in the bedrooms. I wished I could ask 'Atiqa to put a mattress on the floor for me, as she did for her kids. They used to sleep in other rooms, on one shared mattress on the floor. They were warm and wanted to snuggle together beneath the lovely woolly coverlets that roused a nostalgia for some remote time. I wondered whether I had really lived it or just imagined it.

But how could I ask 'Atiqa to do that? She had given me the prettiest room of the house, a comfortable modern room, made to receive guests and designed rather for conjugal nights of love. It would embarrass her, and she would not understand. She took part in our evening chats and had been asking me, the civilized man from Paris, to persuade her brother to give up this 'Arab house' and the old ways of living. She even seemed to apologize sometimes for things that were to me rare or picturesque.

Because I was unable to convince her otherwise and because I was not bold enough to contradict her, all I did was listen to her long arguments with Hassan that almost turned into rows before they went into bed.

Hassan's comments would seem like an apology: "How can you convince a woman that watches *Dallas* on the television to live in a house like this and feel grateful? They should ban these programs as long as they can't provide people with a proper life."

He used to say that in order to be happy, you have to be able to look down on someone else.

"If you have a piece of bread in your hand and you see some-one who has nothing in his hand, you can thank God and be happy. But if you hold your head in the clouds and see someone with a cake in his hand, you won't be content, but you'll die of humiliation. You will be mortified at your discovery."

And so, in Hassan's view, life in such a house, in spite of its negative aspects—sometimes inhibiting with its details of a past age—was better than the lives of tens of thousands who did not have such a roomy house to live in with their women and children. Lots of people had to share a small flat with their extended family for years on end.

That was Hassan. He had a vertical view of things, probably because he learned all he knew as a child at the blackboard. He was happy with this point of view that reflected his standing as a government employee on an income that was as limited as his dreams.

What could he dream of? He was a teacher of Arabic who spent his life expounding literary texts, telling the stories of the lives of the old writers and poets to his pupils, and correcting the faults of their grammar and composition. He had neither the time nor the courage to grasp what was happening in front of him, of correcting the bigger errors in the corruption of language into an auction of slogans.

He was exhausted, absorbed in the problems of his young wife and six children. He tried to hide his bitterness but it was clear in many aspects of his life that he dreamed of a life beyond Constantine. At this time his dream was to meet someone who could help him get a new fridge. I was distressed to discover that not only were we lagging behind France and Europe, we were lagging behind where we had been half a century earlier under colonialism.

Our wishes then were nobler.

Our dreams were loftier.

It was enough today to look at people's faces and to listen to their stories, or to take a look at the displays in bookshops to realize that.

We had dreams and we had culture. The city itself had had more books and newspapers than national institutions would produce today, greater in both quality and quantity.

We used to have thinkers, scientists, poets, wits, and writers, and we had pride in our Arab nation. Today, nobody buys a newspaper to keep, because there is nothing worth keeping anymore. Nobody sits down to read a book in order to learn something. Cultural misery has become a contagious phenomenon that you can acquire just from reading a book. Books in those days were always 'right.' There would be one among us who could speak correctly, like a book.

Today, books too lie. Like newspapers. And so we believe less and less. Our eloquence is dead, since our conversation revolves only around absent consumer items.

When I made this observation one day to Hassan he seemed to look at me in astonishment as he was discovering something for the first time. Then he said rather sadly, "That's true. They have created for us minor objectives that have no connection with the issues of the age. Phantom personal triumphs for some might be getting a small flat after years of being on a waiting list. Or maybe getting a fridge, or being able to buy a car. Or even just its tires. Nobody has the time or nerve to go beyond that and ask for more. We are tired. The complex cares of daily life destroy us. They always need means to solve the simplest detail. How can we think of other matters, about that life of culture that you talk about? Survival is all we care about. Everything else is trivial. We have become a nation of ants, scrabbling for food, or a stone under which we can hide with our children."

"What then do people do?" I asked naïvely.

"Nothing. Some wait, some steal, and some commit suicide. This is a city that offers you three choices under the same pretexts and the same justifications."

I feared for Hassan. I suddenly shuddered. "Do you have friends to go out with?" I asked him without thinking, as if I was asking him which of the three remedies he was going for.

"Some colleagues from school. Nobody else. All those we grew up with have left Constantine." He answered as if he liked my question, or was pleased with my sudden interest in the detail of his life.

He went on to list the names of families we had been close to who now lived abroad or in Algiers, leaving the city to others, mostly from nearby towns and villages. Then he said something that did not give me pause for thought then, but six years later has revealed itself to me in all its stupid dimensions.

"People from Constantine only come back for weddings and funerals."

Then, as if he had overlooked something important, he added, "I'll introduce you to Nasr, Si Tahir's son. He's sure to come to his sister's wedding. He's a fine man now, as big as you are. He often visits me here since he settled in Constantine a few months ago. He's the only one to have moved in the opposite direction. He refused a scholarship to go abroad to study. Can you imagine that? It's unbelievable. When I asked him why he didn't move away as the others did and get out of here, he said he was afraid not to come back. 'All my friends who went away didn't come back.'"

This man's extremism reminded me of you and I laughed. It seemed to run in the family. I wanted to carry on the conversation that was heading towards you, in one way or another.

"What does he do now?"

"As the son of a martyr he got a shop and a truck. He makes a good living, but he is still confused, and can't make up his mind whether to commit himself to business or to carry on his studies. I couldn't give him any advice. Unfortunately, you can't cut yourself off from higher studies: you'll regret that for the rest of your life. On the other hand, as he says, education doesn't count anymore. He sees highly educated young men without a job, whereas illiterates wander around in their Mercedes's and live in luxury villas. This is not the age of education: you've got to be smart. How can you convince any friend or even your own pupils to devote themselves to knowledge when it's no use anymore?"

"One needs to know what he wants out of life. Was money a principal concern? Or knowledge? Or inner balance?"

"What kind of balance are you talking about?" Hassan replied scornfully. "We were a bunch of semi-lunatics. Nobody knew what precisely they wanted or what to expect. That is the real problem in the world we live in. That's why young people are so frustrated. We all lost the initiative. It is the land of lost dreams. Educated people aren't happy. Nor are simple folk, for the rich. What's the point of education when you know you're going to end up working for an ignorant boss who got his job not because of his education but because of his connections? And what can you do with money in Constantine? All you can do is get an uncomfortable flat. Or lay on a wedding where a star singer will perform. Or if you don't have more than 20,000 dinars, either you spend it on drink, paying some local guy who hides behind some government official to buy it, or you get a visa and go to Saudi Arabia for the pilgrimage. You can perform your religious duties and book a place in heaven when this world becomes too much."

"Are you saying that they sold visas to people to go on the pilgrimage?"

"Of course they did. The government limited the number of pilgrims each year because of the high cost in hard currency, especially when they found out that most of them traveled repeatedly for commercial rather than religious reasons. How otherwise can you explain the fact that some have been to Mecca six or seven times with no influence whatsoever on their way of life? I know one drunken pilgrim who had alcohol all over his house, and another who was devoted to business, exchanging hard currency on the black market. They still go on the pilgrimage every year and can easily lay their hands on 20,000 dinars. Where can I get such a sum? My salary is not more than 4,000 a month."

"Do you want to go?"

"Of course, aren't I a Muslim? I went back to praying two years ago and my faith has helped me stay sane. How can you stand firm against all this injustice without faith? It gave me the strength to go on. Look around you."

Everyone here reached this conclusion, particularly the young: they are the real victims of the nation. Even Hassan started praying when he returned to Constantine. Maybe it was because of Constantine, or for some other reason. Maybe faith was like atheism, contagious. If you see them in their thousands heading towards the mosque on Fridays, pressing against the walls, pouring out all over the streets, you would stop and pray without wondering why.

I made no comment on Hassan's strange analyses. He was happy to have me around and happy to start his summer holidays that permitted him to talk at length to me after my long absence. I let him talk and talk, stripping a nation before my eyes, a nation I had cloaked with a crazy nostalgia and passion.

Was he somehow concerned with my disappointment and afraid of losing the joy of my return home and to him? He would stop to shift to another subject, as if he was trying to lure me indirectly back to the faith, to seduce me with redemption. As if just being in France was a sin, to him atheism. That was Hassan.

I could not prevent myself smiling, as I recalled that I had brought him a bottle of scotch as usual. As I went to bed that night I tried to enumerate my sins, but I did not find my vices any greater than those of others, perhaps less so.

I was no criminal, no atheist, no drunkard, no traitor, and no liar. I did not commit adultery. Fifty years of loneliness, half of which I called 'the broken years,' spent with one arm, a mutilated body with mutilated dreams.

How many women had I loved? I do not remember. I have undergone many experiences, from my first love with that Jewish neighbor whom I seduced, to the Tunisian nurse who seduced me. And several other women whose names or how they looked I cannot remember. They came into and out of my bed for purely physical reasons, leaving me empty; then you turned up.

My biggest offence was you, the only woman I never had, the only sin I did not commit. My original offences with you were 'right-handed offences,' the single hand with which I painted you, raped you, but in my imagination.

Will God punish me for the sins committed by the only hand he left me with? I cannot remember who said, "There is no merit in avoiding sin. Merit lies in not wanting to sin." I believed that with this concept only was I not a virtuous man. How could I not have desired you and not embarked on sin with you when love for you had a taste of forbidden fruit and of sanctity? I was sliding unthinkingly towards that love.

What was amazing in my story with you was that the reasons for which I loved you were the reasons that made me abandon your love. I would love you and then give up, more than once a day, and with the same intensity. In the end, I did nothing but try to find a way of stopping the emotional turmoil in which I had constantly been living with you.

I knew that a lover was like an addict who was unable to break his addiction all by himself, but felt he was plunging deeper and deeper into the abyss of death with each passing day. But he could not stand up and escape before he reached the bottom of hell, and feel himself in the depths of despondency and bitterness. It was a strange and bitter happiness. Everything would be decided in the next two days, and I would be through with you in one way or another.

'Atiqa was busy preparing herself for the big event, when she would accompany the women's convoy to the ceremonial bath the next day and then on to the henna night. She was coming and going, busy with us and with her children, packing things in her bag. After all, it was going to be a chance for the women to exhibit everything, including their underwear, in order to show a wealth that was mostly fake, or to convince themselves that they could still win a man over, just like the bride they were escorting whom they eyed in secret envy.

So be it. The rites of your happiness were to begin the next day, and the days we had stolen away from time to time would soon be at an end.

Sweet dreams to you, my lady, as you await the morrow.

And good night to you, my very own sorrow.

The other love woke me up this summer day and threw me down onto the streets.

As soon as I woke up I decided to run away from the house. Away from the never-ending tales of 'Atiqa about the wedding ceremonies and the personalities and big families that were coming especially for an event that Constantine had not experienced for years.

She followed me to the door. "Hey," she said. "People say they brought everything from France by plane a month ago. You should see the wedding dress and the other one she was wearing last night. Goodness me!"

I closed the door behind me, closing off access to my heart at the same time.

Why not? I thought. They own the country and the planes as well. They can import whatever they want, just as they have taken out everything.

Where do I run away to?

The door closed behind me; all that was in front of me was myself.

Without thinking, I threw myself into the mass of passersby, just walking the streets without aim. In that city, you had the choice of walking, leaning against a wall, or sitting in a café watching those walking by or leaning against the wall across the road. I began to walk. I had the feeling after a while that we were all going around this rocky city without knowing what to do with our anger and misery. I kept wondering who deserved to be stoned in that country: the one on top of everybody else, or those sitting on us? I was reminded of the title of a story by Malek Haddad, "Whistling around Yourself." I wish I had read it. Perhaps I might find an explanation for all these riddles we become.

Then my thoughts led me to a vision. I once saw a camel at Sidi Bou Said in Tunisia going round and round, its eyes blindfolded, trying to draw water out of the well for the amusement of tourists. I once caught the eye of those who had placed the blindfold on the camel to deceive him into thinking he was always going ahead. He died without knowing he was just going round in circles and had spent a lifetime doing just that.

Have we become like that camel, hardly ending one round before embarking on another, going round and round on our petty daily concerns.

Our newspapers are full of promises of a better tomorrow, and are nothing but a blindfold keeping us from seeing how the shock of reality, misery, and poverty all around, was lying in wait for half the population.

And me? What about me? Had I become unable to walk straight without looking backward onto the landscape of my memories?

And this homeland. Where did it get this strange ability to turn straight lines into circles and zeros? Memory was a circular fence surrounding me on all sides. These memories stalked me wherever I went outside the house.

I walked backward to the past, blindfolded. I looked for the old coffee houses where every notable or scholar used to have his own circle, where the coffee was prepared on the stone stove and where the waiters never harassed customers for their orders. They were only honored to have you as their guest. Bin Badis in those days used to have a coffeehouse where he stopped on his way to school. It was the Bin Yamina coffeehouse. There was also the Bin Ar'ur coffeehouse that was presided over by Bi'l-'Attar and Bishtarzi. I used to wave to my father there whenever I passed by.

Where could I find a coffeehouse this morning and have a coffee with the best of my memories? How could I find a coffeehouse that was not known by the names of its guests? I saw only a huge number of large cafés, all similar, sad like the faces of the people in that city. You could not distinguish between things anymore, not even those features that used to distinguish Constantine. The elegant white gowns were now rare and faded these days.

The first thing I saw that morning was the uniformity of a city that woke up the way it went to bed, wearing the same sad and gloomy colors, common to both sexes.

Women wrapped in their black veils that revealed only their eyes. Men hiding in gray or brown suits, the same color as their skin or hair, suits they all seemed to have bought from the same tailor. I searched the crowds for a light spot, for a brightly colored dress or a summer suit, and saw one only rarely.

Was I looking at the city that morning only with the eye of an artist, seeing colors and nothing else? Or was it the eyes of the past and the disappointments of the present?

I threw myself into the mass of those men, lost like myself, and I felt for the first time that I was beginning to look like them. Like them, I was a man who did not know what to do with my time or my manhood, and like them, all I could do was walk the streets for hours, burdened with sophistication and sexual misery.

Suddenly, we were similar in every way, the color of our hair and our suits, and the way we dragged our lost steps on the pavement. I was similar to them, but unique in my relationship with you, but what difference did it make?

Your love dragged me to that city, and returned me to my backwardness as well. Your love threw me into this male community, walking slowly under the sun with nowhere to go, people with nothing to do with their energy. Feverish bodies absorbed the heat of the day, and miserable hands spent it secretly at night in private pleasures.

I suddenly stopped at a house that was not like others. It was probably the largest 'closed house' in the city, in a very well-studied location, with three doors leading to different streets and markets so men could sneak in from the city and nearby villages where there were no such pleasures, and then leave stealthily.

That was where my father spent his fortune and his manhood.

That was where men came to seek their pleasures. They came from the nearby towns, from everywhere.

It was behind those walls that presentable but wretched women disappeared, only to reemerge old and ugly, spending their money on orphans and the poor in a final bout of repentance.

I tried not to look at a place that was for years the reason for my mother's private pain and anguish: probably one of the sorrows that killed her.

It also represented a secret ecstasy, repressed dreams I used to dream as a young man but lacked the courage to carry out. Perhaps it was because I did not want to find my father there, or because I was satisfied with the flirtations I managed to have on the roof or in unused attics.

My father was no longer there to inhibit me from entering. He was gone, but he had left an excellent history behind those walls, like any other respected prosperous Constantine man of his times.

Didn't my grandmother say, counseling patience to help Mother put up with his infidelities, "What men do embroiders their shoulders."

Father embroidered his adventures with scars and bruises on Mother's body.

What had happened to this house? I don't know.

They say it had closed down, or probably they kept only one door open, in accordance with the policy of cutting down on the pleasures of the city. It could be out of deference to the dozens of mosques that had sprung out of this rock, and calling out together several times a day, reminding people of the virtues of faith and repentance.

At that moment too, I was like most men in that city, standing on the line that separated lusts of the flesh and the virtues of the spirit. The shady rooms below where sin had a sweet taste called me down; the sounds of the minarets that I had long missed, called me up to pray. The call to prayer severely lacerated the inner parts of my soul, causing me to shudder for the first time in years.

It took me only a few days to become as duplicitous as the city. And it disturbed me to realize that nowhere in this world of contradictions were there any innocent cities. Or cities that were without shame. There were only cities that were, more or less, hypocritical.

No city had only one face, or one trade, and Constantine was a city with many faces and many contradictions. It could invite you to sin and then restrain you with equal strength.

Everything was an invitation for sex. Something in that city seduced you to a stolen love . . . the endless naps, the warm and idle mornings and the sudden lonely nights. Even the paths hanging between the rocks, the secret humid tunnels, the woods and the caves, the wild view of the mountain and the numerous paths around, the laurel and oak woods. You could only watch the age-old heritage of hypocrisy and avoid looking the city in the eye, so as not to embarrass it or be embarrassed yourself.

Everybody there knew the twisted alleys concealed behind the wide streets. They knew about the illicit love stories, the pleasures quickly stolen behind a door or beneath a dignified black veil, where desire slept, repressed for centuries, a desire that gave the women of Constantine a special walk and a special light in their eyes beneath their veils.

For centuries, women have been accustomed to carrying their desire buried in their subconscious like time bombs. They release it during wedding ceremonies, when they surrender to the rhythm of the music, dancing the way they would when they gave themselves up to love. They played the coquette timidly but gracefully, at first waving their scarves left and right, until their stifled femininity stirred from beneath the heavy jewelry and clothing.

They then became prettier in their ways of coquetry that had come to them down the ages. Their breasts would shake along with their hips, and the body that had been emptied of love became warm.

Then came the sudden eruption of a fever that had never been sated by any man. The drums conspired with the heated bodies and beat stronger and faster. Braids were loosened and flew off as the women danced in circles like primitive creatures twisting simultaneously in pain and pleasure, celebrating attraction and alarm. The women lost all contact with their surroundings. It was as if they had left their bodies, their memories and their ages, with no way back to their previous posture.

It was the same as in rituals of pleasure and of torture. Everybody knew that the beat of the drum should not prevent the rhythm from building up, until some of the women had reached a climax and fell to the floor in a swoon. They would then be seized by other women. Some sprinkled them with scent that was ready for such occasions. The women who had swooned would then slowly recover.

That was how women made love in Constantine . . . an illusion.

The city seduced me into an illusory night of love, and I took the bait in exchange for oblivion.

How could I erase memory in Constantine, when pain awaited me at every turn?

Is nostalgia a physical illness?

You haunt me, Constantine.

Our encounter was something I tried to recover from, but it killed me. It seemed that I went beyond the normal allowance of sympathy.

I did not buy you from a drugstore on the road, a purchase that would allow me to sue the retailer that destiny had put you in my way.

I made you by myself. I measured all your details according to my standards. You are a blend of my contradictions, my balance and my madness, my devotion and my infidelity. You are my innocence, my sin, and every decade of my life.

The difference between you and any other city . . . is nothing.

Perhaps you were the only city that killed me more than once, for one reason that conflicted with an earlier reason every time.

So where was the borderline between cure and death? In times of disappointment memory becomes a bitter draught to be swallowed at once, after having been a shared dream to be sipped at leisure.

Shared dreams began there. History dwelt in its streets and was alone. I walked some of those streets with Si Tahir, and other streets with other people. There was one street that bore his name, and there were streets that reminded me of his passing there. And here was I, at one with his steps, continuing down the road. But we did not reach the end together.

My feeling of being an Arab walked with me from one neighborhood to another, and then suddenly I was filled with a mysterious feeling of prejudice.

You could not belong to that city without adhering to its Arab character. The beard and words of Bin Badis still rules this city even after his death. Still he gazes at us from that famous picture: bearded, leaning on his hand, thinking about what will happen to us after he has gone.

His historic cry still comes to us a century later, the only unofficial anthem that we have all learned.

The people of Algeria are Muslims
And belong to Arabism
Whoever says they have moved away from that
Or have died from that—he lies
Whoever wishes to join its root
Will have his wish granted

Your prophecy for us was accurate, Bin Badis. We are not dead. Only our zest for life has died. What do we do, great scholar?

Nobody expected a death of despair. How do a people die, whose numbers double every year?

Youth, you are our hope
With you the morning is at hand

That youth you sang of is no longer the morning at hand, since those who are sitting pretty have crushed us. Our youth watch the boats and planes and think only of getting away. In front of every consulate stands a long line of our dead waiting for visas to get a life outside the country. History moves on but the roles are reversed, and France is the one to reject our people; getting a visa, just for a visit of a few days, has become an impossible task.

We did not die of injustice. We died of desperation and sorrow. Only humiliation has killed people. In the prison cells, we were all united by singing the same anthem. It came from one cell, then was taken up and repeated in other cells by other prisoners who were not there for political offences. The words had a great power to bring us together. By chance we discovered we had one voice. We shook the walls of the prison and our tortured bodies at the same time. Did our voices become hoarse with time? Or was there one voice that drowned the others, when the country became the possession of just some people?

All these ideas passed through my mind as I tramped through the streets and came upon—after thirty-seven years—the prison walls that I had once known from the inside.

Does a prison become something else when we look at it from the outside? Is it possible for the eye to wipe out memory? Can one memory deface another?

Al-Kudya prison was part of my first memories that time cannot delete. It was a memory that made me stop suddenly in front of those prison walls.

I entered them again as I had one day in 1945 with fifty thousand other prisoners who were arrested after the demonstration of the Eighth of May: it is with sadness that I remember.

I was luckier than those who did not enter it that day. Forty-five thousand martyrs fell in a rebellion that shook the whole of eastern Algeria, between Constantine and Setif, Qalima and Kharrata.

They were the first formal group of Algerian martyrs. Their martyrdom came years before the War of Liberation. Can I forget them? Should I forget those who entered the prison and never emerged? Their bodies remaining in the torture chambers? Can I forget those who died the worst kind of death—our comrades who chose to die alone?

There was Isma'il Sha'lan. He was a simple construction laborer. He had the task of looking after the documents and secret archives of the Peoples' Party. He was the first to have a call from the secret police who knocked at the door of his little room, shouting, "Police. Open up."

Instead of opening the door, Isma'il Sha'lan opened the window, the only window, and threw himself out into Wadi al-Rammal. He died with his secrets in Constantine's deep valleys.

Is it possible today, even after half a century, to remember Isma'il without weeping? He died to avoid giving away any names under torture.

Then there was 'Abd al-Karim bin Wattaf whose screams under torture reached our distant cells. Each electric shock they gave him was like a dagger stabbing at our flesh. He swore at his torturers in French, and called them dogs, Nazis, murderers. His shouts came to us, punctuated by the electric shocks. We would respond to him with cries and an enthusiastic rendering of our anthems. His voice then fell silent.

And there was Bilal Husain, Si Tahir's closest friend, one of the forgotten victims of history. Bilal was a carpenter. He was no scholar, but a whole generation learned their nationalism from him. His workshop was under Sidi Rashid's bridge, a base for secret activity.

I remember him stopping me as I was passing his workshop on my way to the Constantine Secondary School. He made me read the newspaper, *al-Umma*, or some other clandestine publication.

I remembered how, during two whole years, I was being politically prepared for becoming a member the Peoples' Party. They put me through more than one field test. Every member was supposed to pass these before taking the party oath. Many started their party activities in one of the cells created by Bilal.

In that workshop, of which no trace remains today, he used to meet the political leaders. Msali al-Hajj gave his last instructions there. It was there that slogans were written onto banners for demonstrations to surprise the French.

Bilal planned a demonstration to take place for tactical reasons on Sidi Rashid Bridge. It was easy to gather people there and then disperse them on all the roads that led to the bridge. The French authorities had not expected the sense of organization and were taken aback at the precision of the planning. Bilal was the first to be arrested and tortured as an example to others.

Bilal Husain did not die as others died. He spent two years in prison under torture. He lost his skin to the machines of torture.

I remember that for several days he was unable to put on a shirt. It would have stuck to his open wounds. The hospital doctor refused to take on the responsibility of treating him.

He left prison and was sent into exile under close surveillance. Bilal Husain lived on as a fighter in unknown battles and on the run after independence. He died quite recently at the age of eighty-one on May 27, 1988. He died in hospital, blind, destitute, and childless.

A few months before he died he told his only friend that when they tortured him they insisted on mutilating him, so he could never have children. At his funeral some people half attached to the government walked behind his coffin to his last resting place. They never asked what he lived on or why he had no family. After the funeral they went back to their government cars without feeling any inward pain. Not one of them knew the secrets he had kept for forty years with the reserve of a man of that generation. Did those secrets deserve such concealment? Bilal Husain was the last man in an age of eunuchs. He lost his sight in an age when those with vision were blinded. Can I ever forget Bilal Husain?

That was al-Kudya prison.

We gazed at it as if we were looking at the walls of the very first prison. We entered it as if we were going into a horrible dream for which we were unprepared.

Many years passed before I entered another prison, but that one was under Algerian control. The prison had no address, and Mother was unable to come and visit me, as she had in the past, weeping and begging help from every prison guard.

That was al-Kudya prison.

How many painful, surprising stories could that prison tell? More than one revolutionary served time there, for the sake of more than one revolution.

In 1955, ten years after the events of May 8, 1945, this prison entered a new phase of prosperity with a fresh intake of prisoners for whom France was preparing an exceptional punishment.

In Cell 8 on Death Row, thirty leading men were waiting for the confirmation of their death sentence. Among them was Mustafa bin Buleid, Tahir al-Zubairi, Muhammad Lafia, and Ibrahim al-Tayyib, the friend of Daidush Murad, and Baji Mukhtar. And others.

Everything was ready for their execution. Then the prison barber told Mustafa, the leading comrade, that they had been cleaning the guillotine the previous day and that he had dreamt they would do the necessary.

This had two meanings for Mustafa who had been planning for some days to escape from al-Kudya. He had been digging an underground tunnel that would lead them to an enclosed yard inside the prison. He went back to digging so he could reach the outside world.

After sunset prayers on November 10, 1955, between seven and eight o'clock, Mustafa and ten others managed to escape from al-Kudya. They carried out the most amazing escape from cells that nobody left but to the guillotine.

After that, Mustafa bin Buleid and the others fell as martyrs on other battlefields where they were no less courageous. Volumes have been written about them, and streets and suburbs in Algeria have been named in their memory.

Meanwhile those left behind, unable to escape, were executed.

Of the eleven who broke out, there are only two survivors. Twenty-eight who shared Cell 8 have died; it was a cell designed for only one inmate.

As I stood in front of the high prison walls, my memory would wander all over the place, seeking out some face, some name, and some executioner. I wanted to open the doors of other prisons that still had secrets. I wanted to redeem the debts of those who had passed through. I once envied a man with whom I had shared a cell for some weeks. Yasin was the youngest political prisoner, sixteen years old, a few months younger than myself. Although they released me because of my age, they refused to let him go. He dreamed of freedom and was hopelessly in love with a woman ten years older: her name was Najma. Six months later I went back to school. Yasin went on to write a book about his love. The idea for this terrible story was born here in that long night, in bitterness and disappointment, but with great national dreams.

Yasin was always amazing. He was obstinate and had a compulsion to provoke and confront. He shifted his aggressiveness from one prison to another. We were his audience but did not realize then that we were with Algeria's Lorca. We were witnessing the birth of a poet who would become the most talented man of his country. Years later I met Katib Yasin in forced exile, in Tunis. His capacity to surprise, I was glad to discover, had not changed. He still spoke with the same enthusiasm, the same aggressive language, declaring war against all who preached submission to France. He was acutely sensitive to cultural humiliation and hostile to those who were by instinct deferential.

One day he was giving a lecture in Tunis and started attacking Arab politicians—and Tunisians in particular. It was impossible to shut Yasin up. He went on denouncing them and they had to switch off the microphone and put out the lights to force people to leave. That night I paid the high price of a police interrogation for sitting in the front row and cheering him.

At that time, nobody paid attention to the faces of those who clapped, but those interested in my movements noticed that my one hand was raised in admiring support. On that day, I discovered another aspect of having only one hand. Because he cannot clap he is fated to be an oppositionist.

After that meeting I saw Yasin and embraced him. "If I have a son, Yasin," I said, "I'm going to call him Yasin."

I had a feeling of pride and pleasure. It was as if I was saying the best thing possible to a friend or a writer.

Yasin tapped my shoulder nervously and laughed as he used to do whenever he was bothered by any acknowledgment given to him.

"You too haven't changed," he said in French. "You're still crazy."

We laughed then. We were to be separated for many years to come. Perhaps I wanted to be loyal to our shared memory, or I just wanted to make it up for my obsession about Najma, the story I would never write but was the story that was, in one way or another, my own story.

In my dreams and disappointments I could see my mother standing on the brink of despair and madness. I saw her running from prison to shrines, offering up sacrifices to Sidi Muhammad al-Ghurab, and cash to the Jewish guard who was also our neighbor. She did this so she could bring me from time to time a basket of food she had prepared. That was Mother, who I hardly knew when I was let out of prison six months later. While Father was preoccupied with his business and his lovers, she would ask God only that I return to her in safety, as if I was the only thing that gave meaning to her life, the only witness to her motherhood and her diminished femininity.

Yes, in the end, we were one generation with one story: a generation taken up with the madness of mothers who were excessive in their love and with the dishonesty of fathers who were excessive in their severity. We experienced love stories and emotional disappointments. Some people use them to create wonders of international literature, others turn them into psychological disorders.

In writing this book aren't I running away from the world of the sick to the world of the creative? Oh Yasin, how the world has changed since that encounter, that farewell!

You were the one who ended your story saying on behalf of the hero, "Farewell, friends! What a miraculous youth was that we have lived."

You were not expecting then that our coming days would be much more wonderful than the days of our youth.

So, tomorrow you get married.

No matter how I try to forget that and walk around the Constantine streets, one alley handed me to another, one memory to another.

Did you not say that you were mine as long as we were in this city? So where are you now? In which street? In which alley of this city that had as many twists and turns as your heart, reminding me of your constant presence, your constant absence, your perplexing resemblance to the city.

You are not mine.

I know they are preparing you for the coming night of your love. They are preparing your body for another man. Not me. I am examining my wounds so as to forget what is happening there.

You are busy, as any bride is busy on her wedding day. And my day is empty like the day of any other retired official.

A long time ago, each of us took a divergent path. We lived in discordant time-scales, one for joy, the other for sadness. How could I forget that?

All roads used to lead to you, even the one I walked in order to forget you and the other where you waited to meet me: all the schools, government and Qur'anic, all the mosques, the 'closed houses,' all the bathhouses from which women would emerge ready for love, all the shop windows displaying fine jewelry and clothes ready for weddings, even the cemetery where I went in a taxi in search of Mother's grave. I had to seek out help from the custodian's records to find the pathway that would lead to the grave, and to you.

Mother: what led me to her that day, the day of your wedding? Did I go just for her sake, or did I go to bury beside her another woman whom I saw as my mother? By her marble grave that was as simple as she had been, that was as cold as her destiny and as cobweb-covered as my soul, my feet felt nailed to the ground and my tears were frozen from a long-suppressed disappointment.

There was Mother, a pile of dust, a marble portrait hiding all the treasures I had held dear. A mother's bosom, her beautiful scent, tresses of her dyed hair, her aura, her laughter. Her sadness and her constant commandment, "Khalid, my son, you can do it. . . ."

A thousand other women took Mother's place and I never grew up. I replaced her bosom with a thousand others, still lovelier, but I never had enough. I replaced her love with more than one love story and I was not cured. She had a perfume that could not be imitated, a face that could not be copied.

Why did I, in a moment of madness, imagine that you were a woman as she was? Why did I go on asking you about things you did not understand, requiring you to play a role you could not play? The marble stone before which I stood was kinder to me than you were. Had I wept in front of it, it would, in turn, have shed tears. Had I stepped on its cold stone, enough warmth would have come from it to comfort me. Had I called it, its dust would have answered me in distress, "What is wrong, my child, what is wrong?"

But I was anxious about Mother's suffering, even after her death. She had, in her life, undergone seasons of disasters. I was sorrowfully anxious for her, even after her death. Whenever I had called on her I had tried to conceal my amputated arm.

What if the dead had eyes as well? What if the cemetery did not sleep? How many words did I need at that time to explain all that had happened to me after her death? I did not cry when I stood in front of her after all that time. I wept unceasingly afterwards. But I simply passed my hand over the marble as if I was trying to brush away the dust that had gathered over the years and to apologize to her for neglecting her.

Then I put up my hand to recite the *fatiha* at the tomb, but some strange surreal feeling passed through my body and I lowered my hand. It seemed as if my hand was asking for mercy instead of offering it. I put it back in my pocket and set off to leave the city of dust . . . and marble.

Hassan and his wife looked forward to the wedding, with its endless preparations. They would be meeting all those VIPs and heads of big families who would be attending. I listened to them sometimes as if I was listening to kids talking about a circus that was coming to a city that had never seen a circus, or clowns, before.

Constantine is a place where the only thing that happens is weddings. For that I both pitied and forgave them. I left them to their happiness waiting for the circus and kept my disillusionment to myself.

Everything was outstanding that day. I knew in advance what his schedule of evening meetings was to be. Hassan would finish his work in the morning, then go to pray the noon prayer at the mosque. After that, he would pass by me with Nasr so we could all go together to attend the wedding.

'Atiqa might in the morning take the children and accompany the bride to the hairdresser. She would stay there with the other women, serve the guests, and prepare the tables.

That day I had an urge to stay in bed all morning and not get up before noon. This may have been because of the problems of the previous day. Or because I was preparing to stay up all night. Or it may have been because of the troubles that were in store for me that day.

Maybe it was because I no longer knew where to go after spending a week wandering around the city that had long been at the back of my mind. You were hiding there for me at every corner. I found out, after a bit of thought, that the bed was the only place which I could run away to from you. Or at least where I could meet you with pleasure and not pain. But then . . .

Did I really dare to call on you at a time when I knew you were getting yourself beautiful for another man? Would I dare to find you that morning? Would my body really forgive you for all your disloyalties: even for those that would in the future come to me in my dreams? Was this not madness inside madness?

But it was not what you wanted in the end when you said, "I'll be yours that night."

I had the desire to possess you that morning, as if I wanted to steal from you everything before I lost you forever. Because after this day, you will not be mine. And this painful, ridiculous game that never amused me will be over. Meeting you this morning would be painful. It would be charged with harsh and strange bitterness. Charged with envy and mad lust.

If only you were mine.

Oh, if only you were mine in that big bed, empty and cold without you, and in that huge house that was haunted by an amputated childhood and with the lust of repressed youth that passed so quickly.

If you were mine, I would possess you as I have never possessed a woman before. I would squeeze you with my one hand in frenzy. I would turn you into fragments, to your basic ingredients, to the fundaments of what a woman was, to a paste that could be used to create another woman, anything that was not you, anything less arrogant and haughty, less of a bully than you.

I, who have never raised a hand against any woman, perhaps would have struck you that day until you felt pain, then loved you until you felt pain and then sat next to your body apologizing to it.

I would kiss you all over, I would kiss away the henna on your body. I would mark you brutally with my kisses so that when you woke up, you would discover me engraved on your body like a tattoo, with that one green color that was painted only on the body.

From where did all that frenzy come? Did I want to be alone with you and possess you before him? Did I know from a basic feeling that I was spending with you the last shivers of pleasure and that after this day you would forever be beyond my bed?

My problem with you was not just lust. If it was, I could have put a stop to it that day in one way or another. There was more than one woman here that a man could have without any effort. There was more than one door half open and waiting for a man to open it up fully. There were neighbors whose steps I often met in those extended Arab houses. I knew their secret desire for love.

I learned with time to decipher the codes of the coy looks of a woman, the exaggerated tidiness, and the careful vocabulary. But I was ignoring their glances, their tacit invitations to sin. I could not know that day if I was behaving like that out of principle or out of stupidity. Or because I wanted to throw up.

I was actually feeling sorry for them, and despising their husbands who strutted like deluded roosters without any justification. Either they owned at home a plump greasy chicken that none had been near, probably out of disgust, or there was another habit, trained by tradition: the man expects that her short wings can still enable her to prance around.

Silly rooster! If all women in the city were pure and the honor of all men was safe, with whom would men commit adultery? All, without exception, when they meet their friends, brag about their love affairs. Wasn't each of them laughing at the other? And didn't each know that there was someone to laugh at him in return?

How much I hated that awful atmosphere full of hypocrisy and baseness inherited as if it was virtue. All this went through my mind when my looks met theirs. I remembered you saying the same thing once when I showed you my admiration for what you had written in your first novel. I quizzed you, seeking evidence of a suspect memory.

"Don't look too far," you said. "There isn't anything behind the words. A woman who writes is a woman beyond suspicion because she is transparent in her nature. Writing purifies what is hung on us from the moment of birth. Seek baseness where there is no literature."

Such inherited baseness is everywhere, in the eyes of most women who are hungry for any man, and in the nervousness of men who piled up their lust until they burst out with the first woman they meet. I had to resist my animal desires that day and not quit the city that was gradually pulling me down. There were instincts I could not ignore no matter what happened. It was as if I was going with a married woman with every justification for doing so.

Perhaps that was the secret of my melancholy. I already knew that another impossibility was being added to the other impossibilities of that day, and that you would never be mine.

I was not ashamed of my right hand that day. I had a feeling of restlessness when I realized that, after all that had happened to me, I still respected my body. What was important in that case was not to lose respect for a body that we may offer to any passerby. And then, where could we be if we insulted the body and He refused to overlook that?

I threw the bedclothes off and went to open the window to let the light in and to cast you out for good. In this haunted city, what if you were a fairy who sneaked in with the night to sleep at my side, tell me stories, promise me a thousand magical solutions for my tragedy, and then disappear at first light, leaving me to my obsessions?

Did your shadow leave my bed that day? My room? Or my memory? Did it escape through that window? I don't know. I know that Constantine came through that same window, a window rarely opened. The call to prayer coming from the various minarets surprised me and rooted me to the ground as people came, rushing in all directions. Sidi Rashid Bridge seemed constantly to be on the move, like a woman preparing for some event, absorbed in daily tasks, looking forward to the weekend. That particular morning I found its lack of interest in my distress a kind of betrayal, a lack of gratitude. I shut the window in her face, and a sudden urge to paint swept me like a hurricane as violent and as extreme as my previous sexual desires.

I did not need a woman anymore. Desire had healed and the pain moved to the tips of my fingers. After all, beds were never the space for my pleasures or my rituals. Only that blank space stretched out on the wooden easel had the ability to drain me. I needed to transfer my accursed energies onto that and to pour out a lifetime's disappointment onto the canvas.

I unloaded a memory that inclined to the color black, for I had been partial to this city that had been stupidly wrapped up in black for centuries and, paradoxically, had hidden itself beneath a blank seductive trinity.

Help, you impossible triangle. Help, you city that lies hidden beneath that respected trinity—religion, sex, and politics.

How many men beneath your black cloaks have you swallowed up? Not one of them expected that you would undergo the ritual of the Bermuda Triangle with its self-destructive urge.

Depression and anger were growing in me that morning, building up as the hour approached for Hassan and Nasr to escort me to the house of your wedding.

I walked up and down the room nervously, like an addict restless for his opium. Anger and distress had paralyzed my hand and I was unable to shave and get myself ready for this unique event.

How could I have failed to expect the need to hold a brush in my hand, to have an overwhelming urge to paint? That desire was becoming a pain in my fingertips and my whole body was becoming nervous. I wanted to paint and paint until I dropped dead, or collapsed from exhaustion and ecstasy.

I would certainly not paint any bridges or arches on that occasion. It would probably be women in black veils . . . and white triangles, with deceiving eyes and promises. The color black usually meant dishonesty. Just like white. But then, I might not paint anything, and might die as I was standing, impotent before a virgin canvas. It was magnificent sometimes to sign a blank space with a white signature and slip away on tiptoe, because in the end only destiny signs our lives and does what it pleases with us.

What good would cheating do in such a case? Why prevaricate? Were you not my painting? What was the point of my painting you a thousand times?

Today, someone else is going to place his mark on your body and his name next to your identity papers. What was the point of my covering scores of canvasses with you, when I consider the bed that will contain your body and immortalize your femininity forever?

What would I gain in painting when there was always someone else who signed the picture?

While I was in that advanced stage of depression the phone rang and jerked me out of my self-obsession. I ran to answer it in another room. Hassan was on the line.

"What are you doing?"

"I was still dozing," I answered with complete frankness.

"All right then, I thought you'd be ready and waiting for me. I rang to tell you I might be a bit late. I've got a little problem I need to take care of."

"What problem?"

"Just imagine what has got into Nasr! He doesn't want to go to his sister's wedding."

My curiosity was roused.

"What? Why?"

"He's against this marriage. He doesn't want to meet the guests or the groom. Not even his uncle."

"He's right," I almost said. But what I actually said was, "Where is he now?"

"I left him at the mosque. He told me he prefers to spend the day there, instead of being with those bastards."

For the first time for ages, I laughed heartily.

"Nasr's great," I could not stop myself blurting out. "My God, he's great."

Hassan was shocked. "What's got into the two of you?" he interrupted. "How can you say that? Shame on you! How can anyone not attend his sister's wedding? What will people say?"

"People? What people? Let them say what they want. Who cares?"

"Stay at home, then. I'll pick you up as soon as I finish. We'll talk about it later. I'm calling from a café. There are people around. Know what I mean?"

Then he added, "You'll find something in the kitchen 'Atiqa has prepared for you."

I put the phone down and went back to my own room. I had a morning thirst and my bitterness had, after that phone call, had a tang of strange joyfulness. It made me feel I was not alone in my sorrow. Someone else was in similar pain and was actually, in his own way, making a stand against that marriage.

His solution was worthy of a son of Si Tahir. I had not yet met him but I expected him to be strong-minded like his father, stubborn and straight like him. If that was the case, Hassan would never get him to change his mind. I remember Si Tahir's stubbornness, his decisiveness, and his resolve from which nobody could shift him.

Once a position had been taken, I found there was a touch of authoritarianism and arrogance in The Leader. Then I realized that in those early days the revolution needed men like Si Tahir, with that stubbornness, that absolute self-confidence, and that ability to impose his views and authority on others. It was not out of love of position or power. It was to bind the revolution together and to stamp out any factionalism. It was to allow the flame of revolt not to die but to spread with the winds.

Si Tahir's memory emerged all of a sudden, at a moment that I had not put aside for him. The memory was painful, like the bullets they emptied into his body. They put an end to him just months before independence. He did not live to see Algeria free, and he was not going to be there for you either. Was it his destiny to miss these two joyous events?

He left the way he came, ahead of his time. It was as if he knew he was not made for the coming days.

I suddenly became bitterly aware that all those who loved you would not be attending the wedding: Si Tahir, Ziad, and now Nasr. Why did it have to be only me? Fate was leading me there. Luring me there for the sake of memory, nostalgia, and crazy love. You once came out with a sentence that inspired me with dreams and fantasies: "I will be yours so long as we are in Constantine," you said.

I believed you and came here, although I knew you were lying, offering white clouds for a long summer. But who could resist the pretty drizzle of lies?

There are lies we try to believe. We may not like the weather forecast. Who can dry sublime tears when we feel them inside us?

You were really a sadist and you knew it.

I realize I once told you, "You'd have been Hitler's daughter if he'd had one."

You laughed then. You laughed. It was a bully's laugh, confident in strength. I commented with the grimness of a victim, "I don't know what made me love you. I'm going to escape from control by bullies. Have I fallen into the clutches of some tyrant woman?"

You suddenly smiled and then after a pause, "You're amazing when you speak," you said. "You open up more than one topic I could write on. I'll write all this up one day."

Write it up then. It really is the stuff of fiction.

Drinking was all I could do that morning to make me forget my disappointment over you. Between an empty bed, a window overlooking minarets and bridges, and a table without any paint brushes, my only lifeline was paper, pen, and the bottle of whisky I had brought for Hassan: it was still in my briefcase. I then decided to drink it to the memory of Ziad and Si Tahir, and to Constantine. I recalled a play I had once liked. At the top of the page was written, "Here's to you, Constantine."

The city that prevented you from drinking but gave you every incentive to do so. I laughed at the role that was waiting for me here.

I did not know then that I was planning some words that would suit this book as an escape from disappointment. The idea of writing it was perhaps born that day. I wanted to challenge you and to challenge the city, and the lie they call my homeland. I raised my glass that was filled with you. To you I drank! To your forgetful memory and your eyes that were created for deceiving.

To the joy of that night that was prepared for tears, for my frozen tears. Once you reconciled me to God and the rites of worship. Today you betray me and shoot me in the back. So why should I not drink? Which of us is the greater unbeliever?

Drinking is not my thing actually. Drinking was for the extremes of happiness or grief. Now it was tied up with you, and your crazy mood changes. Every time I drank I noted the event as a chapter in our never-ending story.

So here I am, opening my last bottle in your honor. I am committing my final act of folly. I do not suppose I will get drunk after today because I am washing my hands of you. I am burying you in my own way.

I thought of Nasr, your brother who was praying at one of the city's mosques, at this moment trying in his own way to forget. One misfortune after another at your wedding party tonight. One of us will relish that.

Look at us, Nasr. You and I are sons of a city that conspires with us in acts of extremism and madness, that enjoys the sadism of torturing her children, that bears us effortlessly and drops us like a sea turtle dropping its young on the sea shore, then passes on, leaving us to the mercies of the waves and the predatory birds of the sea. Just think! Only God makes you think.

Here we are, unthinkingly seeking out our destinies between bars and mosques. Look at us! We are like an upturned turtle, unable to escape, fighting against logic. How like death is birth in these ancient cities. We are born and die in the gusts of winds that blow from different directions. There are so many orphaned turtles in this city.

Hassan's eyes went red when he surprised me and came and saw me sitting at the table writing, a half-empty bottle of whisky beside me. He almost cried out as if he had seen a ghost. It was as if by opening that bottle I was defying him in his house; I could have shot him in my madness.

I tried to humor him. "Why are you hanging around like that?" I said mockingly. "Haven't you ever seen a bottle like this before?"

But he did not want to be humored. He took the bottle and went straight to the kitchen, mumbling and cursing. He seemed tired and sad.

"For God's sake," he said when he returned, "What's got into the two of you? The whole country is being screwed while one of you is praying and the other getting drunk! What am I going to do with you both?"

My ears caught an expression I had not heard for years. "The whole country is being screwed." It was a purely sexual expression that meant that the country was upside down, or you were witnessing something extraordinary. I smiled, realizing how capable that city was of suggesting sexual imagery everywhere, and with amazing innocence.

I was unable to hold back my black sense of humor and looked up at him. I said, "This is Algeria, Hassan. Some pray, some get drunk, while others screw the country in any possible way."

He was not interested in carrying on that kind of conversation. He was too tired after all that time arguing with Nasr.

"I'll fix you a coffee," he said. "It'll wake you up and clear your head and we can then talk. Some of the people waiting there haven't seen you for ages. You can't see them in this state."

He made some coffee and when he brought it in I asked him, "What happened to Nasr?"

"He promised to show up at the dinner for my sake, but only

for a short while. Even so, I doubt whether he'll actually come. I don't get it. He's so stubborn. After all, she's his only sister. How can he behave like that? He should be standing at her side in front of everybody. It's crazy."

I was drinking my coffee 'to clear my head,' as Hassan put it, but I was getting more and more drunk and crazy just by listening to him explaining why Nasr was boycotting the wedding. His talk was taking us to more than one subject.

Nasr had accused his uncle of abusing the name of Si Tahir, and not really being interested in his brother's family. The only object of this wedding was to give a hand to upstarts. It was simply political. He was against his uncle's choice of this bridegroom whose reputation, both morally and politically, was bad. Everyone talked about the various deals he had made, about his offshore accounts, his Algerian and foreign girlfriends. Not only that, his children from his first marriage, were the same age as his bride.

"Do you find this marriage normal?" I asked.

"I don't know by what criterion you want me to judge. Certainly, as things are with us, it's natural. It's not the first and it won't be the last. Most big shots have their girlfriends. In one way or another, they all gave up their first wives for a younger model, prettier and better educated. You can't stop a man who's just added a new star to his shoulder from adding a new woman to his house. You can't forbid a man who's finally made it to an undreamed-of higher post from looking for the girl of his dreams."

He went on: "I tried to persuade Nasr that his uncle had, of course, no wish to destroy his sister's future with this marriage. Anyone else would wish for such a relationship. They would run after it. It was the only way to solve his problems and also his niece's at the same time. It would remove lots of the things that trouble her."

"Would you have done the same?"

"Of course I would have. Why not? The marriage is legitimate. It would be against religion to do what many people do today. It's as if one of them is sending his daughter or his wife or his sister to fetch a paper from the office. Or getting a flat or a license to trade. People know you don't get something for nothing. The poor open up another source of income for their needs. 'Bring me a woman, and have whatever you want.'"

"What are you trying to say?"

"This is what's happening in more than one city, especially in the capital. Any girl who goes through any office in the main branches of a political party can have a flat or any other service. Everybody knows the address. Everyone knows the one who hands out services and flats to women, and slogans to the masses."

"Who told you that?"

"I've seen it with my own eyes," he mumbled, "and heard it with my own ears when, a few months ago, I went to see a friend who worked for the Party. I wanted him to help me get out of teaching. Just imagine. Even the janitor, who welcomed all women, wouldn't talk to me. I explained that I had come all the way from Constantine. In vain. Only women were able to get any attention there. When I complained to Comrade Janitor, he testily replied that most visitors were employed in the party units or were women fighters. I almost asked them with what parts of the body they fought but I held my tongue.

"Hey, mate, wake up! Everything nowadays goes through women or through private deals. Yes, if I had the choice I would marry my daughter to someone who could get her anything through one phone call. It's better than giving her to someone like me living in misery as I do, someone who would make her unhappy or send her knocking on doors."

All this was more than I could bear. Hassan noticed the sense of shock on my face. He tried to soften the blow.

"It won't happen anyway. Even if I were to present my daughter to some Si, he certainly wouldn't take her. They only marry their own kind, to keep 'the oil in the flour,' as the saying goes. They make sure power keeps in circulation with them. So don't worry. But tell me, how can a simple chap like me build his own life around here? All the girls are looking for men in positions of power and authority, men who are on the way up. These men know their worth and make their conditions each time. And the number of unmarried women is on the increase. It's the law of supply and demand.

"If you saw things like this you'd feel that what Si Sharif did was OK. The important thing is that he's looking after his niece, providing security for her, and for himself as happy a future as he can. As for the groom being someone who's dipped his hand into state funds, they've all done it and are still at it. Some have been exposed and some know how to keep a low profile."

I almost had to admit that he was right. And that Si Sharif was right too. I did not know anymore. But there was something in this marriage that refused to enter my mind or to convince me.

SIX

I PUT on my black suit for your wedding.

An amazing color! It is just right for weddings . . . and funerals.

And why black? Perhaps because when I loved you I became a mystic: you became my sect, my way of life, and black became the color of my silence.

Colors have their language too. I have read that black clashes with patience. I have also read that black carries its own opposite in itself. I heard once of a famous dress designer who replied, when asked about the secret behind his always designing things in black, replied, "It's a color that puts up a barrier between myself and other people."

Today I can tell you a lot about this color, but I will settle for the words of that designer. On that day I wanted to put up a barrier against all those people I was going to meet, all those drones coming to land on your wedding table.

A barrier also between you and me.

So I put on my black suit, that would face in silence your white dress aglow with flowers and pearls, a dress, they say, that was specially made for you by a French designer.

Can an artist be neutral about the choice of his colors?

Sorrow had its own elegance too. I was elegant. The mirror confirmed that and the eyes of Hassan told me that too. His confidence in me was suddenly restored.

"Yes. Khalid. That's my brother!"

He looked at me and I almost said something, but I remained silent.

At the wide-open door Si Sharif welcomed me with open arms.

"Si Khalid, welcome! We are honored to receive you. Thank you for coming. You have made us so happy."

And for the second time all I could say was, "Congratulations!"

I forced myself to look joyful and tried to maintain this look all evening.

The house was filled with women's shrill cries of celebrations and my lungs filled up with the smoke of cigarettes. My heart was full of sorrow, but I managed to fake a spontaneous smile. I chatted with people I knew and people I did not know. I made myself laugh, talked about what I knew and what I did not know. I did not want to be alone with you. I did not want to arouse the you inside me and crumble.

As I came forward to greet the bridegroom whom I had not seen for some time, he pulled me to him and kissed me like an old friend.

"You've at last come back to Algeria, Si Khalid," he said. "If it weren't for the wedding we'd never have seen you."

I try to forget that I am talking to your husband, to a man who is just being polite with me, and that all that matters to him is to be alone with you at the end of the evening. I look at the big cigar he has chosen for the occasion, at the blue silk suit that he wears—or that wears him—with the elegance of one who is used to wearing silk, and try not to look at his body. I try not to remember. I amuse myself by looking at the faces of other people.

A group of women came in and you appeared. The group radiated joyfulness and a sense of glory, just as I give off a sense of the grief of an artist. I am seeing you for the first time after many months of absence. You pass by, so close and yet so far, like a shooting star. Heavy steps in heavy dresses. Ululations, the beat of the drum, and a song, one that takes me back in memory to a child running among the old Constantine houses in another group of women following a bride about whom I knew nothing.

I used to love those songs. For the bride they are unforgettable, but today they bring tears to my eyes.

Open wide the door, mother of the bride . . .

They said it even brought tears to eyes of brides when they heard it.

Did you cry that day? I wonder . . .

Your eyes are so far away. The mist in my eyes and the crowds of guests make you seem even further away. I turn away, ignoring my own question. I am content to watch you play your last role, moving forward like a princess of legend, alluring, surrounded by admiring looks, artless, proud.

There you are, desired by every man, as always, envied by every woman, as always.

And there I am, staggered by you, as always.

There is Faraqani singing for the people in the front row, people with stars on their shoulders. As always.

His voice becomes more beautiful and his violin stronger as the top brass and the fat cats celebrate. The voices of the choir rise as one to greet the groom:

Faith, how fair for me is this music-marked marriage
May they never be separated
Or have cause to fear. Five and fifty years should be their lot

More ululations and money is tossed to the music makers.

Strong and loud are the voices of those specially-hired throats. Generous are the hands that give, as easily as they take.

There they are. All of them, as always.

Big bellies, Cuban cigars, and double-breasted suits. Friends of every regime in any era, people with diplomatic bags and shady missions. Excellencies and debasement. People without references. Thus are they known.

There they are, once and future ministers, once and future thieves, opportunists, administrators, and other opportunists looking for something to administer, former spies, and soldiers disguised as ministers.

There they are. Men with revolutionary notions and the fast buck, bull-headed empty heads living in fancy villas. One speaks for all, sharks around the bait of dubious banquets.

Birds of a feather, I know them. I ignore them. I pity them. How sad they are in their wealth and their security. In their knowledge and in their poverty. In their rapid rise and their fearful fall. How wretched they are, that day, when one stretches out his hand to shake that of another. In attendance, this is their wedding.

Let them eat and make merry, let them scatter money right and left, as they listen to the song of Faraqani that is sung at every Constantine wedding—Salih Bey, a song that has been sung for centuries, to remind citizens of the power of Salih Bey, of the deceptions of rulers, of the pomp that does not endure. It is a song traditionally sung today for amusement. The words do not allow a single person pause or thought.

They were sultans and ministers . . .
They have now departed and we have mourned them
They had piles of wealth and treasure
It gave neither honor nor riches, nor did it bring them joy
Oh Salih! The Arabs said over and over
"Call no man happy till he is dead"
What good was power or money in the end?
What good was it before you, God?

As I listen I recall another contemporary song I heard with dance music on the radio. It was a song that wooed Salih. Another Salih.

Salih, Salih, how I love your eyes

Oh Constantine! You had a Salih Bey. But not every Salih is a bey. Not every bey is a Salih.

Here was my homeland finally before me. Was this really my home?

In every room there was somebody I knew a lot about. I sat and looked at them and heard their complaints and their mutterings. Not one of them, it seemed, was happy.

Was it not ironic too that they complain and criticize and curse the nation? Extraordinary! They have all crawled into high positions. Are they not part and parcel of the corruption? Are they not the cause of all the disasters that have happened?

I greet Si Mustafa, who had become a minister on the day he called on me to buy one of my pictures. I refused. Si Sharif was right to put his money on a good horse.

"How's everything, Si Mustafa?" I ask.

Straightaway he started complaining, "Believe me, I'm up to my ears with problems, you know."

I remembered what General De Gaulle once said, "A minister has no right to complain. After all, no one forced him to be a minister." I kept that to myself. Instead I just said, "Yes, I know."

I also knew about the huge sum of money Mustafa had received as commission on a Canadian contract to renew the equipment of a national company. I was too ashamed to remind him of that, knowing that those who had been in office before him did not do any better. I just listened to his complaints as if he was any ordinary citizen.

My eye caught Hassan also busy talking to an old friend, a teacher of Arabic before he suddenly became the ambassador to some Arab country. How did that happen? There was the matter of a legacy and an old friendship that brought this teacher together with one of these people. And that was not the only diplomatic case.

Then there was Si Husain whom I knew well as a colleague when I was in the press office. Suddenly, out of the blue or because of his rotten ways, he became an ambassador, after his reputation circulated in high places. With his criminal record they wrapped him up in the Algerian flag and sent him abroad with the appropriate diplomatic honors. He is here today. In his natural environment. He was called home after a case of fraud and misuse of state funds abroad. He came back without any scandal to a post in the Party, albeit a minor post.

In such cases as his, there are always honorable waste paper baskets.

In another corner you can see someone holding forth—as if he is a revolutionary thinker—explaining theories of revolution. One of *his* revolutions was that he had made it to the front row in dubious circumstances, by supplying young girl students to an old notable who was besotted with young girls.

That was the nation.

That was your wedding, to which I had been invited, my lady, a circus reserved for clowns and acrobats who specialized in vaulting over values and other people, a circus where a handful poke fun at everybody, and a whole nation is being trained to be stupid.

I envied Nasr for not attending this carnival. I only guessed that he had not come, but where was he now? Was he still praying in that mosque to avoid meeting people and seeing what was going on? Would his prayers or my drunkenness change any of that?

Oh Nasr, stop praying. They too have started praying, wrapped in their cowls of piety.

Stop praying and let us think a bit.

Stop praying and let us think a bit. Flies are all over the place and are demolishing this banquet.

I feel sad as the evening advances and as the festivities go on, and as the notes shower down at the feet of the chorus girls who have given themselves up to dancing to the music of the most famous of popular songs.

As the night sways where will I lay
On a silk bed, on a pillow . . .oh wishes, oh wishes!

Yes, Faraqani sings.

There is no connection between this song and the housing crisis as may be seen from the beginning. It simply glorifies nights and silky beds unavailable to most people.

Over the dead, oh eyes, don't cry . . . oh!
Don't weep over the dead
Oh wishes . . . oh wishes

I will not cry, I will not cry. This is not a night for Si Tahir, not a night for Ziad. Nor is it a night for martyrs or for lovers. It is a night for public deals celebrated with music and ululation.

Out of the bath she flows . . .
And the perfume glows . . . O God!
To whom? Who knows?
Or mine will she be? Oh wishes . . . oh wishes!

I will not ask myself that question. I am now aware that you are for someone else, not me. That song—and that crowd who took you away with ululations for your night of licit love. When you pass by me . . . when you pass by me, walking like a bride, I feel you walking over me, not with perfume but just with your hennaed feet. Your ankle bracelets ring inside my chest. There is a ringing inside me that awakens memoirs. Stop, Constantine, slow down. Poetry is not read in that way, in such a hurry.

Stop. Gold-embroidered and gold-sequined dress, allied to the poetry written in Constantine generation after generation. The golden belt squeezing your waist and exposing your feminine ebullience, that was what set off your enchantment of me.

That was the beginning and the end of all that can be said about Arab poetry.

Slow down. . . . Let me imagine that time stopped and you belong to me.

I may die without having a wedding, without having ululation. How I would love today to make away with these women's ululations and think that they are blessing my obsession with you.

If only I were a bride-snatcher, that hero of legend who ran away with beautiful brides on their wedding nights, I would come and take you with me on a white horse, away from them.

Had you been mine, we would have blessed this city. A saint would have set forth from every street we crossed and would have burnt incense on our path. But how sad this evening is. Constantine! How wretched are its saints. Alone, they sat at my table without any clear reason and occupied the front seats of the theater of my memory.

So here I am spending my evening greeting them one by one.

Greetings, Si Rashid! Greetings, Si Muhammad Ghurab! Greetings, Sidi Sulaiman! Sidi Bu 'Inaba. Sidi 'Abd al-Mu'min. Sidi Musid. Sidi Bu Ma'za. Sidi Jalis.

Greetings, those of you who have ruled the streets of this city, their alleyways and their memories.

Stay with me, saints of God. I am tired this evening. Do not abandon me. Was not my father one of you?

'Isawi, was my father the son of his father?

You who were in one of those closed circles of Sufis in those marvelous rites, you used to implant that red-hot skewer into your body. It went through your body from one side to the other. You then took it out without there being a single drop of blood. The red-hot metal used to pass through your body as if it was a piece of burning coal. You would then cool it down with your spittle and you would not be burnt.

Instruct me today how you suffered without bleeding.

Instruct me how I can recall her name without burning my tongue.

Instruct me how to rid myself of her, you who used to repeat with the 'Isawi brotherhood in gatherings of religious intensity, you who used to dance under the influence of fever: *I am Sidi 'Isawi who injures and heals.*

Who can heal me, father, who?

And I love her.

At that late hour of pain, I realize that I still love her and that she is mine.

I defy them all—the pot bellies, the bearded ones, the bald ones, those with countless stars on their shoulders, those to whom I have given much and for return they have raped you before my very eyes.

I defy them with the arm that was no longer mine, with the memory they have stolen from me, with all they have taken away.

I challenge them to love her as I did.

Only I love her for no reward, and I know that at that very moment someone else was quickly lifting her dress, carelessly removing her jewelry, and running into her body with the breathlessness of a fifty year-old lying with a young girl.

I wept over you and over that dress. How many hands had embroidered it? How many women had worked on it so that one man might enjoy lifting it, tossing it onto some chair as if it was not our memory, our homeland? Was it the fate of nations that all the generations would prepare it for a man that would come to enjoy it all by himself?

That night I wondered why I stopped at those details. I was discovering now the meaning of everything that never had a meaning before.

I wondered—does love for this country, or an aspect of it, does it give ordinary things a sacred value that is only appreciated when we no longer possess it?

Nowadays the ordinary routine of life kills the dream and removes that sacred value. It was one of the companions of the Prophet who advised Muslims to leave Mecca as soon as they had concluded the rites of the pilgrimage, so that the city may retain its mystique and sacred value in their hearts, and so that familiarity would not turn it into any other city where anyone can steal, commit adultery, or commit any other outrage.

That is what has happened to me from the moment I set foot in this city. I am treating it as an extraordinary city.

I look at every stone with love. I greet every bridge, one by one. I ask news of families, of the saints, and of their menfolk, one by one. I look at them as they go by, as they pray, as they make illicit love, as they indulge in madnesses. Nobody understands my madness or the secret of my link with a city from which everybody dreams of escaping.

Do I find fault with them?

Do the citizens of Giza in their misery and wretchedness feel that they live on the slopes of miracles and that the pharaohs are still with them, ruling Egypt with their stones and tombs?

Only outsiders who read Greek and have studied pharaonic history treat these stones with reverence. They come from the ends of the earth just to be near them.

Should I linger here and commit the folly of being near dreams until they are burnt out? Day after day, one disappointment after another, I was getting relief from the burden that was weighing on me, and draining the pain away with the sweetest illusions.

At this moment I do not want this city to be more than a stab of sympathy.

The few ululations of joy that came after dawn to celebrate your soiled nightdress were the final blow I received in that city. I took it on the chin. I did not move and I made no protest. I stood like a corpse as I saw people around me clambering to touch your nightdress that was exposed to view. They came to present you to me, a canvas stained with blood, another proof of my impotence, another proof of their crime.

But I made no gesture, no protest. It is not the right of a spectator at a bullfight to alter the logic of things and to be on the side of the bull? Otherwise he would stay at home and not attend a sport that was created to glorify the matador.

Something in this atmosphere heavy with the cries of the women, with makeup, and the music celebrating the night of the consummation of the marriage, the shouts at the sight of the blood-stained dress, reminded me of the rites of the bullfight. They come to the arena and consider beautiful the bull's death to the beat of the dance music. The bull dies to the slashing of the decorated blood-red sword wielded by an elegant killer. Who among us is the bull now? You or me? Who is suffering from color-blindness? The only thing I see then is red, the color of your blood. A bull turns in the circle of your blood with the arrogance of a beast that can only be overcome by humiliation. He knows he is already condemned to death.

All this confused me, embarrassed me, and filled me with contradictions.

Was I not burning to know the end of your story with him, the one who took you away from me? Did he take everything from you?

A question had obsessed me like mad ever since I put Ziad before you and put you face to face with another destiny: did I open up your citadel to him? Did I reduce your lofty towers? Did I surrender you to the appeals of his manhood? Did you leave your childhood to me and your femininity to him?

Here was the answer before me, after a year of pain. Here it was finally: soft, red, and a few seconds old. Here was the answer that I had not anticipated. So why the sorrow? What upset me most this night was that now I know that he died without enjoying you. He is the one who most deserved you tonight. Or were you just a city conquered by military force like any other Arab city?

What hurt me more that night? Was it to know your puzzle at last? Or that I would know nothing about you from today on, even if I talked nonstop to you, even if I read your books over and over again?

Were you a virgin then, were your sins only on paper? Then why did you make me believe all those things? Why did you offer me that book, giving me a pretext for jealousy? Why did you teach me to love you, line by line, lie after lie? Why did you teach me even to rape you on paper?

So be it.

My consolation today is that you were my most delicious defeat—among all my other setbacks.

"Why are you sad this morning?" Hassan asked.

I tried not to ask why he was happy that day.

I know that the absence of Nasr at yesterday's wedding did upset him a bit, but it did not stop him from enjoying Faraqani's music, laughing and talking to people he had not met before. I was somehow glad to see him so naïvely happy, to have opened for him those doors, rarely opened up to ordinary people, to be invited to the wedding that he would talk about for days. He would answer people's questions and tell them who was there, what they ate and what the bride was wearing.

His wife could forget that she had borrowed jewels and clothes from neighbors and friends. She would start boasting to everyone about the luxury as if she had suddenly become part of it all, simply because she had been invited to be a witness to the good things of other people.

"We're having lunch with Si Sharif tomorrow," Hassan said. "Don't forget to be at home at noon so we can go together."

"I'm going back to Paris tomorrow," I replied distantly.

"How can you go back tomorrow?" he shouted. "Stay at least another week. What is there in Paris?"

I tried to say I had some commitments and that I had been in Constantine long enough, but he insisted.

"You can't do that. At least have lunch with Si Sharif. Then go."

"It's over. I'm leaving tomorrow," I said with a resolution he did not understand.

I relished saying this in a Constantine accent. I could feel with every word that a long time would go by before I could adopt the accent fully. He then said, trying to persuade me of the importance of accepting such an invitation, "He's a fine man. You know he's still loyal to our old friendship in spite of the heights he's reached. You know, some people say he might be made a minister. Then God will end our misery."

He murmured the last sentence as if he was speaking to himself. Poor Hassan! Poor brother! God would never bring an end to his misery.

Was it naïve to think that the wedding had been nothing more than a deal? And that Si Sharif never did anything without getting something in return? We do not make alliances with senior officers unintentionally.

As for what Hassan might get out of Si Sharif's promotion—dreams, simply dreams. The believer starts with himself, and years may pass before he reaches the stage of Hassan, and takes some crumb of what he wants.

"Have you dreams of becoming an ambassador?" I joke.

"Oh dear, my friend," he said, as if he was hurt by the question. "'Take what you can as soon as you can.' All I want is to quit teaching, to get a respectable post in some educational or cultural organization, any job on which I and my family can live a decent life. How can eight of us survive on this income? I can't even afford a car. Where can I get the millions to buy one? When I think of all those posh cars lined up there last night, I feel sick and lose the appetite for teaching. I'm fed up with a job that has no reward, moral or material. It's not like the old days when the teacher was a prophet. As one colleague put it, 'We're just poodles in tatters.' We're everyone's doormat. The teacher gets on the same bus as his pupils. He has kids and cooks just like them. People curse him in front of them. He then goes home like this colleague of mine, prepares his lessons and corrects papers in a two-roomed flat he shares with eight or more others. Meanwhile one person owns two or three flats thanks to his job or through influence. He can entertain his lovers or he can lend the keys to someone who can open up other doors. I envy you, Khalid. You are a long way away from all this, living in your classy quarter of Paris. Not a care in all the world."

Oh, Hassan, I feel a lump in my throat every time I remember that conversation. It is a wound, a tear, it becomes remorse and regret. I could have given you more help. I really could have.

"Ask them for something, Khalid," you used to say, "since you are here. Aren't you an old militant? Didn't you lose an arm in the war of independence? Ask them for a shop, a truck, a small plot of land. They won't refuse you anything. It's your right. If you want, leave it for me to take advantage so I can survive with my children. They know you and they respect you. But nobody knows me. It's crazy not to take from this country what belongs to you. It won't be charity they're giving you. There's more than one person carrying the certificate showing he was a militant though they may have done nothing for the revolution. You carry your certificate on your body, in your flesh."

Oh, Hassan, you did not understand that this was the only difference between them and me. You did not understand that it is no longer possible, after all these years and all that suffering, to bow my head to anyone, not even for a gift from the nation. I might have been able to do it straight after independence, but today, with the passing of time, it has become impossible.

I want to stand like this before them, to be a thorn in their conscience. I want them to be ashamed, to lower their heads when they meet me and ask me my news, when they know that I know all their news and that I can bear witness to their contemptible conduct.

Oh, Hassan, if only you knew. If only you knew the pleasure it is to walk in the street and to talk to them with your head held high, meeting them, any of them, great or small, and feel no embarrassment. Some of them cannot walk two paces down a street on their own two feet. Instead they go in an official convoy.

I said none of this to Hassan. I only promised as a first step to buy him the car he was dreaming of.

"Come along," I said, "and choose a car that suits you. Get it from France. I won't let you live in this way any longer."

He was as happy as a child. I felt that it was an impossible dream come true. He could not have asked for it. But how could I have known that when I had not seen him for many years?

When I remembered Hassan that day the look he gave me filled my heart with a deal of happiness. I gave him pleasure and comfort for a few years. But I did not know that they would be his last years.

"Do you insist on leaving tomorrow?" Hassan asked.

"Yes, I've really got to go."

"Then you must call Si Sharif and apologize. He could get the wrong impression and be upset."

I thought for a moment and realized he was right. "Call him, and let me have a word with him," I said.

I had expected things to end up that way, but Si Sharif welcomed me and overwhelmed me with his courtesy. He insisted on my calling on him, straightaway.

"Let's have lunch today then. We've got to see you before you go, and besides, you can give your wedding present to the bride and groom in person, before they leave tonight."

There was no way out. Again I found myself face to face with you, after I had decided to get away as soon as possible, to run away from these people who were orbiting around you in one way or another.

There I was, wearing the same black suit, holding a painting that was the reason foreverything that had happened to me, as I went off to lunch with Hassan: my feet once again leading in your direction.

I knew I would definitely see you this time. An earlier idea made me feel we would not miss each other today. What did everybody talk about? Who did I meet? What did I say? What did we have to eat? I can no longer remember. I was enjoying some last moments of my love for you. All that mattered was to see you and finish with you at the same time. But I was afraid of your love. I was afraid that your love would flare up from the ashes again. Great love is frightful even at the moment of death. It is a threat to the end.

The most painful moments, and the craziest and most ironic, were when I planted two innocent kisses on your cheek. And then having to employ all the right words that I could remember, I managed to congratulate you.

Did you know how much effort, self-control, and patience I used to give you the impression that I had only once met you fleetingly, and that you were not the woman who had turned my life upside-down?

The woman who shared my empty bed many months ago and was mine only until yesterday.

Oh, the act I had to put on to make me give you that painting without making any comment, or gesture. As if that painting had not been the beginning of my story with you twenty years ago.

You too were fantastic in the act you put on. You unwrapped it and took a close look at it as if you were seeing it for the first time, and all I could say was what I had once said before, "Do you like bridges?"

There was a short silence. To me, it seemed so long, like the moment preceding the pronouncement of a death sentence. Or a pardon.

You spoke before raising your eyes to me, "Yes, I do."

What happiness you bestowed upon me with those words. I felt you were sending me one final love signal. You were presenting me with more than one idea for more paintings, for more than one night of fantasy. It was as if, in spite of everything, you would be faithful to our common memories and to a city with its bridges that had brought us together.

Were you really my love at that moment, when another man was beside you, devouring you with his eyes, eyes not sated with a complete night of love, and talking about the places you were visiting on your honeymoon? I was bidding you farewell with silence, to your final exit from my heart.

Was that your first defeat at my hands? Everything is finished then. Here is my final encounter with you.

Was it worth waiting all that time for this meeting? All that pain?

How beautiful my dream was. How pretty, but in reality now how flat.

It was full of anticipation for you, but in your presence became a painfully empty reality.

Was that half-look we exchanged worth all that pain, all that yearning and all that madness?

You want to say something and you mutter some words. You mutter glances.

Your eyes forget to talk to me. I no longer know how to decode you.

Did we go back to that day to the role of being strangers without realizing it?

We parted.

Two more kisses on your cheek. A glance. Two glances. A lot of acting, and then a silent hidden pain.

We all exchanged words of politeness, congratulations and final thanks. We exchanged addresses, and your husband insisted on giving me his home and office phone number in case I needed anything.

We parted from each other with our illusions, resolutely.

When I went back after that to the house, I looked long at the business card that I had been fingering on the way back with some anxiety and a semi-humorous bitterness. It was as if you had moved from my heart to my pocket under a new name and telephone number. But without much hesitation or reflection I decided at once to tear you to shreds as long as I had the strength to do so and as long as you wanted everything to come to an end in Constantine. And that is what you wanted, and so do I today.

What did you want that evening when you phoned me suddenly to take me out of the whirlpool of my thoughts and conflicting emotions?

That night Hassan handed me the phone.

"A woman is wanting you," he said.

You were the last person I expected.

"Haven't you set off yet?" I asked in surprise.

"We're leaving in an hour. I wanted to thank you for the painting. You've given me unexpected joy."

"I've not given you anything. I gave you back a painting that's been ready for you for twenty-five years. I have another present for you that you'll get one day. I think you'll like it."

"What are you going to give me?" you asked in a very low voice. It was as if you were afraid you may be overheard or someone might take the painting away from you.

"It's a surprise. Suppose I wanted to *give you a gazelle*?"

"That's the title of a book."

"I know. That's because I'll give you a book. When a man loves a girl, he gives her his name. When he loves a woman, he gives her a baby, and when he loves a writer, he gives her a book. For your sake I'll write a novel."

In your voice I detected joy and confusion, bafflement and a mysterious distress. Then, suddenly, you spoke in a very affectionate tone that I had not encountered in you before.

"Khalid, I love you. Did you know that?"

Your voice broke off suddenly, uniting with my sad silence. We stayed like that for some moments, wordless. Then you added, pleadingly, "Khalid, say something. Why don't you answer me?"

"Because *the pavement of the flower does not answer anymore.*"

"Do you mean you don't love me anymore?"

"I don't mean anything in particular," I answered distantly. "That's the title of another novel by the same writer."

What did I say after that? I don't know. That was probably the last thing I said before I hung up. We parted for several years.

Malek Haddad wrote: "Don't bang at the door so violently. I'm no longer here."

Do not try to come back to me through the back door, through the gaps in memory, through the murk of dreams or through windows that have been blown open by the wind.

Do not try anymore.

I abandoned my memory the day I made the amazing discovery that it was not exclusively mine. It was shared. I shared it with you. Each of us had our own version even before we met.

My dear woman, do not bang away on the door. I do not have any doors anymore.

The walls gave up on me the day I gave up on you. The roof tumbled in when I tried to salvage my property after it had been torn apart and scattered about after you.

Do not keep going round a house in this way, a house that was once my house.

Do not try to sneak through the window like a thief. You have stolen everything from me and there is nothing left that makes the risk worthwhile.

Do not keep banging so painfully at the door.

You strike at the innermost core of a memory that is simply empty without you. Echoes come back, full of pain and alarm.

Didn't you know that the valley became my home after you? Like a pebble that lies in the hollow of Wadi al-Rammal.

Then slow down, my lady, as you cross the bridges of Constantine because one false step will hurl a pile of stones at me. A slip will bring you tumbling down on me.

You were a woman disguised in the clothes of my mother, in her perfume and in her care for me.

Like the bridges of Constantine, suspended between two cliffs and two roads, I became weary.

Why all this pain? Why are *you* the biggest liar among mothers, and *I* the dumbest fool among lovers?

Do not knock at the doors of Constantine, one after another. I do not live in this city. It lives in me.

Do not look for me on the bridges. They never once carried me. I carried them.

Do not ask for their songs about me. You came, panting, with news old and new, with songs that were sung for sadness and then became songs of joy.

The Arabs said. The Arabs said. What we give Salih is not money.

The Arabs came. My goodness! What we give Salih is the Bey of Beys.

I knew by heart what the Arabs said and what today they dare not say.

And I know. Salih was the first mourning dress you wore, even before you were born. He was the last of the beys of Constantine. I was his last testament.

Oh, Hamuda, ah, my child. God be with me at home, ah, ah.

What house, Salih? What house do you bequeath to me?

I visited Suq al-'Asr and saw your house emptied of its memory. They had even stolen the stones and the iron windows. They destroyed the corridors and smashed up its carvings. The house remained standing, a yellowing skeleton against whose walls young men and drunkards pissed.

What country is this that pisses on its memory, Salih?

What country is this?

Here then is a city clad in mourning for a man whose name they can no longer remember. Here you are a child whose ties with this bridge nobody knows.

Remove your veil from now on. Show your face and stop all that knocking. Salih is no longer here. Nor am I.

We then separated.

They were wrong when they said that love never died.

Those who wrote love stories with happy endings, to give us the idea that Laila and Majnun were emotionally exceptional, understood nothing about the laws of the heart. They wrote literature, not love.

Passion was only born in minefields, in restricted areas, and its victories were not always with beautiful and harmonious endings. It dies as it was born, in beautiful destruction.

We then separated.

Farewell, beautiful destroyer. You, the rose of volcanoes, the jasmine that grew out of my embers, farewell!

Oh, daughter of earthquakes, your destruction the most horrible. You killed a whole nation inside me. You sneaked in through the corridors of my memory and then blew everything up with one small match.

Who taught you to play with the fragments of memory? Answer me. From where did you bring all those burning waves? And all the devastation that followed afterward?

You were actually not dishonest with me. You were not a lover and not really unfaithful. You were not my daughter, nor were you my mother.

You were just like my homeland, with all its paradoxes.

Do you remember that distant time when you loved me and were looking for a substitute father in me?

You once said, "I have waited so long and so intensely for you, just as people wait for good men, for prophets. Please, Khalid, do not be a false prophet. I need you."

I noticed that you did not say, "I love you." You only said, "I need you." We do not necessarily love prophets. We only need them at all times.

So I replied, "I didn't choose to be a prophet."

"Prophets don't select their own mission," you joked. "They simply perform it."

"Nor do they select their followers. So if you ever discover that I am a false prophet, it may be because I was sent to unbelievers."

You giggled, and with the stubbornness of a woman who loves a challenge, you said, "You're only looking for a way out to justify your probable failure with me, aren't you? I won't give you that. Give me your ten commandments and I will apply them."

I gazed at you. You were too beautiful to submit to the commandments of any prophet, too weak to bear the burden of divine teachings, but there was an inner light in you that I had never experienced in a woman before. A pure seed I did not want to ignore. Was that not what prophets were supposed to do, look for good seeds inside us?

"Put the ten commandments to one side and listen to me. I have the eleventh for you."

You laughed and then, with some candor, said, "Give it to me, you worthless prophet. I promise to follow you."

At that moment I felt a desire to take advantage of your promise. I would say, "Just be mine," but that was not what a prophet would say. Without realizing it I had begun to play a role that I had chosen for myself. I was going to look into my mind for something a prophet could say that would validate his mission for the first time.

"Carry this name of yours with greater pride, not necessarily with arrogance but with the deep awareness that you are more than just a woman. You are the consciousness of a nation. Do you understand? Symbols are not supposed to shatter. These are ignoble times. If we are not biased to values, we'll find ourselves on a rubbish tip. Be biased only to principles. Consider only your conscience, because in the end it's the only thing you live with."

"That is . . . your commandment?"

"Don't underestimate it. Applying it is not as easy as you think."

You had to mock the commandment of that broken prophet and undervalue it to the end.

Six years have passed since that trip, that meeting, that farewell.

In the meantime, I have been trying to bind my wounds and forget. Trying since my return to put some order into my heart, to put things back into place without too much noise or complaint, without breaking a vase or moving a painting or the position of old values on which the dust of time had gathered.

I tried to turn the clock back, without any grudge or any forgiveness either. We do not forgive all that easily those who give us a transient happiness that disintegrates only to expose our earlier misery. We even forgive least of all those who, with no sense of guilt, murder our dreams before our eyes.

I did not forgive you or them. I tried only to treat you and the country with less nostalgia. I treated you both with indifference.

News of you would come to me by chance whenever I heard about your husband's continuous success and his deals, open and secret. The news of the nation reached me also sometimes through newspapers and sometimes through meetings and sometimes during the visits of Hassan when he came to pick up the car I had promised him. And each time I dealt with what I heard with that indifference born of terminal despair.

I began to attach myself more and more to Hassan. It was as if I was just discovering his existence. I became concerned with his well-being after realizing that he was all that was left to me in this world, and especially after observing at first hand his wretched life. I had known nothing about that before my visit to Constantine.

I called him regularly, asking about his children and their needs and about the repairs needed in the house and that I agreed to pay for. His mood fluctuated at different times. He seemed enthusiastic about the contacts he was making and his schemes to move to Algiers, but then he would get discouraged. I used to feel it when he asked, "When are you coming here, Khalid?"

I saw him as a shipwrecked vessel, sending out emergency signals to me. However, I went along with him and promised each time to come the following summer. I knew in my heart I was lying, and that I had broken my links with my own country. In fact, I had assumed an attitude of hopelessness. I was moving in the opposite direction at a speed I could do nothing about, nothing at all except be confused and wait for some catastrophe.

I was packing up my heart's belongings. Without realizing it, I was moving away in the opposite direction from my own country.

I clothed my exile in oblivion. I created another country in my exile, perhaps an eternal country in which I had to make adjustments to live.

I made peace with the things around me, starting with a healthy relationship with the Seine, with the Mirabeau Bridge, and with all the landmarks I saw from my window and that I had for no reason regarded with hostility.

I had more than one short-term affair. I filled my bed with crazy pleasures, with women I impressed every time, using them to obliterate you until there was nothing left of you anymore.

This body of mine forgot its longing for you. It forgot its obsession and folly and its escape from any but fantasy pleasures. I was intentionally emptying women of their basic symbols.

Who said that some women were exile and others home? It is a lie. There was no space for them outside the body, and memory was not leading the way to them. In fact, there was only one way of which I was certain today.

I learned something I must now tell you.

Desire is, strictly speaking, a cerebral matter, nothing more than an imaginary act, an illusion we create in a moment of insanity when we become slaves to one person whom we deem magnificent for some reason that is beyond reason. A desire that is created from something unknown, that may take us to another memory, to another fragrance, to a word, to another face. It is an insane desire born somewhere outside the body, in the memory or perhaps in the subconscious, or in other places where you sneaked in once and became the most wonderful person, the epitome of womanhood.

Can you understand now why I killed you the day I killed Constantine in me?

Why was I not shocked to see your corpse stretched out on my bed?

The two of you were only one woman in the end.

You may ask yourself why I am writing this book. Well, my lady, I will answer that I am borrowing your practice of ritually killing others, and I have decided to bury you in a book. There are dead bodies that should not be kept in our hearts, for love after death stinks, especially when that love is criminal.

Note that I have not even mentioned your name in this book. I have decided to leave you without a name. Let us suppose your name is Hayat. Perhaps there is another name. Is your name really important?

Only the names of martyrs accept no distortion. We owe it to them to speak their full names just as we owe it to our nation to expose those who betray it. They build their glory over its destruction and their wealth on its misery, so long as nobody holds them to account.

Critics would probably say that that is compensation for other things, that it is not the full story. That is only the ravings of a madman who has no idea of literary form. I can assure them in advance of my own ignorance and of my scorn for their criteria. My only criterion is pain. I have no ambition but to astonish you and to make you cry when you finish reading this book. There are things I have not told you yet.

Read it, and get rid of all those half-baked books on your bookshelf, books with incomplete men and lovers.

Literature is born only from wounds. To hell with all those who have loved you reasonably and have not bled or lost their balance.

Flip through my pages timidly, as if it is an album of yellowing photographs of the child you were once, just as you look through an old dictionary about to be thrown away. Just as you read some private correspondence you have stumbled upon one day in your post. Open your heart and read me. I want to tell you all the things you did not know about Si Tahir and Ziad and others. But Hassan died and there was no more time to talk about martyrs, when each one of us might be the next to fall.

I am distressed that I did not give you a gazelle. *Gazelles are only gazelles when they are alive.* I have nothing left to give you today.

You took away from me all the ones I had ever loved. One after the other, one way or another. My heart became slowly a mass grave where loved ones slept randomly, as if a mother's grave was extended to contain them all.

I was just a memorial plaque to Si Tahir, to Ziad, and to Hassan. A memorial plaque to the tomb of memory.

I used to know a lot about the folly of fate, about its oppressiveness, its obstinacy when it insisted on marking someone out.

But could I have anticipated what did happen?

I used to think I had paid enough to stupid fate. Fate caught up with me later, after the years following the disaster of Ziad, after the disaster of your husband, and then finally came to rest.

How could fate come back to take away my brother, whose death made no logical sense? He was not at the front. He was not on the battlefield to die the death of Si Tahir or of Ziad. He too was targeted by bullets.

That day in October 1988 the news of his death came as a bolt from the blue over the crackling telephone. Tears got in the way of 'Atiqa's voice.

She kept weeping and repeating my name as, in my shock, I was asking her, "What happened? What happened?"

I knew how Algeria was shaking, and about those events the French press were competing to report with pictures and in detail, with a concern not devoid of glee. I knew the details and that, on the second day, trouble was still confined to the capital. But how could I have expected what happened? 'Atiqa kept repeating in short bursts, "They've killed him. Oh, Khalid, they've killed him."

How did Hassan die? Did it matter now, when his death was as simple as his life, as trivial as his dreams? I read all the papers to understand how my brother had died between dreams and illusions. What took him to Algiers to meet a group there, Hassan, who hardly ever went to Algiers? He went on the weekend and found his own end. Constantine was strangling him; its many bridges led him nowhere. They told him that he would find the thread in Algiers. The road would take there. The bridges would not. Hassan agreed and went to Algiers to meet 'someone' through 'somebody else.' It was decided that his case would be finally sorted out this time, after it had been dealt for years by intermediaries. At last he was going to leave the teaching profession, get a transfer to the capital and get a job with an information outfit. But fate had taken his file this time, and between this someone and that, he died by a stray bullet on the pavement of his dreams.

Dreams are not within the grasp of all, my friend. All you can do is dream.

Really, wretchedness knows how to select its ingredients. And so it chose me and selected for me all these terrible things, for me alone. All I wanted was to give you a gazelle. How could I do that? And all you are rewarding me with is utter destructiveness.

Suddenly, an old conversation we had came to mind.

Six years have passed since that conversation. At that time, you found in me some resemblance to Zorba, the man you loved most as you said, and about whom you used to dream of writing a novel—his story or the love of a man like him.

I wonder, was it because you were incapable of writing such a novel, that you were content to turn me into a version of him? And make me, like him, learn to recover from things I liked by eating them until I threw up?

You made me love beautiful destructiveness. And I learned, like some killer bird, to dance in my pain.

This is the fair destructiveness that you told me about one day with such amazing enthusiasm that I had no doubts.

"It's amazing," you said, "that mankind copes with disasters by dancing. We also make a distinction between disappointment and defeat. Not every defeat reaches everyone. You've got to have extraordinary dreams, happy times, and outstanding ambition, so you can transform these emotions of yours into their opposite."

Oh, my lady, if only you knew how big my dreams were. How massive the destructiveness that the television channels competed to transmit and show today! How terrible the destructiveness, and how distressing it was to consider the dead body of my brother on the sidewalk, struck by stray bullets!

Sad and cold is Hassan now, waiting in a morgue for me to identify him and to accompany him to Constantine.

That tyrant mother, lying in wait for her children, and swore to take us back to her, even if it was only as a corpse!

Constantine, you win, bringing us back together when we thought we were healed, when I thought that I had cut any remaining sentimental ties with you. Hassan would never leave for the capital anymore, and I could no longer run away from you.

There we were, back with you, one in a coffin, the other the remains of a man.

You have delivered your sentence, City of Rock, Mother City. Open wide your graveyard and wait for me. I am bringing in my brother. Find some small space for him alongside your saints, your martyrs, and your beys, because he was all those in a way. He was a gazelle.

And you, my lady, as you wait, come and watch all this

beautiful destructiveness. Zorba will be here any minute to hold my shoulder and start the dance.

Come over! You cannot miss the scene because you will be able to see how prophets dance when they are really bereft of ideas.

Come! I will dance as I have never danced before, the way I wished I could have danced at your wedding but did not.

I will dance as if I had wings. I will dance as if my missing arm was restored to me.

Come, so my father may apologize—he who never took part in the 'Isawi rites, in its gatherings or crazed dancing when a man would plunge a skewer through his body, drunk in an agony that is next to ecstasy.

Grief has more than one ritual, and pain has no precise home. Let the prophets and the holy saints apologize to me. Let them all make amends. I do not know exactly what they do when they grieve. What did they do when people rejected the true religion? Did they weep or did they pray? I decided to dance, since dancing was also a prayer.

Look at me, Great One! I will dance to you with one arm.

O God! How difficult it is to dance with one arm, my Lord! How unsightly it is to dance with one arm! But . . .

You will have to excuse me, for you took it away from me.

Excuse me, you took them all away.

Excuse me, for you are taking me too.

Is the believer really right? Or is that something said to teach us to be patient, to win us over, to replace misfortune with a declaration of faith?

Thank you, Almighty God! You who are the only one who may be praised.

You who are concerned with the setbacks only of your believers and the godly.

I acknowledge that I have not dreamt of a declaration of good behavior like this.

A Greek rhythm filled me up and cast you out, my lady. The music of Zorba approached me, an invitation to extreme insanity.

It came on a tape I used to listen to and always enjoy, but today it comes in the midst of death and destruction, and suddenly takes on its original meaning.

I get up from my couch as it comes over me. I shout, as in the story, "Up, Zorba, start to dance."

Here then is the beautiful destructiveness that seduced us. I did not realize it was as ugly as this.

Theodorakis' music reached me and penetrated every pore.

Note by note, and wound by wound.

Slow . . . then fast like sobbing.

Shy . . . then bold like a moment of hope.

Sad . . . then joyous like the moods of a poet in his cups.

Hesitant . . . then sure as the pace of a soldier.

I surrendered myself to it, dancing like one crazed in a vast room furnished with paintings and bridges. I stood in the middle of the room as if I was standing on a high rock and was dancing amid the destruction, while five bridges of Constantine crumbled and tumbled into the rocks and rolled down the valley.

Oh Zorba . . . don't you know?

She married! The woman I loved, while she loved you. I wanted her to like me, but she made me look like you.

Ziad was gone! My friend Ziad who bought this tape because he loved you through it, and maybe because he anticipated such a day for me, but, in his own way, prepared for me the details of my future. Perhaps he received it as a present from you. And I inherited it from among the pile of sorrows he left.

Hassan was gone! My brother who never cared much about the Greek gods. He had only one God and some old records. He died with no other love but to Faraqani and Umm Kulthum and the recitations of 'Abd al-Basit 'Abd al-Samad.

His only dream was to visit the holy city of Mecca and have a refrigerator at home.

Half of his dreams came true in the end. The nation gave him a refrigerator. He awaits me in it in his usual cool way, so I can mourn for him on his way to his final resting place.

If he had known you, he would perhaps not have had that foolish end.

If he had read you carefully, he would not have looked at his killers and dreamed of having a job in the capital, a car, and a smart house.

He would already have spat in their faces, cursed them as he cursed anyone, refused to shake hands with them at that wedding. If he had known you he would have said, like me, "Bastards, thieves, killers, you can't steal our blood as well. Fill your pockets with all you want, furnish your houses, and build up your bank accounts. We'll keep our blood and our memories and hold you to account, pursue you and then build up our country anew."

Oh Zorba, Ziad is dead, and now Hassan has died treacherously as well. If only you knew, my friend. None of them deserved to die.

Hassan was as clean and as clear as mercury, utterly innocent, afraid to dream, and when he started to, they killed him.

Ziad was like you. If only you had heard him laugh, talk, blaspheme, curse, cry, and get drunk! If only you had known the two of them, you would this evening be dancing with me in grief as you have never danced before, as in the novel after you cursed the priest who came to take you as the holy sacrifice before death.

But no matter. I know you will not be there tonight, my friend, and I will not blame you. Maybe you never existed on this earth. Because you are a creature of fiction at a time when people talk about such legends, about new gods from Greece. You taught them mad defiance and the fruitlessness of life.

Does it matter that you are not here tonight? Any more than all the others?

I do not blame you, my friend. Ultimately you are not responsible for all the follies that can be committed because of a novel.

Just tell me one thing. You killed Turks and they killed many of your comrades. Is there any distinction between killers?

Si Tahir died at the hands of the French. Ziad at the hands of the Israelis. Here is Hassan who dies at the hands of Algerians today.

Are there degrees of martyrdom? What if the nation is both the killer and the martyr at the same time?

And how many Arab cities have entered history with massacres, with secret cemeteries still bolted and barred?

How many cities are there whose citizens have become martyrs before they became citizens?

Where do we place all these? Victims of history or martyrs? What name do we give death when it is committed by an Arab dagger?

As soon as she saw me, Catherine cried, "You've got the face of a man with a hangover."

She then added, teasingly, "What did you do last night, you wretched man, to be in this state?"

"Nothing. Perhaps I just didn't get any sleep."

"Did you have friends in?" she asked, glancing round the room and searching with a woman's curiosity for evidence of people I had passed the evening with.

She was right that time. I became cynical and my sorrow was close to madness. I smiled at her question and wanted to answer, "Yes."

Sometimes grief is next to madness and it becomes self-parody.

"Did they stay over?" she asked.

"No, they left," I said, and added after a moment's silence, "My friends always leave."

It may be that she was not convinced, or she became more curious. Her eyes continued to look for something among the chaos of the living room and the two open suitcases in the hall. Women are always like this, unable to see beyond their bodies, and Catherine was unable to detect the traces of Ziad and Hassan and Zorba in that flat. She was actually on the margins of my own grief. Perhaps because of this she was persuaded without much talk that I had woken up after a night of love.

"Why did you call me and rush me here?" she asked.

"For many reasons."

Then after a short silence, I suddenly said, "Catherine, do you love bridges?"

"Don't tell me you brought me here to ask me this question," she said with disbelief.

"No, but I would like you to answer it."

"I really don't know. I've never asked myself such a question. You know I've always lived in cities that had no bridges. Except Paris, of course."

"It doesn't matter. In the end, I prefer you not to. It's enough that you like my paintings."

"Of course. I love your paintings. I've always thought of you as an exceptional artist."

"Then so be it. All these paintings are yours."

"You must be mad," she shouted. "How can you give me all these paintings? It's your home town. You might want them one day."

"I've had enough of nostalgia. I'm going back there. I'm giving them to you because I know you appreciate art. With you my paintings won't get lost."

There was a new tone in Catherine's voice, a tone that was full of sadness and strange joy.

"I will keep them all," she said. "No man has ever given me anything like this before."

I cast a final glance at her body, hidden as always beneath light flowing clothes.

"And no woman has given me such a sweet exile," I said.

"I'm afraid you might regret it and miss one of your paintings. I want you to know that you will always find them with me."

"I might. In the end we always regret something."

She suddenly realized how serious the situation was.

"*Mais ce n'est pas possible.* We can't just leave each other like this."

"Oh, Catherine, let us part, still wanting each other. History has decreed that we are not to have enough of each other and that we don't really love each other. For more than one reason. You've got more than one version of me now. Hang my memory on your walls even if it is the antithesis of my memory. After all, I was part of it."

She was unable to grasp all the secrets and symbols that I had not explained to her. Maybe she did, but her body refused to understand. Her body that was always missing the point, the body of a French official always protesting, always demanding something more, always exaggerating in freedom of speech and freedom to strike.

How could I find the words to explain my grief?

Where would I get the silence that would explain to her, without my saying anything, that Hassan was in another city waiting for me in a refrigerator? How could I tell her about his six children who had nobody else but me?

How could I explain to her my cold feet and the ice crawling into my body as time marched by, when she undid my shirt buttons, out of force of habit?

"Catherine, please, I don't feel like making love now. Forgive me."

"What do you want then?"

"I just want you to laugh, as you usually do."

"Why should I laugh?"

"Because you can't be sad."

"And what about you?"

"I'll wait until you've gone to be sad again. My grief is, as always, only postponed."

"Why do you tell me that today?"

"Because I'm tired. I'm leaving in a couple of hours."

"You can't. They've cancelled all the flights to Algiers."

"I'll go and wait at the airport and take the first plane. I've got to go today or tomorrow. I'm expected."

I could have told her, "My brother is dead, my only brother, Catherine," and then burst into tears. I needed to weep in front of someone, but did not do so. I could not do it with her around.

Perhaps an old constraint. Grief is a personal matter and sometimes becomes patriotic. I kept my wound to myself but decided to carry on the conversation as usual. Perhaps I could tell her some other day about it all, but not today.

Suddenly I felt as if I had harmed a butterfly.

"Catherine," I said. "We've had a beautiful story, haven't we? Complex, but beautiful. You have been the woman who was always almost my biggest love. Being away from each other might achieve what years of being together failed to do."

"Will you love me when we part?"

"I don't know. I'll certainly miss you. It's the logic of things. It was more than habit with you. I'll have to change my habits from now on."

"Will you be back?"

"Not for quite a while. I've got to learn the other aspect of oblivion. It's also hard to cross the bridge that divides us from exile."

"Khalid, why do you surround yourself with all these bridges?"

"I don't. I carry them inside me. Some people are born on a suspension bridge. They come to this world between two pavements, two roads, and two continents. They are born in crosswinds and grow up trying to reconcile the contradictions inside themselves. I may be one of those. Let me tell you a secret. I've just discovered that I don't like bridges. I hate everything that has two sides, two directions, two probabilities, and two controversies. That's why I'm leaving them to you. I wanted to burn them."

That was the idea but I didn't have the courage of a Tariq bin Ziad to do so. But still, I wanted to burn them until I had a return route engraved on my heart. I did not want to spend the rest of my life going backwards and forwards on this bridge.

I want my heart to have a final destination.

I want to return to that city perched on a rock as if I am conquering it afresh, just as Tariq bin Ziad conquered that mountain and gave it his name, Jabal Tariq, Gibraltar.

I had lost all sense of direction from the day I left home. I had cut myself off from history and geography and from the challenging years that were outside latitude and longitude. Where was the sea and where was the enemy? What lies before me and what is there behind me? Only the homeland is beyond the sea. Before me is only the whirlpool of exile. Only I am between them. Who am I declaring war against when around me is nothing but the frontiers of memory?

Catherine was looking at me, uncomprehendingly. Our relationship had always been a complete misunderstanding and without any vision. We separated as we met, more than a century ago, strangers to each other, not really knowing one another, without really loving one another, but always attracted to each other.

You once said, "What happened between us was real love. What didn't happen was the stuff of romantic novels."

Yes, but . . .

And between what happened and what did not, other things did happen that had nothing to do with love or literature, because in the end we only make words in both cases. Our own homeland made the events and wrote us up the way it wanted. Were we not after all merely the ink used for writing?

I left my homeland when I was banned from breathing, and I came back in the last minutes of a curfew.

I faced the airport and the mourning city alone that day. I remembered something Hassan said six years ago: "People of Constantine come back only for weddings and funerals."

I was surprised when it occurred to me that I, the legitimate son of this city, had been forced to return twice: first to attend your wedding, and secondly, to bury my brother. What is the difference? I died the first time and he had died now: both killed by our dreams. He died because his dreams got the better of him, and I died for having given up on my dreams and grieved their passing.

An ill-tempered customs official, as old as independence, stood at his desk. He was unmoved either by my missing arm or by my grief. He spoke in the tone of one who is persuaded we only go into exile in order to make money and are all smuggling things through in our suitcases.

"What have you got to declare?" he yelled in my face.

"Why do you have to shout?" I asked.

We stood close to each other, but he could not read me. It happens that nations become illiterate. Others were at that moment coming in through the big doors, carrying elegant diplomatic suitcases.

His hands dug deep down into Ziad's modest bag and going through a bunch of papers. I held a tear back but he did not notice.

"I declare memory, my son," I did not say.

I held my tongue and gathered up the draft of this book that were scattered around in the bag, fragments of a book, fragments of dreams.